"COME OUT OF THAT DREAM WORLD YOU'RE IN," DASH CHIDED HER.

He knew he was losing her with each step they took inside his opulent home. "Do you like it?" he finally asked.

Lotus looked up at him, wanting to tell him to get lost, to let her go. "Your money came to you on the backs of shattered people, shattered dreams. Do you honestly expect me to admire you?"

"I'm considered to be an honest businessman."

"By whom? The mob?" She stepped back when she saw the pain on his face. "I didn't mean to hurt you. I'll leave."

Dash grabbed her hand. "Don't go." He kissed her. "We have a long way to go and the road's going to be rough, but I don't want you to leave me. Please."

Lotus looked at him, her heart racing. She felt so confused, but one fact was certain. She didn't ever want to leave him.

CANDLELIGHT ECSTASY SUPREMES

37 ARABIAN NIGHTS, *Heather Graham*
38 ANOTHER DAY OF LOVING, *Rebecca Nunn*
39 TWO OF A KIND, *Lori Copeland*
40 STEAL AWAY, *Candice Adams*
41 TOUCHED BY FIRE, *Jo Calloway*
42 ASKING FOR TROUBLE, *Donna Kimel Vitek*
43 HARBOR OF DREAMS, *Ginger Chambers*
44 SECRETS AND DESIRE, *Sandi Gelles*
45 SILENT PARTNER, *Nell Kincaid*
46 BEHIND EVERY GOOD WOMAN, *Betty Henrichs*
47 PILGRIM SOUL, *Hayton Monteith*
48 RUN FOR THE ROSES, *Eileen Bryan*
49 COLOR LOVE BLUE, *Diana Blayne*
50 ON ANY TERMS, *Shirley Hart*
51 HORIZON'S GIFT, *Betty Jackson*
52 ONLY THE BEST, *Lori Copeland*
53 AUTUMN RAPTURE, *Emily Elliott*
54 TAMED SPIRIT, *Alison Tyler*
55 MOONSTRUCK, *Prudence Martin*
56 FOR ALL TIME, *Jackie Black*
57 HIDDEN MANEUVERS, *Eleanor Woods*
58 LOVE HAS MANY VOICES, *Linda Randall Wisdom*
59 CLOSE ENOUGH TO TOUCH, *JoAnna Brandon*
60 FINDERS KEEPERS, *Candice Adams*
61 FROM THIS DAY FORWARD, *Jackie Black*
62 BOSS LADY, *Blair Cameron*
63 CAUGHT IN THE MIDDLE, *Lily Dayton*
64 BEHIND THE SCENES, *Josephine Charlton Hauber*
65 TENDER REFUGE, *Lee Magner*
66 LOVESTRUCK, *Paula Hamilton*
67 QUEEN OF HEARTS, *Heather Graham*
68 A QUESTION OF HONOR, *Alison Tyler*
69 FLIRTING WITH DANGER, *Joanne Bremer*
70 ALL THE DAYS TO COME, *Jo Calloway*
71 BEST-KEPT SECRETS, *Donna Kimel Vitek*
72 SEASON OF ENCHANTMENT, *Emily Elliott*

LOTUS BLOSSOM

Hayton Monteith

A CANDLELIGHT ECSTASY SUPREME

Published by
Dell Publishing Co., Inc.
1 Dag Hammarskjold Plaza
New York, New York 10017

ISBN: 0-440-14907-X

Printed in the United States of America

First printing—May 1985

To my two grandmothers, Ethel Hayton Monteith and Ellen McAnally McMahon, who raised very large families but who had enough wisdom left over to coat the life of one redhaired freckle-faced girl who must have driven them crazy with her questions. I will never forget the love they gave to me. I dedicate *Lotus Blossom* to them.

To Our Readers:

Candlelight Ecstasy is delighted to announce the start of a brand-new series—Ecstasy Supremes! Now you can enjoy a romance series unlike all the others—longer and more exciting, filled with more passion, adventure, and intrigue—the stories you've been waiting for.

In months to come we look forward to presenting books by many of your favorite authors and the very finest work from new authors of romantic fiction as well. As always, we are striving to present the unique, absorbing love stories that you enjoy most—the very best love has to offer.

Breathtaking and unforgettable, Ecstasy Supremes will follow in the great romantic tradition you've come to expect *only* from Candlelight Ecstasy.

Your suggestions and comments are always welcome. Please let us hear from you.

Sincerely,

The Editors
Candlelight Romances
1 Dag Hammarskjold Plaza
New York, New York 10017

CHAPTER ONE

Lotus Sinclair had never broken into someone's office files before; in fact, she had never tried burgling anything. "And I don't think I'm very good at it," she muttered to herself as she rubbed her hands down the sides of her net stockinged legs. She hadn't had time to change out of the skimpy black satin costume she wore as one of the roving photographers at Cicero's, the high-style gambling casino that had taken Las Vegas by storm. In the few short months since it opened, it had become *the* place to see the best shows. It had also turned into the hottest gambling facility in the area, and the Las Vegas experts predicted that it couldn't have gone any other way. Hadn't Dash Colby, born John Dasher Colby to an old-money family in Boston, done the same thing in Atlantic City at the Xanadu and at a casino in the Grand Cayman Islands? Hadn't he also done well in the restaurant business in San Francisco, London, and New York?

Lotus had no interest in Dash Colby, the boss she had never seen. Three short weeks ago she had come to work here for one purpose only. She was going to find out who had forged her uncle's signature and used his credit card to run up monumental debts not only in Cicero's, but also in Atlantic City at the Xanadu. Lotus knew the signatures had to be forgeries because her uncle, Silas Sinclair, was an honorable man who would never do such a thing. The thought of what her uncle had gone through is what steadied her hand. She hated doing anything illegal, but she hated gambling more. And it was a gambler who had forged her uncle's name on all the IOU's, and she was going to find out who did it.

Swallowing her fear she tried to concentrate on what she was doing. Still, she shivered as she thought what her brothers, Todd and Rob, and Jeremy, her brothers' friend and her sometime date, would say if they knew what she was doing.

With the tool Petras had given her she attacked the lock on the file cabinet. Petras had been her brother's bosom friend in Vietnam and was like a brother to her. He was married now, and though confined to a wheelchair, he ran a camera shop that was doing very well. He had assured her that the tool he had given her would easily pick any simple lock.

Lotus could still recall the shock on his and Martha's face when she had arrived at their doorstep. She had landed in Las Vegas from Rochester, New York, that morning and had already checked into an inexpensive rooming house several blocks from Petras's house.

"Petras!" Martha had cried when she saw her. Then she was embracing Lotus. "Come inside!"

The whir of the wheelchair preceded his exclamation. "Lotus doll! What are you doing here?"

Petras tried to crane his neck to see around her. "Are Todd and Rob with you?" He reached up with both arms to hold her, his eager smile fading as he saw the look on her face. "What is it?"

"I . . . I . . ." Lotus bit her lip, then broke down. "Oh, Petras, it's been so awful. I thought perhaps Rob or Todd might have told you."

Petras gestured to his wife to take their children into another room. "Come with me, Lotus," he said as he wheeled his chair around to precede her into the living room. He waited until she was seated in a chair, then he moved closer and took her hand. "Rob called me about what happened to your uncle. He said the family was torn up about it, that Lee and Will were like zombies after your uncle's stroke." He paused. "Your uncle is still holding even, isn't he, Lotus doll?"

"If you mean, is he alive? Yes, he's breathing, but he seems to have shrunk." Lotus gulped a breath to steady herself, then stared out the window. "That's why I'm here."

"What do you mean?"

Lotus looked back at him. "I mean that I know my uncle was deceived and victimized. He didn't sign those IOU's. He'd never embezzle funds to gamble at casinos here and in Atlantic City. While I was in Rochester, I answered a newspaper ad to be a roving photographer at the Cicero."

"What?" Petras gripped the arms of his wheelchair. "Lotus, tell me what you're planning?"

"I'm . . . I'm going to get a hold of the records of the casino and find out who signed Uncle's name to the IOU's."

"No!" Petras thundred. "Lotus, are you mad? I can't believe that Rob and Todd allowed you to—"

"They don't know I'm here and you're not to tell them. Give me your word. Don't you see I have to do this. Uncle is dying and my aunt is fading away. Our whole family is being destroyed by a lie. I can't live with that. You must give me your word . . . because I need your help."

"Lotus . . ." Petras lifted his hands in a helpless appeal.

"Will you help me?" she persisted.

Petras stared at her then nodded. "But you must tell me everything you're going to do. If it's too dangerous I can't—"

Lotus kneeled in front of him, taking his hands in hers. "It won't be. I've thought it all out. Once I'm a camera girl at the casino I can break into the office . . ."

"God, Lotus!" Petras groaned, his hand gripping hers. "Do you know who you're dealing with? Dash Colby! The man makes granite look like cotton! And he's damn smart. Even here in Las Vegas, where the high-rollers congregate, he's considered a gambler's gambler, a risk taker. He'll face any odds and take on any challenge. Do you think you can put anything over on a man like that? Very sharp and dangerous men have tried and failed." Petras shook his head as he looked at her determined face, aware once again that the youngest child of the Sinclairs' might look Oriental, which she was, but she still had an Irishman's determination. "Can't I talk you out of this?"

Lotus shook her head, her black silky hair swinging around her face. "I've decided to use my natural parents' name, Weston. That way no one in the casino can make the connection to Sinclair."

Petras nodded, wincing. "I don't know what Mr.

Sinclair will do to me when he finds out I aided and abetted you in this. I should be horsewhipped for even considering it."

"If you tell my brothers, I'll still go through with it, and you know if Rob, especially, comes out here, he is liable to create more trouble than we can handle." Lotus referred to her very hotheaded brother who was the second oldest of the three Sinclairs. Lotus had been adopted by the Sinclairs when her parents had died, and she felt every bit a member of the family.

"Rob would be likely to take the casino apart." Petras gave her a rueful smile. "What made you think of this scheme, Lotus doll?"

"I was desperate." She pressed her hand to her mouth. "You can't know what it's like to witness the slow destruction of a person. Because that's what's happening to Uncle . . . and Mother and Dad aren't much better. I just had to do something."

"Where does your family think you are?"

"They think I'm on a raft trip. I have a college friend who is on a rafting trip right at this very moment. When she wrote and said she was going and would be out of touch with civilization for a week, the idea came to me that it would be a good cover for me so that I could come to Las Vegas. So I did."

Petras sighed and closed his eyes for a minute. "I suppose one of the things you want me to do would be to copy his file"—his eyes snapped open—"that is, if you can get it out of the office."

"I can. I know I can." Lotus felt a surge of hope. Petras was not rejecting her!

"I have a friend, Richard, who works at the casino." Petras went over to the phone. "He's another Vietnam vet." He looked at Lotus after he dialed. "He owes me a favor. . . . Yes, Rich. It's Petras. I was wondering if you could come over to the house this evening. Good. Sure. Eight o'clock is fine."

That evening, after dining on one of Martha's delicious meals, Richard, Lotus, and Petras went into the living room to speak privately.

"I can't believe you think she should do this," Richard said after he had heard Lotus's plan.

Petras shrugged. "I don't think she should do this, but since I can't stop her, I'm going to try to make it as safe for her as possible. Will you help us?"

Richard looked irritated. "It's not 'will I.' It's 'can I?' Petras, you know that the security surrounding Cicero's is the best." He shook his head. "And Hans"—Richard shuddered—"God, he'd give his life for Cicero's and that's not even mentioning Colby." He shivered again. "Dash Colby is tough . . . the toughest I've ever known—and I thought we knew some hard guys in Nam. . . ."

"I'm going to do it, with or without help, Richard," Lotus said.

Petras smiled at his friend. "See what I mean?"

Richard nodded. "All right, Lotus. Petras has told me all about your family and what they have done for him and what they mean to him." He looked at his friend as he spoke. "And if it hadn't been for you, I would be dead or in prison now, hung up on drugs and booze. So if the three of us can pull it off we will." He turned to look at Lotus. "You say you have a job at Cicero's?"

Lotus nodded, feeling her hope returning.

Petras patted her hand. "Don't be too confident that we can pull this off, little sister."

"I know whatever we do, it will be better than standing idly by and watching my uncle die."

Petras exhaled a breath. "All right, so we wait for Lotus to start her job and get accepted. I think you should speak to Lotus as little as possible, so send all messages through me."

"Right."

"We can do it. I know we can." Lotus was filled with determination now.

"I hope so," Richard muttered. "I don't relish Hans, the head of security, strangling me."

Petras glared at his friend, then squeezed Lotus's hand. "I don't like what you're doing but I understand it. If only I hadn't promised I would help you. . . ."

"Too late," Lotus said, smiling as she gave him a quick kiss on the cheek.

That had been three weeks ago. And now she was in Colby's office trying to pick a lock by herself!

Snap! The lock gave! The sound scared her and she looked toward the door, hoping no one had heard the noise. She exhaled after a few moments, her breathing the only sound in the austerely decorated room. It was a large office with cream walls and beige leather and oak furnishings. Not one extra piece of furniture crowded the area, giving the rectangular room a very spacious look. With great care, she eased open the door that fronted the file drawers and choked. *Damn! Each of these drawers has an individual lock!* She gritted her teeth and pressed the tool into the file marked S-U, praying that it would contain what it implied—the files from the letter S to the letter U. It took a few long seconds before there was a pop and the drawer opened.

With hands shaking, she pawed through the file until she found the folder with the name SINCLAIR typed on the flap. She didn't bother to open it. All she wanted to do was get out of the room. She shoved the folder into the shoulder bag she had brought along for just such a purpose and then quickly closed the file. She fiddled with the tool until she heard the click telling her that the file was locked again. Then she closed the wooden front door and locked it. Next she very carefully sprayed the wooden front of the cabinet with odorless cleaner and wiped the door. *Petras was right. It does take away most of the marks the tool made.* She tucked the tool and the cleaner in her bag, zipped it closed, and walked toward the door.

She stopped dead in the middle of the room when she heard the sound of the latch. Frozen, she watched the handle turn. She looked for a way to escape, but the door opened before she even had a chance to move, and she was facing a very tall, slim but muscular man whose ash blond hair had a silvery look from the strands of gray running through it.

He saw her at once. Pocketing the key, his eyes moved from her face to her feet and back up. "So that's why the door was open. Did Hans send you in here?"

"The door was open. I came in myself." Lotus told the truth. It had been Petras's friend, Richard, who had managed to get Hans away from the office, after the office manager had unlocked it, so that she could sneak into the room.

"I'm Dash Colby. Are you looking for a job?"

"I'm Lotus . . . ah . . . Weston, and as you can tell from my costume, I already work here. I'm one of the roving photographers. I start my shift in fifteen minutes so I'd better go." She tried to smile, but her face felt like solid dry ice, and she moved past him.

He caught hold of her upper arm. "Weston! That's an unusual name for an Oriental, isn't it?"

"I was born in New York. My father was an American professor of history at Tokyo University when he met my mother, but they came to America before I was born." Lotus explained, finding it difficult to hold his gaze. If she asked her to open her shoulder bag, the game was over!

"And you're a China doll," Dash whispered, inhaling her fragrance as he leaned over her. "Is that Joy you're wearing?"

Lotus was surprised. "Yes, it is. Are you so familiar with French perfume?"

He shrugged, closing the door as he moved into the room to stand closer to her. "Somewhat."

She'd bet on that, Lotus thought. He probably has the damned stuff piped into his home for his cupcakes. Then she blinked as another thought crossed her mind. "What made you call me 'China doll'?" Most persons assume my origin is Japanese."

"But you are Chinese, aren't you?" Dash reached out a hand to touch her tiny nose, running one finger across her high wide cheekbones. "There's both strength and fragility in your heart-shaped face."

"My mother was born in Peking. She went to Tokyo to study." She paused. Why was she telling this man her life story?

"Go on." Dash urged in soft tones.

"Ah . . . well, there isn't much to tell. My parents were killed in an auto accident after we returned to Japan. I was seven years old at the time. . . . You don't want to hear all this . . ." Lotus felt embarrassed. When had she become so confiding? She was actually babbling in front of a stranger.

"Yes, I do," Dash answered honestly. He had often told women he wanted to know more about them, then he would find himself bored before the story was finished. But now he found himself intrigued with every word she said. "Were you named after the creaminess of your skin? It's like a lotus."

Laughter rippled from her throat, bringing his glinting gaze there. "I was called Lotus because of the beautiful flowers that abounded in our garden in Tokyo. What's wrong? You have a strange look on your face."

"Do I?" *What a smile and laugh she has! What a sweetheart!* He could feel his pulse rate increase. "Have dinner with me tonight?"

"I can't," Lotus told him, wishing for a moment that she could. "I have to work." She glanced at her watch. "Oh, Lord, I'm late now." She moved toward the door, but again he stopped her.

"Have supper with me after your shift."

"I can't. I'm almost engaged," she lied, wondering what Jeremy, her occasional escort, would say to that. She stepped back as she watched the smoky blue of his eyes turn to azure steel.

He lifted one of her hands. "No ring."

"I'm just going to have a wedding ring. We'll probably marry in a couple of years." She babbled, compounding the lie. She clamped her lips together, angry with herself for talking so much.

"He's a fool," he muttered, irritated at the relief that filled him knowing that no marriage was imminent. What the hell was she doing in his office in the first place? "You never did tell me why you're in my office."

"No, I didn't, did I? Ah, you see, I was going to ask you if I couldn't audition for the chorus." She gulped. Well, she could dance, and music had been her minor in college. In fact, she had sung the lead in "Flower Drum Song," when her university had put it on.

"I see." He looked her over again, enjoying his leisurely perusal of her more than he had enjoyed looking at anyone in a long time. "I think you wouldn't fit in with our showgirls, Lotus. Most of them are five feet eight to six feet in height. You can't be more than five four."

"I'm five five." She lifted her chin. Wasn't it enough that her brothers called her Small Change without hearing it implied from a stranger?

He leaned toward her. "So tiny but so tough. Tell me about your family."

"I was adopted by friends of my parents right after my parents' death. Daddy had been named in my father's will as my guardian in case of such an eventuality. They had two boys, Todd, who was twelve, and Robert, who was ten. I'm the youngest child." *Why do I keep on talking?* Lotus agonized taking a step backward. *He's a man who could put me in prison!* "I have to go to work."

"All right, darling." He leaned down and kissed her lightly on the mouth. "I'll see you after your shift."

Lotus could feel her lips moving but no sound came forth. She finally walked toward the door. If Dash hadn't reached around her and opened it, she would have walked right into it.

She kept on walking, feeling his eyes on her, but she never looked back.

The casino and restaurant were jammed with people, some laughing and shouting and dancing, but most serious and quiet, never lifting their eyes from the dice, cards, or roulette wheel.

Lotus moved among the people, taking some pictures, but not as many as she would have liked. It was hard to make a living doing this. Most casino devotees concentrated on gambling. The last thing they wanted to spend money on was pictures. It was tough going, but little by little Lotus was making the quota she needed in order to make any profit on the straight commission job. As it was, she lived in a tiny room on the top floor of a rooming house. She had to go down to the third floor to use the bathroom and shower facilities. Many times it troubled her that she had been so secretive with her family, but if any of them even guessed what she was doing, she would have been whisked away from Las Vegas in a flash. She shrugged as she thought of the room she was renting, but knew that it wouldn't be for much longer. She had put her shoulder bag in her locker before she had started her shift. So all she had to do was take the file out after work, bring it to Petras to copy—and then she could leave Vegas and return home.

"Hey, sister, get over here. Me and my wife

want a picture with our friends." A heavyset man in an open-necked shirt waved at Lotus.

"Yes, sir. Coming." Lotus hurried over weaving in and out of the tables in one of the casino's restaurants.

After she had taken the photos and noted that there didn't seem to be any other customers in the restaurant, she made her way back to the gaming rooms to see if there would be any work there. "Just a few more and I'll make the rent money," she mumbled to herself.

"Would you mind taking my picture?" Dash touched her arm, smiling down at her.

Lotus smiled back. "You don't need me to take your picture."

"But I do." He looked past her and gestured to someone. "Lana, come here."

Lotus turned around to see Lana Dalbey, one of the showgirls, sway up to Dash and put her hand through his arm, reaching up to kiss his mouth at the same time. Lotus had a burning wish to kick her right in her high instep.

"Lotus wants to take our picture." Dash lifted his head and turned the tall lissome blonde to face Lotus. "Go ahead."

"Sweetie, why don't we have Harry take it? After all, he's in charge of Foto for the casino," Lana drawled, her eyes flicking over Lotus, then away again. Foto was the company that had hired Lotus.

Lotus froze in position, her camera ready for shooting, taking deep breaths to keep her temper in check. *This inscrutable Oriental is about to smack you with this camera, Lana,* Lotus fumed.

"Go ahead, Lotus." Dash grinned at her, then

laughed when she continued to stare at him. "Kill me later. Take the picture now."

Lotus snapped it, then looked down at her camera in the pretense of checking the film. She knew if she looked at the people in front of her, the fury building inside of her would erupt. Who the hell was Dash Colby to patronize her? She wasn't that hard up for money that she needed his or his girl friend's clever remarks.

"Lotus. Look at me, Lotus," Dash put his hand under her chin, the softness of her skin stirring him.

She jerked her head away, her shoulder-length black hair swinging around her face like a velvet curtain. "I have to develop my film. Excuse me." She wheeled away from him and stalked from the room, along a corridor leading off the lobby to the rear of the club. The locker rooms, dressing rooms, and storage areas were there, as well as the small darkroom Lotus shared with the other photographers.

She slammed the door of the darkroom and flipped the switch so that outside the door a red light flashed. No one would enter the room until the light was off.

Mumbling to herself, Lotus readied the liquids and pans. "It's a good thing I wasn't working the instant camera at that moment. If I'd stayed one more minute I'd have smacked her," she fumed, automatically performing the tasks she had learned as an undergraduate student in the graphic arts department of Rochester Institute of Technology. She used her photographic skills as a free-lance photographer at weddings and other celebrations while she worked toward finishing her master's degree in Graphic Arts. She intended to become a full-time photographer when she graduated. "But not until I finish what I started . . ." she spoke out loud, hanging the negatives up so that she could look at them. Then she began to print her work. "Uncle Silas would never have taken money from the firm." The firm Lotus referred to was Sinclairs, Inc., a photographic company selling camera equipment and also doing photographic work in the field of sales, publicity, and public relations. Sinclairs was a respected firm. She had worked there part time while in college, and though she felt very comfortable at Sinclairs, she planned to try her wings in New York. Her family had not said they would be against her going, but Lotus knew they would prefer her to stay with the family company.

She sighed as she thought of the family and how her uncle's problem had worn them down like water on a stone. *Great-Grandpa Sinclair was even a friend of George Eastman, the founder of Kodak in Rochester. No one who knows our family would ever think that one of them would steal or embezzle. . . .* She slammed her small fist on the counter as she looked at the smiling faces of people in the prints she pinned on the line to dry. "I don't know who did this, Uncle Silas, but I will find out." A dry sob wracked her as she thought of the man who had aged twenty years almost overnight, who'd had a mild stroke as a result. Her mother and father walked around like somnambulists, their faces white and strained. The happy homes, always filled with people, were like tombs now and had been that way for the past nine weeks, ever since the first news broke in the Rochester newspapers. "I will not let our family be destroyed. I won't. I won't." Lotus spoke into the darkness, her low voice seeming to echo in the gloom.

When she was finished printing all the photos she had taken, she left them hanging to dry. With a little luck she might be able to take pictures of some of the latecomers, but it had been her experience that it was the early evening people who were more apt to want pictures. She flipped the red light switch off and grasped the handle of the door. Before she could push it, it opened.

"Hi."

"Hi," Lotus said, looking up into Dash Colby's face.

"I could see you were offended by Lana's actions. That's why I was waiting here, to apologize. I didn't want you to think I was denigrating you or your work. I know how tough it is to be a Foto girl, and how important it is to make quota just so you'll get some pay." He touched her cheek with one finger, then dropped his hand. "Please have supper with me."

She felt such a rush of heat she thought her knees would buckle. "I'm . . . I'm not through. I was going in to work the rooms again. . . ." She inhaled a deep breath.

"Fine. I have a little work to do. How would it be if I came looking for you in, say, an hour?"

Lotus wanted to tell him to disappear. "All right," she answered him, flustered. She walked around him to go back down the hall to the main part of the casino, hoping that he wouldn't notice her trembling knees.

"You have marvelous legs, darling, such trim

calves, sweet ankles . . ." he murmured behind her, "and that little black ruffle shows off . . ."

Lotus whirled around to glare at his laughing face, then she was almost running to get away.

As she walked through the tables, she was conscious of the skimpiness of her costume for the first time. It had not bothered her previously because it had certainly covered her as well as the bikini she wore to the beach. "But you don't wear black pumps and net stockings with that . . ." she mumbled to herself, nodding to a customer who hailed her.

By the end of the hour she had told Dash she was tired. To her surprise, there had been many requests for pictures, and she had used both her instant camera and the larger commercial one she carried around her neck.

At the last minute there were two more customers, so she had to hurry to the darkroom to develop and print out her last works of the day. These photographs she would drop by the concierge's desk where the customers were instructed to pick up their prints. While the work was drying, she hurried to the locker rooms and changed into her street clothes. She would be dining with Dash Colby in slacks, but they were her best linen ones. The coral color repeated in the linen vest was a foil for her dark hair. She shook her head at her mirror image. "You look Oriental, but that skin is a little too Irish looking. No wonder it takes you so long to tan." She grimaced at her reflection, brushed some coral lip gloss on her mouth, checked the tote bag she carried to see if the folder was still inside the zippered bag, then she walked toward the door. "I feel short in my linen slip-on flats but what the heck? I didn't know I was going to dine and I couldn't ride a bike with heels," she said aloud as she left the ladies' area.

"You must have money in the bank. Do you always talk to yourself?"

Lotus jumped and nodded as she noticed Dash propping up the wall in the corridor. "Usually I'm so busy with my conversations with myself I'll walk right by friends."

"I know. You didn't see me until I spoke to you."

"I'm a little casually dressed for supper. Would you like to put it off until another day?"

"I think you look lovely." He stood close to her.

Lotus studied him. "You're taller than my brothers and they're over six feet."

"I'm six feet four inches."

"Lord," Lotus whispered as he took her arm. She hoped he didn't notice how she stiffened when he touched her tote bag.

"What do you carry in that thing?" he grinned down at her.

"I carry my lunch in it, reading materials, and sometimes a change of clothes." She told him the truth, just omitting that tonight she also was carrying a folder stolen from his files!

"You could carry your bed in it."

"It is large," she agreed.

"Yes." *Why is she so nervous?* he wondered.

When he led her toward the Crystal Room, she dug in her heels. "What is it, love? You'll like the food."

"I know, but I'm not dressed for it."

"You look wonderful. Believe me. I wouldn't bring you here if I thought you would be embarrassed."

"If you say so," Lotus reluctantly gave in.

The maitre d' saw them coming and almost ran to get to them. "Your regular table, sir?"

"Please, Alain. Alain, this is Lotus Weston. She may wish to eat here other evenings," Dash said.

"There will be a table for her," Alain said, smiling.

When Lotus hung back, Dash put his arm lightly around her shoulder and urged her to follow Alain.

The table was on a low dais, sheltered by plants but had a clear view of the small stage.

"I didn't know they had shows in here," Lotus whispered as Dash seated her, then himself. Alain melted away.

"Small stuff. Piano players, trios, that sort of thing. I don't like loud sounds with my meals. . . ."

"Neither do I." Lotus smiled at him.

He leaned toward her. "You have the most beautiful face."

Lotus drew back, feeling her eyes widen. She came from a loving family, but there had always been a little restraint when it came to deeply personal things. She wasn't used to someone speaking to her the way Dash did. "Thank you." She could feel her lips lift in a smile.

He grinned at her. "You're welcome." He moved closer to her. "Your skin doesn't have the olive tones of an Oriental."

"My mother says that just my eyes and skin are of the West. The rest of me is Eastern." Lotus smiled as she thought of her adopted mother with the fading blond hair. Her thoughts carried to her adopted father and brothers, then to her cousins, her aunt . . . and then to Uncle Silas.

She heard Dash speak to the waiter, but she

didn't listen to what he had ordered. When the waiter left, Dash turned to her.

"Why are you frowning?" Dash's breath lifted the fine hair that swept across her forehead.

"I was thinking of my uncle. He's been ill. He had a stroke." Lotus struggled from her painful memories to look at her dinner companion. She had forgotten for a moment why she was here, what had happened, to her family and Uncle Silas. She had even blanked her mind to Dash being a gambler, and owning the casino that held so many of the bogus IOU's attributed to her uncle.

"I'm sorry." He watched the play of emotions across her face. Pain, incredulity, then a slight acceptance. He lifted her fine-boned hand and kissed the palm. "I am sorry that your uncle is ill."

"Thank you." Lotus didn't want to believe him. Wasn't it to his gambling houses that much of the embezzled money was sent? Wasn't it his accounting department that had sent the bills found in her uncle's personal files? "I believe you," she whispered. When his hand tightened on hers, she turned it over so that their palms were together.

Their food came and as they ate, Lotus didn't remember what she put in her mouth a moment after she swallowed it, yet she knew it was food for the gods. When he opened his mouth for a taste of her food, she lifted her fork with a piece of fish and pepper on it. "Oh, dear, I dropped the pepper." She laughed, then bit her lip when she saw him watching her.

"Your laugh is beautiful."

She chuckled. "Can't be. You said my face was beautiful." She giggled, then covered her mouth.

Dash pulled her hand away, leaning over to

place his lips on hers. "Let me cover your mouth." Never in his life had he felt so carefree. *You're a damn fool, Colby,* he castigated himself, but he couldn't stop his pulse from jumping into overdrive when her mouth quivered under his.

Lotus pulled back. "Have to eat my dinner," she babbled, feeling as though her heart had leaped from her body. Everyone in the busy supper room seemed to have faded away. She and Dash were alone!

"Yes. Do you like the swordfish?" He fought a desire to pick her up and carry her out of there.

Lotus's head shot downward. Swordfish! So that's what they were eating. Delicious! "Yes. Thank you."

"You're very polite." Dash smiled at her, and his stomach dropped a thousand feet when dimples appeared at each side of her mouth when she smiled back.

She nodded. "In our house you were either courteous or you received lecture Number 233 as my brothers called it. It could last for two days." She leaned her chin on her hand when the waiter removed her plate. "Mother is a stickler for good manners."

"You love your family. Did you say you were adopted?" Dash noticed her stiffen. "Is that a sensitive subject? Your adoption?"

So that's what he thought? Lotus mused, hoping he hadn't noticed her sigh of relief. The man was sharp! She should stay out of his way! Playing around with him was like waltzing with a tiger shark. She nodded, hoping he wouldn't pursue the subject.

"Shall we have the cheese board and fruit, or would you like a sweet?" Dash changed the subject.

"Fruit is fine."

After they finished the dessert and drank some coffee, they left the Crystal Room.

"I'd like to dance for a little while. Would you?"

Lotus looked at her watch and was about to shake her head.

"Don't say no, Lotus. I'll drive you home after a few dances, I promise."

"No need. I have my bike." She had purchased the rather battered five-speeder from a second-hand shop. It gave her the exercise she needed, and it was faster than walking to work.

"We'll put the bike in the trunk of the car. I won't let you ride it home so late." He led her toward the nightclub section of the casino.

Lotus opened her mouth to protest, then closed it. Why should she? She wanted to dance with him.

Again the maitre d' hopped forward when he saw them, and they were led to a secluded table that had a fine view of the stage and the orchestra.

Lotus lifted her hands to remove her jacket. When she felt Dash's hands there, pushing hers away, she allowed him to remove it. She turned to smile her thanks and saw him looking down at her, the jacket still in his hands.

"That vest is . . ."

"Beautiful. I know." Lotus chortled, breaking into a laugh when she saw the appreciative gleam in his eye.

Dash felt his mouth lift in response. She was a darling! Totally unaffected! He felt a surge of sensual interest that he hadn't felt in years. "How old are you, Lotus?"

"Twenty-five. How old are you?"

"God, you look about eighteen." Relief coursed through him, glad that she wasn't as young as she looked. The theory that dark-haired women looked more mature than their lighter-haired sisters just went out the window, he mused, all at once realizing that blondes and redheads seemed bland next to Lotus's luscious exotic coloring and features.

"Well?"

"Well, what, angel?"

"How old are you?"

"Thirty-seven. Tell me about this engagement of yours while we're dancing." Dash helped her from her chair, not seeming to notice the persons who tried to get his attention as they wended their way to the dance floor.

Dash turned her and took her in his arms, bending low so that he could hold her comfortably.

"Won't you get a crick in your back?" Lotus said, out of breath, feeling curtained from the world by his body.

"Not to worry, darling. Now, tell me about your engagement."

"There isn't much to tell." *And that's the truth since there isn't an engagement, not even an understanding,* she thought, wishing he would change the subject. "Jeremy went to the university with my brothers. That's how I met him. After graduation my brothers went into, ah . . ." She had been about to say Sinclairs, but she caught herself. If Dash made the connection between that name and the same one in his files, it would be trouble. ". . . the family business. There was a job opening. It was offered to Jeremy and he took it." Lotus shrugged. "We began dating."

Dash watched her all the while she spoke. "And are you sleeping with him?"

Lotus stopped dancing, but when she would have turned away, Dash caught her around the waist and held her. "I have to go, Mr. Colby," she said.

"I was out of line. Forget I asked. Turn around, love, and don't be angry. They're playing a great love song."

Lotus hesitated, aware that other dancers were looking at them curiously. "All right." She turned in his arms, feeling comfortable when his arms closed around her. "But I won't answer questions like that. You're my employer, not my mentor."

"Right," Dash agreed, knowing he was going to go crazy thinking of her with Jeremy. With great effort he masked the thought from his mind and concentrated on the words to the song, "Stardust," which the musicians were playing.

"It is a lovely song," Lotus whispered.

"Yes." Dash tightened his hold, feeling her tiny boned but strong body against him.

They danced until the club closed, only sitting down for short periods to sip their drinks.

"Do you always drink mineral water and lime?"

She nodded her head. "Alcohol gives me a headache."

"I don't think I've ever tasted Saratoga water, even though we sell a great deal of it."

Feeling daring, Lotus offered him her glass.

He accepted, turning the container until he was drinking from the same spot that she had. Sipping, he watched her, the blood fluctuating in her face. It satisfied him that he could disconcert her. At least she wasn't indifferent to him! The fact that he cared so much bothered him and he literally stiffened in his chair.

"What is it? Have you a headache?" Lotus noticed the deep scowl on his face that had appeared suddenly—and had just as quickly disappeared.

He looked at her. "It's nothing. Let's dance." He rose to his feet and came around to help her from the chair.

As she led the way to the dance floor, his eyes seemed to fix on the flowing motion of her hips and legs. *She doesn't walk, she floats,* he thought.

Later when he was walking with her through the casino to his office and all the clubs were closing, she paused in front of the gaming rooms, which never closed. "Do they ever go home?"

"Some don't seem to have a home." He gave a hard laugh. "Not that I'm complaining. A man lost a million, seventy-five thousand at a twenty-hour session of baccarat last month."

"You're joking." Lotus choked. That made her uncle's so-called debts of a half a million dollars, in this casino and in the Xanadu in Atlantic City, seem almost natural. At least it hadn't taken place in just one day! "What size installment payments does he have?"

"None, love." Dash led her down the hall to his office, unlocking it with his key.

Lotus felt crimson from head to toe as she stood in front of the office door. It embarrassed her that she had broken into his files. Fear that he would discover that she had done it before she could copy the file and return it to its rightful place filled her as she watched him

"He wrote a check for the entire amount, and

we deposited it in our bank the next day. We didn't expect it to bounce, and it didn't."

"I see." She tried to smile at him as she walked past him into his office. She faced him. "I really should go, and it's no problem for me to ride my bike. I ride at night all the time."

"No," he rasped, glaring at her, fear filling him at what could happen to her if some creep stopped her. "No, I don't want you to do that. I'll drive you from now on when you work at night. You ride your bike when you work in the daylight hours only. If you work at night, I'll drive you home."

Lotus could feel her mouth drop open. "Don't be silly. I usually work at night and I always use my bike."

"Not anymore." He pulled a lightweight cotton pullover from a closet. Then before she could blink, he had dropped his trousers and hung them on a hanger on a portable valet near the closet. He grinned at her. "You're blushing again, love. Haven't you ever seen a man undress?"

"Don't be ridiculous. I have two brothers."

He would have bet the casino that she hadn't seen any men undress in front of her. What brought an innocent young woman to Las Vegas to work? The thought caught in his brain like a burr until he shook it loose. He would think about that some other time. The best news, he thought, was that if she ever did sleep with that fiance of hers, it wasn't more than once or twice; otherwise, she wouldn't have looked so uncomfortable when he changed his trousers and shirt in front of her. "It's not as though I've stripped down to the buff, Lotus, is it?"

"Not as if you've stripped to the buff," she echoed him, feeling her stiff lips lift in a smile. God, he was beautiful. Even if she never saw another man peeled down, she would know that she had seen the best there was in physiques when she looked at the man in front of her. She blinked, trying to clear the picture of him from her head. "Ready?"

"Ready." He slipped on the cotton pullover, hooked a blazer over his shoulder, and led her out of the room. When she would have turned left, he urged her right. "This is the way to where the car is parked."

"But my bike is this way," Lotus explained.

"Not to worry." Dash backtracked to his office, unlocked the door, and went over to the phone on the desk. He punched out a few numbers, then barked instructions into the instrument. "There," he said after he hung up. "The bike will be locked up until tomorrow."

"But, don't do that," Lotus sputtered. "That's my transportation in the morning."

"I'll pick you up," Dash said soothingly. "Not to worry." He was leading her to the parking lot as they spoke.

"And do you want to get up at five and ferry me over to Mac's cafe for the early shift?" Lotus expostulated, trying to loosen his grip from her upper arm.

Dash stopped dead, his eyes narrowed in fury on her. "Why do you work there?"

"Because I get breakfast that way and the few tips I get help keep the Reaper away," Lotus snapped back. "Now, do we get my bike?"

He continued to walk and she followed. "No, I'll

drive you home, then I'll pick you up tomorrow morning at four-thirty."

"Four-thirty . . ." Lotus wheezed, thinking about the two alarms clocks needed to wake her at five, so that she could be at the cafe, one block away, at five-thirty. "I don't need to get up half an hour early."

"You can at least jog with me as long I'm taking you to work, then waiting to bring you to Cicero's."

"Waiting?" Lotus gasped.

"Of course. How else would you get to work?" He helped her into the passenger side of the car.

She had taken no notice of the car until she was inside of it. "Goodness. Is this a Ferrari?"

"Yes." His teeth gleamed in the dark interior of the car.

"Marvelous."

"Would you like to drive it someday?"

"Is the pope Catholic?" Lotus muttered.

Dash laughed. "Fine. The next time we go out . . . which will be . . ." He shot his left hand in front of him for a moment to look at his watch. ". . . This evening I will let you take the wheel."

"We don't have a date for tomorrow," Lotus ventured.

Dash lifted one hand from the steering wheel and placed it on her knee. "Yes, we do, love." He pressed a switch and a tape player slid into view.

The music combined with the flashing lights of Las Vegas had a soporific effect, and Lotus felt the weightlessness that comes between consciousness and sleep.

"Lotus," Dash whispered. "You'll have to give me more directions."

"Huh? Oh, yes, turn left, then right, then to the end of the street. It's the large white house. I live on the fourth floor."

Dash's car quickly made the trip, then he parked it in front of the house. "You live on the fourth floor?"

"Yes. I have a room. It's cheap. Of course I hate going down to the third floor to shower and use the bathroom." Lotus clamped her lips closed. She was chattering to him again.

"I don't see a fire escape."

"There's a rickety one in the back. I tried it, and it's a scary trip down, but I think it will hold me."

"You think?"

"Yes." She stared at him. "You're grinding your teeth."

"Am I?" He exhaled a shaky breath. "This is no place for you."

"It's fine." She didn't tell him that she wasn't staying in Las Vegas long enough to worry about her accommodations. Just long enough to get a copy of that file. . . . "Oh no . . ." Lotus groaned aloud, remembering that she wouldn't be able to get the file copied if Dash was going to be on her tail every minute. How could she get in touch with Petras and get him to pick up the folder?

"What's wrong, love? Did you forget something at the casino?"

"Ah, yes, that's as good as any . . ." Lotus answered, distracted, her mind churning with the problem.

Dash came around to the passenger side of the car, opened the door, and leaned in, his face having a look of wary amusement. "And what do you mean by that remark, love?"

"Huh?" Lotus bent her head back to look up at him. "What did I say?" Then she remembered. Trying to fight the blush she knew was creeping up her neck, she smiled at him, noticing that his face was all silver angles and planes in the shadowy light from the interior of the car. "I was thinking about copies," she told him, which was true. "Some of my customers like two or three of a frame. I was hoping I marked them correctly." That was not the truth. She had marked the negatives as carefully as she always did, the moment they were developed and dried, notching the edge of the negative to indicate how many copies.

"I see." Dash almost lifted her out of the car. He didn't believe her. His angel was lying! *She's holding out on me! But why and about what?*

He walked her up to the front door. "It's been a while since I kissed a girl good night on a front porch," he drawled.

She would bet a check on that, Lotus mused. No doubt he just follows them inside and to bed. Not tonight! "Quaint custom," she said out loud as she opened the squeaky screen door that sagged on its hinges.

Dash frowned at the obvious neglect of the house. "I don't like you staying here."

"You're repeating yourself." Lotus dared to reach up and touch his nose with her index finger.

"Brat," he rasped, leaning over her, then lifting her straight up his body, so that her feet dangled several inches off the floor.

"Not true. You said I'm beautiful." Lotus had never been so outspoken, so open with anyone.

"Yes. You're a beautiful brat." His mouth grazed hers, then fastened. The kiss lengthened and deepened.

Lotus had the sensation of being in a free-fall from the planet Venus.

CHAPTER TWO

To Lotus the next three days were kaleidoscopic chaos. She and Dash were together every waking minute. She had to pinch herself many times to remind herself exactly why she was here—that she had a mission to accomplish in Las Vegas. She felt guilty about putting Petras and her mission on the back burner. She knew she had to get the file to him. He would be worried sick since Lotus had insisted he not get in touch with her, that it was safer for her to contact him. She had to find the time to get the file to him, but somehow Dash's image kept getting in the way.

Finally on Friday, when she was finishing up a morning stint at Mac's cafe, she looked over to the corner of the counter where Dash always sat waiting for her. She walked around and down the narrow aisle behind the counter to pause in front of him and smile while filling his coffee cup. The coffee was one of the things at Mac's that made the trip into the diner worthwhile. "Dash, I have to work another hour. Mac asked me if I would, and since I don't start my stint at the casino until eleven, I said yes. . . ."

"Why did you do that? You work hard enough the three hours you're here," he said, leaning over and taking her hand to his lips. "I saw the grease spatter hit your hand."

"Cool water and baking soda took care of it." Lotus felt breathless as she often did these days. It happened whenever Dash looked at her, grinned at her, touched her, kissed her. The list was endless and none of Lotus's hard-and-fast reasons for being sensible seemed to change the status quo. "Didn't you say that you had an important meeting at nine-thirty this morning?" Lotus quizzed, trying to regulate her heartbeat by taking deep breaths.

"Yes, but I'll put it off. . . ."

"No." She put her hand on his lips, feeling his mouth move against her fingers. "I'll ride my bike. It's a lovely day. The sun is shining, there's a breeze. And I need the exercise."

Dash watched her for a moment. "I don't like you being out on the highway—"

"Bike path," she interrupted him.

"Whatever," he said, snarling, not losing his scowl when she chuckled. "Promise me you'll be careful."

"I promise."

He shot out his hand to look at his wristwatch. "I should get to that meeting." Concern made a muscle jump at the side of his mouth. God, even in that simple, starchy waitress outfit she was wearing, she looked adorable. "All right. I'll meet you and we'll lunch at one."

"Fine." Lotus almost collapsed when he leaned over the Formica counter and kissed her full on the mouth.

"See you later, darling."

"Yes," Lotus promised not even noticing when another customer called to her.

At the end of an hour she left the cafe, feeling greasy, the odors of pancakes and eggs filling her nostrils. "First I'll ride over to Petras's shop, then I'll go home and take a quick shower . . ." she muttered to herself as she pedaled down the street to a more trafficked thoroughfare where the honking and screeching of the cars seemed to go right through her.

After traveling the ten blocks to Petras's camera shop, she parked her bike in the stand out front and went in the store, the bell over the door announcing her.

"I'll be right there," a voice said from a speaker placed in front of a curtained door leading to the back room.

Lotus knew it was Petras's habit to keep his cash box in the back room and his display case locked while he was in the back. She heard the whir of his wheelchair just moments before he came through the curtain. "Hi, friend," she greeted him.

"Lotus! Where have you been? I've been worried sick. I've tried to call three times, and the third time I called you were so mysterious. Weren't you able to get the file?"

"You weren't supposed to call." She tried to smile at the man who had been more like another brother to her. "I have it." She patted her tote bag. "I've been carrying it around in here for three days."

"What?" Petras looked up at her. "Are you crazy? If anyone at the casino discovers that file missing . . ." His lips compressed as he looked at her. "Richard has been very concerned about you too. You haven't been in contact with him either. My God, girl, do you know what could come down on you if anyone at Cicero's suspected?"

"They won't," Lotus said with more confidence than she felt. Now that she knew Dash better she was sure that he was tougher than either Richard or Petras had even guessed, but she didn't dare tell Petras that she had been in such close contact with the man he considered to be so dangerous. She wondered if he knew that Dash was sexually dangerous as well. She shook herself to clear her mind. She had to concentrate on the job at hand.

"Do you think you'll be able to copy it for me, so that I could get it back by tomorrow?" She pulled the folder from her bag. "I haven't had a chance to do anything more than glance at it, but this is the Sinclair file. I hope we can discover something."

Petras snatched it from her hand and wheeled his chair around with the agility of long use. "Put the sign in the window. I'm going to copy this now." He glared at her. "And I don't want you to return this to Colby's office. I want you to slip it under the door or leave it where someone will find it. You could even get it to Richard and let him return it. I don't want you involved in this any longer. Do you understand me?"

"But, Petras, I . . ."

"No buts, Lotus. This has gotten out of hand. Gamblers can play rough, and from what I understand of Colby, he is one tough cookie. He was in Vietnam like me, but he was a Huey pilot not infantry like Rob or me. . . ." Petras referred to her brother, Robert Sinclair, who had fought beside Petras in Vietnam and carried him back to their lines when Petras had been wounded. "Those

Huey pilots had the chutzpah of Satan himself. They flew those things right into the enemy guns. They would land and pick up our guys with the Vietcong breathing right down their necks. They had more than guts, Lotus; they had a Viking's flirtation with death. Are you getting the picture?"

Lotus nodded, biting her lip. More and more she realized that Petras mustn't ever know how involved she had become with Dash. She coughed, trying to smile. "Has the business been doing well?"

Petras stared at her another moment then nodded. "Better than even I expected. Martha has been doing the books for me now that the kids are in school. I owe your family a great deal, Lotus doll."

It had been her father who had insisted on starting Petras in his camera and film business in Las Vegas. Petras was devoted to her family, and though Lotus had sworn him to secrecy, she had no doubt that he would get in touch with her brothers if he thought there was any chance of her being in danger.

"Lotus, if I hadn't given my word that I would help you in your scheme and keep silent, I would get Rob out here to shag you back to Rochester," Petras iterated sternly as though he had been reading her mind.

Lotus smiled at him weakly, and followed him back to the big copying machine in the back room. "No need to do that. I intend to go home to Rochester as soon as possible." She sighed. "I was thinking that now might be the time to go to New York to try my luck as a photographer there." Lotus shrugged. "I always said I would do that."

The words dribbled away as though they had no substance. *Is that my escape from Dash Colby?*

Petras's eyes narrowed. "Is something wrong, Lotus?"

She shook her head, forcing a smile. What would he say if she told him that she thought she was in love, not only with a gambling man, but with the one who ran the business?

"Feeling a little smothered working in the family business? You've worked at Sinclair's since you were a teen-ager."

"That could be it," Lotus offered.

"I thought Rob told me you were dating Jeremy?"

"Now and then, but it's nothing serious." Lotus said no more, but she knew by Petras's scrutiny that he was trying to read her expression. She knew she was going to tell Jeremy she couldn't continue to see him when she returned home. How could she even date one man when she couldn't stop thinking about another? It wouldn't be fair to Jeremy or to her, and that's what she would tell him. "How are Martha and the kids?"

"Jeannie has a strep throat, and it looks like Kevin might come down with it. Other than that we're doing well. Stop trying to put me off, Lotus doll." Petras positioned the first paper of the file on the copier, pushed down the top, locked it, and pressed a button. He used a nickname her brothers had called her when she had been a baby. "You're like a kid sister to me, and I won't have you getting yourself into trouble. Now promise me you'll get rid of this file as quickly as possible, and you won't endanger yourself." He patted her hand. "And Martha wants you to come to dinner."

"Promise. And I want to come to dinner." Lotus leaned over his chair and kissed his head. "And I feel like your sister too. Rob was so afraid you would resent me because of my Oriental background, but you never have."

He smiled at her, before putting in the second sheet of the file. "Some of our guys resented Orientals after Vietnam, but most of them realized that we were all victims of greed and bad judgment." Petras was the head of the local Vietnam war veterans, and he often gave speeches about the needs and circumstances of former buddies. "Besides, you are just like your family whom I love. In fact, you're so like Rob and Todd that it's spooky." He put in the last paper of the file, then put the original back in the file and handed Lotus the copy. "Now promise me that you'll get on that plane tomorrow and get out of this town before anything happens that could tie you to this." He frowned up at her. "You could go to jail . . . and I think that might be the best thing that could happen to you if Dash Colby found out about all this."

Lotus shivered, her mind flashing to the happy moments she'd spent with Dash in the last three days. He had been happy, carefree, and relaxed, but she hadn't deluded herself that it had denoted weakness. She had watched him with others. She saw him eject an obstreperous person from the premises. His cold, implacable strength intimidated not just the man but many of the other people around him. "I know he's tough."

Petras's head shot up and he stared at her. "Don't you involve yourself with him, Lotus. He's a plastic explosive in Savile Row suits. Don't mess with him."

Lotus nodded, knowing that the smile she gave him was weak.

"By the way, Lotus, I have a connection in New York City, another vet, who's a photographer. If you decide to go, I'll get in touch with him."

She nodded. Then they talked for a few minutes about Christmas when Petras and his family would be coming East.

She left his shop, promising that she would have dinner with Martha and him and the children tonight before she flew East.

As she bicycled toward Cicero's casino, she pondered what Petras had said to her. "Maybe it would be better if I just threw the file in a corner and let someone find it . . ." she muttered as a motorist careened around her and blasted his horn. "Same to you, fella. I'm where I should be," Lotus shouted, the tough but fair Yankee upbringing she'd had never letting her back down, even to a disgruntled driver.

She was still arguing with herself when she reached the casino and put her bike in the stand, locked it, and carted her tote bag on her shoulder into the huge building.

"About time you got here, Lotus. Melanie's sick. She wants you to take her shift at noon," her boss, Harry, told her, rubbing his hands together agitatedly.

Lotus groaned and nodded. She owed Melanie a favor. No lunch for her today. She went down to the locker room, changed into her costume of black satin with the net ruffle across her backside. Impulsively, she shoved the folder in the bottom of the carrier for her camera equipment. *I can't just put this any old place. What if the person who finds it doesn't give it back? What if Dash decides to launch an investigation on how it got out of his office?* She shivered at all of the ramifications of her deed. *No. The best way is to return it to the office so that no one will know it has ever been removed.*

She strolled up the long corridor leading to Dash's office, trying to give the impression that she was where she belonged. She smiled at the other staff members hurrying past her. She had reached the short hall, more lavishly decorated than the corridor she had just traversed, when she saw Amy Blaisdell step out of Dash's office. The bespectacled Amy was a valued employee at Cicero's, but not one that Lotus would have chosen to see. She was the accountant!

"Hi, Lotus," Amy called to her when Lotus paused. "The boss said you might stop by his office. Did you want to go inside?" Amy gave her a knowing look. "He said you were to be allowed in at any time."

Lotus gave a weak laugh, not able to look Amy in the eye. "I just want to talk to him for a minute." She didn't, but she supposed she could tell him that she couldn't meet him for lunch which was true, since she was filling in for Melanie.

"Oh, he isn't there. Neither is Hans, but you can go in, if you like. . . ." Amy's lips compressed a bit.

Lotus knew Amy resented anyone else having access to the private offices but herself or Hans. Amy was very conscious of the pecking order. Lotus blinked as Amy's words sank home. The office was empty! "Well, maybe I'll just leave him a note. Shall I lock it when I leave?"

"The automatic lock is on."

"Fine." Lotus let the door of the office swing

shut in Amy's face, heaving a sigh of relief that neither the outer or inner sanctum was occupied. "Luck, you are a lady." She gave a giddy laugh, then almost ran into the inner office to the file cabinet. She didn't have a key! "Damn, damn, damn," she mumbled to herself. She hoped the ice-pick that Petras had given her would be in her camera bag. She ransacked the bag and was about to give up when she felt a sharp jab against her finger. "How like me to find it that way," she muttered, sucking her finger where a dot of blood showed.

Grimly, she attacked the door and hastily scratched it with the sharp instrument, gouging the finish on the wood. "Damn. I hope I still have the cleaning liquid in here," she muttered.

It seemed to her that it took longer to open the door than it had when she'd done it the first time, but she kept at it until it popped. Then, without taking a breath, she tackled the individual lock on the drawer. After an eternity of jabbing and turning, it, too, snapped open. Her hands were trembling so much that when she lifted the folder to slide it between the ones marked SIMMONS and SIPPEL, she had to try three times before the folder dropped into place. She closed the drawer, her sweaty hands slipping on the surface of the metal, then as quietly as she could she closed the outer door.

After she'd sprayed the cleaner and wiped the area, she shoved the bottle back in her bag and closed it. Then she wiped her perspiring face with a tissue she'd pulled from her bag. "Get out of here, Lotus," she warned herself.

As she scampered across the inner office to the

reception area, she remembered that she hadn't left the note she told Amy she was going to leave for Dash. When she scuttled back to the office, her trembling hands made it difficult for her to hold the pen. It took twice as long to write the message. "I can't see you at one o'clock for lunch because I have to take Melanie's shift." Finally she scratched out her name, then lifted a paperweight and placed it on top of her note. Finally, she replaced Dash's gold pen in its holder

"What are you doing in here?" It was Hans Melford, Dash's righthand man. He scowled at her and she jumped. His eyes shot from her to the desk and back again.

"Ah . . . Amy let me in so that I could leave Dash a note," Lotus said and struggled to control her breathing. The man was a threat! He never seemed to do anything but frown, and he moved like a wraith! "You could ask Dash . . ." Lotus continued.

"No need. He said you were to come in here whenever you chose." He stood against the open door, more or less inviting her to leave.

Lotus shivered as she walked by him. He didn't trust her! She prayed he wouldn't look in the file drawer and see the scratch on the door that not even the cleaning fluid masked completely. "Good-bye," she said, and hurried away.

She barely noticed her growling stomach as she photographed the flux of customers in the early shift. It was a good shift for a Foto girl because the diehard gamblers didn't arrive until much later. There were more tourists in this shift.

While she worked she thought about what had happened.

She had stayed too long in Las Vegas, and should never have involved herself with Dash. He represented everything she feared and hated. If it hadn't been for men like him, her uncle would not have been charged with a crime he hadn't committed. She must never forget that. She had the copy of the file. She had stayed longer than she should have, and right at that very moment Hans Melford might have discovered the scratch and be piecing things together. She shuddered at the thought, then smiled at a customer who raised a quizzical eyebrow at her.

"That's a great picture." A round man with eyes like agates smiled at her, then showed the instant camera print to his equally plump wife

"Thank you, sir. Ah, excuse me just a moment." Lotus left the gaming room where she had been taking pictures and went out to the lobby to the rows of public telephones. She dialed and waited. "Petras? Yes, it's Lotus. I'm ready to leave, if I can get a flight out tomorrow. You will? Oh, that's nice. Of course I'll get over to the house. Yes, I'll be here, if you want to call me back. They'll page me. Thanks."

When she hung up the phone, she stood there staring at the receiver, listening to the signal that told her the connection was broken. Tomorrow she would be leaving Las Vegas, leaving Dash. Her heart seemed to squeeze in her chest, sending a pain of loss through her whole system. She was losing Dash!

"Aren't you going to hang up the phone?" His silken laugh coiled around her as he took the receiver from her hand and replaced the instrument. "You're pale. What is it? Aren't you feeling well?" He lifted her, cameras and all, up his chest so that he could scrutinize her. "You're working too hard . . . and now you want to give up your lunch. No way. You're eating with me. Do you want to make yourself ill?"

Lotus looked into his eyes and shook her head. *I want you,* she said in her mind, her hands coming up to clutch his neck. *I'm losing you and I don't want that.* Her eyes felt damp.

"Lotus . . . baby." Dash felt her panic. "I'm getting you out of here."

"Can't." Lotus gulped. "Have to work." Where had all her restraint gone? What had happened to the stiff-upper-lip theory she had always subscribed to? She rubbed her hair against his chin.

He let her slide down his body, keeping her sheltered from the curious eyes of passersby, but not releasing his hold on her. "I'm getting you out of here. Hans will find someone to fill in for you."

Lotus felt immobilized, disoriented. "Can he do that?"

"Yes." Dash looked around him, his face a polite mask as people gazed at him. "Let's go." Keeping his arm around her, he led her to the office, went through the outer office to his own, then punched a few buttons on a console. "Hans, I want to see you, please."

When the stocky assistant entered, his eyes narrowed on Lotus, but other than that he made no sign that he even knew she was there. "You wanted me, Dash?"

"Yes." In short sentences Dash told Hans what he wanted done. "Get Harry to find a substitute for Lotus." Then he dismissed him. He looked at Lotus. "You're still white. I don't like that." He punched a few more numbers on the console then spoke again, his voice muffled when he half turned away from her. When he faced her again, he was smiling. "You're coming with me. I'm taking you to my house."

"But I can't, my own shift starts in a short time and . . ." Lotus bit her lip. She had been about to say that she had to wait for Petras to call and tell her what time her flight was tomorrow, but she caught herself in time. "Well, you know . . ." she finished weakly, wishing she could go with him and stay with him all day. How could she think such a thing! Petras would be calling soon! She couldn't stay with Dash.

"Your job is all taken care of," Dash informed her, his eyes roving over her. "That costume is too brief. I don't like all the men who come through this casino seeing you that way."

"Most of them don't see me." Lotus smiled. "They're thinking about gambling." It surprised her that he would say that! Many of the show girls wore even skimpier costumes than hers. Then she remembered what she had to tell him. "Dash, I can't come . . . anywhere with you. After my shift, I'm going to a . . . that is, I was just going to have something simple and go home."

"I'm taking you home with me." Dash was adamant.

"Ah . . . but . . ."

"And don't try to figure me out, Lotus. I can't work out why I feel the way I do about you." His rueful smile lifted a corner of his mouth, giving his lips a mysterious satanic style that made her catch her breath.

"Where are we going?" Lotus wondered if she

should try to get a message to Petras, then she decided that it might be too risky. But he and Martha were expecting her for a meal! She groaned inwardly. There were so many reasons not to go with Dash. How was she to get a message to Petras? And more important, how was she to prevent herself from falling more in love with Dash?

"My home. It's on the edge of the desert and very private. We'll have a swim and some canapes, then we'll have a dinner." He grinned at her. "That I will cook for you."

"Oh. Will I survive it?" Lotus couldn't chase away the lightheartedness she felt. Her voice of reason was buried as she thought of being with him. She would be spending hours with Dash! She would be leaving tomorrow, but for now she would savor the moment. From the time she'd been a child, she had always projected into the future, her goals and aims always in front of her, but now she was going to put it all aside. Today, this minute, was all she would consider.

Dash bent over her, kissing her nose. "You will not only survive. You will enjoy it."

Lotus laughed out loud.

Dash's smile disappeared. He cupped her face with his hands. "That is also a very beautiful thing about you, China Doll." His mouth nuzzled her lips, parting them, letting his tongue quest gently over her teeth to the roof of her mouth

Lotus's heart dropped to her feet, then soared up and out of her body. Even as her eyes closed and she sagged against him, she knew that he was the One who had walked her dreams when she was a child. He was the Knight, the Warrior, the Hero who would sweep her away and keep her safe all her life. As her rational mind told her she was a fool, that he was gambler, a womanizer, a high-road freewheeler, her heart told her that she loved him. Even if she never saw Dash again, she knew that there would never be anyone who would come close to taking his place.

"Open your eyes, darling." Dash's voice was hoarse. "We have to get out of here." He grasped her hand in his and pulled her along behind him, his long strides making her run. "Now hurry and change." He left her in the locker room.

She changed in record time, curses escaping her lips when she fumbled with a snap or zipper. She had to get to Dash! She thought this as she rushed from the locker room and he was there, waiting to grasp her hand again. They ran from the building like children.

When they reached his Ferrari parked behind Cicero's, she was out of breath. "Whew! I'm glad you weren't parked blocks away . . ." Lotus wheezed, bringing Dash's gaze around to her.

He frowned, then his brow cleared and he looked contrite. "Sorry, love. I forgot for a moment how tiny you are."

"Five feet five is not tiny," Lotus said, after he seated her in the front seat, then went around to climb in under the wheel. "Only a giant would make that statement. How ever did you get so tall?"

"I come from an old Boston family. Being tall is a prerequisite."

"You come from an old Boston family!" Lotus exclaimed incredulously . "I'm sure they're delighted they have a gambler in the family."

Dash's mouth lifted in hard amusement. "Oh, yes, they're delighted."

"Are you joking about your family?" Lotus asked.

He glanced at her for a second, then back to the road as they sped out of the city proper into the countryside. "No. I'm not joking. You're right about one thing. Two of my sisters would definitely have consigned me to the devil long ago if I weren't holding some of the purse strings in the family." His grin widened. "My assorted cousins have degrees to their armpits, but not much common sense. It has been my dubious honor to bail them out from time to time." His voice deepened into a broad Boston accent. "One does not give up one's box at the opera because one is temporarily out of funds."

Lotus chuckled. "They don't talk like that. Do they?"

"They do. Now tell me about your family. Where are you from? Why did you come to Las Vegas?"

He had asked the question in a friendly way, but all Lotus's fears about what she had done, and what her family had gone through, rose like choking smoke in her mind. Did he suspect her? Was he masking his real feelings? And was he just stringing her along until he had her dead to rights? Would he call the police? Have her arrested?

"Love, you're pale again." Dash reached for her hand, bringing it to his lips. "I want you to be happy, healthy. I want to take care of you."

His warm voice melted her paranoia and washed her fears away. He was Dash . . . and he was special. She leaned her head back and looked at him, then let her gaze wander.

Lotus was about to ask him more about his family when she became aware that they were out in the desert. Being a Northeasterner, she had never been to a desert. She forgot what she was going to ask him as she stared at the rough, coarse beauty of Nevada.

"Like it?"

"Oh, yes," Lotus whispered. "I've never seen anything like it. It must be wonderful to explore it."

"It is, but don't you try it alone. Getting lost out here is anything but funny. Someday I'll take you out into the desert camping."

Lotus's heart wrenched. *No, you won't, because I won't ever see you again after today.*

"Darling? Whatever you're thinking about can't be pleasant. Look at me." Dash had stopped the car in front of a three-car garage that looked as though it had been built into the side of the hill. "We're here."

"So we are." Lotus felt her smile wobble off her face. She turned in the seat to face him because he seemed to expect it as he leaned his left arm on the steering wheel and watched her. "I was just thinking about . . . about"—her mind went blank—"about nothing," she finished, seeing the flash of disbelief on his face before his hard smile replaced it.

"Out of the car, China Doll. I want to show you my home."

"Is it underground?" She stepped from the car, delighted to lean against him when he pulled her to his side.

"It looks that way from here, and I do have this side recessed in the hill, but the other overlooks a shallow valley and dry creek bed. You can see for miles."

"Do you own much of the land around here?'

"About seventy acres."

Lotus could feel her lips parting. "That's quite a bit of land."

"Yes." His answer was noncommittal. *What are you hiding from me, my sweet? I can't figure you out, but I'm not letting go of you. You intrigue the hell out of me and I want to know what makes you run, because you are running, my China doll, and running hard.*

"I'm not the only one who daydreams," Lotus said and looked up at him, thinking how handsome he looked with the sun flashing silver in his ash blond hair.

"But I was thinking about you, China Doll."

There was silken menace in his voice. Lotus pulled back from him and stared up into his face. "Why do I feel threatened?"

Animosity toward her melted away. He stared down at the brave look of her, her chin in the air, her small hands curling into fists. "I was angry, that's true. I sense that you're not being open with me. I hate that, but I'm not going to let it stand in the way of our beautiful day. Sorry. Truce?"

"Truce." Lotus breathed a sigh of relief. She had today and she would use it to get to know him, to build memories with him, that she could pull out of her mind and scan when she was unhappy.

Lotus was stunned when she saw his house. It was very modern, with simple decor. All the wood was cedar and pine. There were no painted walls, not even in the bathroom, as she discovered. The ceilings were high and vaulted and the open side of the house looked out over the valley with floor-to-ceiling glass, yet there was privacy, since all the land as far as could be seen belonged to Dash.

"It's lovely, so wild ... and free ..." Lotus whispered, feeling him come up behind her as she looked out the window wall of the living room into the spectacular valley.

"Come and see the kitchen, so you'll trust me when I tell you that I can cook."

"How many women have you cooked for here?" The minute the question was out of her mouth, Lotus regretted it. "Sorry, don't answer that. It's none of my business."

"No, it isn't, but I will tell you that I mostly entertain other women at my apartment above the casino and that I don't cook for them." Dash leaned down and kissed her neck. "Come and see the kitchen."

Lotus could feel her entire body blush as she imagined the things he did other than cooking in his apartment.

The kitchen gleamed with chrome and steel. There were three ovens and a microwave, and built-ins everywhere. It was when Dash led her to the well-stocked pantry that she gasped. Every herb and condiment that could be thought of was there. Dried peppers and herbs hung in bunches from the ceiling along with pots and pans. There were more pots and pans that hung above the work island in the middle of the kitchen.

"I like it. I'll help."

"That's the idea. Would you like to wash up? My bedroom suite is through there. Use that."

Lotus's gaze slipped across his face and away. "I can use the guest room."

"I know. I would like you to see mine, and I know you would be more comfortable seeing it alone rather than with me."

Lotus nodded, relieved that he had made it easier for her. She walked the length of the deck bordering the sunken living room and dining room to the hall leading to his bedroom suite.

His room was in earth tones. It was as though the desert continued right into the room. The vivid orange and greens of the throw pillows were a welcome foil for the browns, tans, and beiges of the rest of the area. She looked at the sitting room with its floor-to-ceiling bookshelves filled with volumes of prose and poetry, and some on ethics, economics, and engineering.

Lotus used the very masculine bathroom all in beige, with turquoise and blue azulejos on the floor and walls and delighted in the feel of the fluffy towels after the thin ones she had been using at her rooming house. She ran a covetous eye over the hot tub and wished she could use it; instead, she washed her hands, and then wandered back into the main part of the house.

She found Dash in the kitchen, an open cookbook in front of him "What shall I do?" She felt shy suddenly.

"Tear the spinach for the salad. We're going to have hot spinach salad. It's very good."

Lotus swallowed as her mouth began to water. She hadn't had much to eat because she had been in a hurry and concerned about returning the file to Dash's office.

The bell on the stove rang and Dash opened one of the upper stoves, a thick glove on his hand. "Here we are. Artichoke canape. We can munch these while we get the other things ready. I hope you like lobster."

"I don't like it. I love it." Lotus watched him put

the hot dish on the wooden segment of the island work area. The rest of the surface was tile with orange and green azulejos interspersing to carry through the color scheme of the front room.

Dash walked toward her with a section of artichoke canape in a napkin, watching her face. *She's still very shy with me.* "Taste." He held the piece up to her mouth, feeling his heart beat as she bit into the hot food. "Good?" he asked her.

Lotus nodded, one hand fanning her mouth as she chewed, then swallowed. "Hot. Good." She smiled up at him, feeling her face go flaccid as he bent toward her and kissed her, his tongue running along her lips, then entering her mouth. Lotus was sure her legs were going to buckle.

He took her full weight against him, loving the feel of her. He lifted his head a fraction, his body bent over her. "There was a crumb of food at the corner of your mouth. Waste not, want not, my Boston Yankee grandmother taught me."

"Wise maxim," Lotus said and gasped, still leaning on him. "Haven't finished the spinach yet."

"Shame on you," Dash muttered, not releasing her.

Lotus pushed back from him with shaky hands. "I'm hungry."

He grinned at her, masking his own excitement, delighted that she would be as affected as he was by their embrace. "You win." When she turned away from him to the small sink where the washed spinach was set in a collander, he let his one hand feather down over her small but rounded backside. "Very nice," he whispered in her hair as she arched toward the sink. "Very, very nice."

"Thank you." Lotus babbled, then could have kicked herself for sounding so inane.

They finished the preparations in companionable silence to the strains of the love ballads that were coming from the stereo system that seemed to be in every room.

The last thing they did was broil the lobster tails over the open hickory fire

Dash fitted an apron on her as she stood next to him watching him turn the seafood. "I don't want you to get too close to the fire. You could be burned again like you were this morning when the grease spattered on you." He frowned down, then lifted her hand to his mouth, kissing the red mark. "You got this when you went too close to the grill."

"It doesn't hurt anymore," Lotus said. But she didn't want him to stop kissing her hand. It drove her crazy.

Dining with Dash was fun! This continually amazed Lotus. It was so diverting and relaxing to be with him. Not even her brothers, whom she loved, made her feel so comfortable . . . and they certainly didn't bring out the other feelings she experienced with Dash!

"What are you thinking, love?" Dash asked her as he put another broiled lobster tail on her plate and proceeded to cut and lift the meat from the shell.

"How nice this is." She could feel laughter brimming inside her as she watched him. "But I feel I should tell you that I've been cutting my own meat and feeding myself since I was quite small." She opened her mouth and took a forkful of food from him.

"How innovative of you! Now feed me," Dash told her, leaning toward her and opening his mouth.

Right through the cheese and fruit they had, they fed each other. Lotus told herself to stop, put on the brakes, and that this man spelled danger with a capital *D*. He wasn't good for her and she could list the reasons why he wasn't. All her adjurations to herself had substance and she found them valid, but she felt caught in Dash's web . . . and she didn't want to free herself. She wanted him to be hers . . . for just a little while.

Dash watched the play of emotions over her face. He could read the struggle within her. It irritated him to think that he was holding his breath lest she decided to leave him, because he knew that if she rose and told him that she didn't want to stay, he would take her back to her little fourth-floor room in that ramshackle house.

"Stay with me." He hadn't wanted to say such a thing. Pride had always dictated his moves with women. He had never asked any of them to stay with him. If they did, fine; if they wanted to leave, they could do that too. He had wanted no ties, no commitments, neither had the women with whom he had involved himself. But he knew he didn't want Lotus to go. "Stay with me tonight."

She looked into the azure richness of his eyes, ready to tell him that she would be going as soon as they finished eating. "Yes. I'll stay," she heard herself tell him.

"You will?" Dash questioned, not sure that her soft response had been what he'd heard, or if it had just been what he wanted to hear.

"Yes," she repeated, feeling the rush of blood

up her face. She had just told him that she was going to spend the night with him. She had never said such a thing to any of her other boyfriends, Jeremy included, and yet she considered some of those relationships pretty serious. Her only sexual experience had been when she'd been twenty and a junior in college. It had been uncomfortable and unrewarding. She was not anxious to repeat it, and none of the urgings of her friends at school to try it again had changed her mind. But now she was telling a man that she barely knew that she would spend the night with him . . . and she was delighted, not apprehensive, with the idea. She stared at her wineglass.

"You haven't had that much champagne, darling, just half a glass." He leaned over and lifted the palm of her right hand to his lips. "If you change your mind . . . at anytime, at any moment, tell me. It will end then. Just say a simple no."

She looked at him and knew that he would take her home at anytime. She smiled at him and leaned toward him and kissed the fingers that were curled around her hand. "I know that."

Dash felt as though he were crumbling, yet he had never felt so buoyant, so alive . . . so conceited, because she trusted him. He was proud and humble at the same time. "Thank you for the lovely compliment, China Doll."

"You're welcome."

He rose and went behind her chair to direct her toward the living room.

Lotus balked. "We should do the dishes."

"I have help come in every day."

"I still think we should rinse them. It's an awful

job to clean hardened-on food. If we run water on them, it will be easier."

"We rinse the dishes." *What a love she was,* he thought, watching her as she preceded him into the kitchen carrying the cutlery, *and what a darling shape.* His pulse kicked into overdrive just watching her.

They stood hip to thigh as they rinsed the dishes, smiling at each other often.

"If anyone had told me that rinsing dishes in my own kitchen could be fun, I would have had them certified; but it is a delight," he murmured as he led her out of the kitchen into the living room area, his one arm around her.

"I never thought of it as fun before . . . but that's because I was always arguing with my brothers about whose turn it was to do the dishes." Lotus smiled up at him, then caught herself. She mustn't talk about her family! She might slip and tell him too much. Dash Colby was a very sharp man. He needed very little information to add two and two and get a conclusion.

"Tell me more about your family." He could feel his eyes narrowing on her. He had sensed her withdrawal. What was bothering her?

"There's not much to tell. Most of the time we're happy with each other." She took a deep breath. "Besides, I told you a great deal about myself; yet, you haven't told me anything about you."

She's putting me off again, he thought smothering his irritation. "Ask away."

"Are you an only child?"

"No. I'm the middle of five children. I have two older sisters, a younger brother and sister. They all live in Boston. The three girls are married. Alan is still looking."

"Like you."

"No. I've stopped looking." The sensual twist to his smile had Lotus blinking.

"Then you two will be the only single ones." Lotus couldn't hold his gaze. "Watch out, your mother will be after you."

"Not to mention my father, my uncles and aunts and my cousins. . . ." Dash grazed her cheek with his lips.

"It sounds as though you have a large family." She gave a breathless laugh.

"A mob scene." He watched her, amazed that her laugh could bring him such a good feeling.

"Was it your parents who called you Dash?"

"My mother calls me Dasher, but that's an old family name and she would never think of shortening it to Dash. My sisters and brother shortened it, as I recall, though when my sisters are angry they call me Dasher."

"I like Dash," Lotus said, settling on a long couch set at right angles to the oak-manteled stone fireplace.

He walked to a sideboard, poured thimbleful sizes of liqueur, and sat very close to her on the furry white settee. "I hope you like Dash, and not just his name." He handed her a glass and sat down again, his arm along the back of the settee.

Lotus sipped the strong liquid tinged with the taste of orange and wrinkled her nose. "Different."

"Grand Marnier, love. Don't you like it?"

"I've never had it before, but I think a couple of sips is fine." She leaned back against the overstuffed upholstery, happy when his arm dropped to her shoulder and he scooped her into the curve of his body.

"Then leave it, sweet. You can't be tipsy on half a glass of champagne and a thimble of liqueur," he told her, his soft voice ruffling the hair on her forehead

"I know." She closed her eyes and sagged against him. When he sighed, she could feel her pulse rate jump. In lazy excitement she watched him place her tiny glass on the coffee table in front of the couch along with his. It was her turn to sigh when he put his other arm across her waist and pulled her even closer to him.

"I know this must seem too quick to you, angel, but I want you so much. I have wanted you from the moment I saw you in my office the first day." He tilted up her chin. It both jolted and gladdened him to see the serene acceptance in her face. "Do you want me?" He had never asked that question in his life! He had always assumed that the women he pursued wanted him as much as he wanted them. He never had had reason to suppose that such a supposition was incorrect.

"Yes, but don't expect too much." She felt calm. "My experience hasn't been as extensive as you might think for someone my age. . . ." She lifted her hand and rubbed it on his chin. "You have bristles already."

"Which I will shave off, my darling." He felt his face crease in concern. "Are you a virgin, love?"

"No . . . but I can't say that I've enjoyed sex." *Which was only once,* she told him in her mind, *and Alex Venet was a flop as a lover.*

He watched her for long minutes, his mind turning over, computing the small amount of information she had given him and coming up with the full picture. *Some clod was her first and only lover,* Dash grated, *and though my China doll doesn't say it, she is a little afraid of making love.* "If you are at all unsure we won't do anything but kiss a little, hug, nuzzle." He punctuated each word with the action, feeling her small frame wriggle against him. "You don't mind that, do you?" His voice was thick.

"I like it when you touch me," Lotus told him, her hands coming up to rub up and down his skin, the light bristling of his cheeks an erotic stimulation to her being.

Dash rose to his feet, pulling her with him. "Come with me while I shave."

"I'd like that." Lotus meant it. Doing the most mundane things with Dash were fraught with excitement, she mused.

They ambled out of the living room, across the tiled foyer and along the corridor to his suite.

"You've decorated this house with American Indian artifacts. I like that," Lotus said in lazy happiness when he led her into the master suite, through the sitting room to the large cream-colored bathroom. "I like your hot tub." Lotus leaned against the vanity while he shaved.

With half his face covered in shaving cream, he smiled at her, leaned toward a console and flipped a switch. The hot tub began churning at once, and in minutes, the steam on the surface was being carried through vents in the tiled ceiling. "Be my guest."

Lotus looked from him to the hot tub and back again. "All right." She left him and went into the dressing room, closed the door, and removed her clothes. With a towel wrapped around her, she returned to the large bathroom, smiling at Dash who was waiting for her freshly shaven . . . and naked except for a towel around his waist. "That didn't take you long," she told him.

"The thought of getting into that hot tub with you speeded things up considerably."

Lotus went right up to him, her eyes never leaving his, even when he leaned down and lifted her up, his one arm across her shoulder blades, the other under her buttocks. "I feel very tall," she whispered, her mouth less than an inch from his.

"I feel able to leap tall buildings myself, my sweet lady. By the way your towel is slipping."

"Is it?" Lotus whispered.

"Yes." He bent his head and began to kiss her throat, her collarbone, then her breasts.

Lotus's fingers dug into his skull. She couldn't have suppressed the groan that escaped her if her life had depended on it. She was still holding him that way when he pushed the towels away from both their bodies and then stepped down into the tub and lowered them both into the hot swirling water. Lotus was sure her body was filling with helium as Dash continued to caress her, to love her. Their bodies bent and swayed in the current of water yet their mouths clung, then quested over each other's form. She wanted him to love her so much all earlier qualms left her.

Finally after an eternity of loving, when Lotus knew that her blood was bubbling faster than the water, Dash lifted her in his arms and stepped out of the tub to rub her body with an exotic emollient, then pat her dry.

"Your skin is delicate. It needs protecting," he told her as he carried her through to the bedroom. "I will protect you in all ways, my China doll, even from my love."

"That's good because I didn't come prepared," she told him out of breath.

He chuckled into her hair, his hands tightening on her.

She had a moment's earthbound sanity. How could she be making love with a man who could destroy her uncle and others like him? She hated gambling and gamblers. She stared at the face so close to her own. Does he know who I am? Would he set a trap for me this way? She clutched at him, her mouth seeking his. Her uncomfortable thoughts melted away and there was only Dash.

Nothing in Lotus's life had prepared her for the sensual onslaught as Dash loved her body from her ankle to her chin, not missing a pore as his mouth went over her. With mounting impatience she resorted to a similar attack as instinct guided her hands and mouth. When she heard him groan, her blood pressure went through the roof and she wriggled against him with joy.

"Darling! Don't! Let me love you . . ." Dash told her thickly.

"I am. And I am loving you."

"You are indeed," he murmured.

His tongue explored into her body, surprising her, arching her against him. She called out his name as passsion filled her.

When he parted her legs and slid between them, she was ready and eager to be joined with him. She had the feeling of soaring on a meteor as the rhythm of the love took them, propelling them past the sun and the stars. "Dash! Dash!" Lotus called to him

"I'm here with you, darling."

They spiraled together, poised above Venus, to fall in gentle plummet back to earth and each other.

"I love you. I love you." It stunned her when he said that to her.

"I love you too." That shocked and delighted her too, when she answered him back.

"Marry me," Dash groaned in her ear.

CHAPTER THREE

"Marry me, marry me, marry me, marry me . . ." the jet engines on the plane sang as Lotus flew east from Las Vegas to Rochester, New York, with a stopover at O'Hare in Chicago. The words that Dash had said to her filled her mind. She couldn't concentrate on anything else. And she had told him she loved him back! He had made love to her all through the night, and she knew before morning that she belonged to him for all time. She groaned in her mind as she stared sightlessly out at the clouds scudding past the wing of the plane. And she did love him! Her eyes were dry but tears coursed through her being as she thought of Dash and all she had given up when she fled from Cicero's.

Petras had booked her flight and she had taken a taxi from her rooming house after telling Dash she had to change for work and that she would see him later.

It was as though she were with him still on that huge bed of his, lazy eyes alight with fire as he looked down at her.

"Cat got your tongue?" he had whispered as he

stared down at her after loving her and making the declaration.

"Marriage is a very serious step," Lotus had replied from the circle of his arm, her one hand caressing his fresh shaven cheek.

"Very." Dash's smile had been white heat. "I heard you say that you loved me."

"Did you hear that?" Lotus's voice had tremored. "I heard you say it too."

"Yes." His mouth had begun a slow search of her breast. "So when shall we marry?"

"Could I have a little time to think about it?" She wanted to tell him no, that she was going back home, but she couldn't destroy what was between them with such words. She wanted to hold it, cherish it, keep it . . . forever.

"Five minutes?"

She had smiled up at him and shook her head. "Let me think about it."

Dash could feel his being stiffen in resistance. He didn't want her to think. He wanted her to say yes, then they would find someone to marry them at once! He wanted to keep her. "All right." He expelled a big sigh and nodded. He didn't think there was a someone like Lotus for him on the planet and now that he had found her, he didn't want her out of his sight.

When Lotus tried to rise from the bed, he'd urged her back again. "I want to love you," Dash had told her.

Lotus ran every reason why she should get up from that bed, dress, and leave around her head. They dissipated like smoke in a wind as she lifted her arms to hold him, embrace him, and lock him to her body.

They had made love again. The gentle frenzy generated by Dash had left her gasping with delight and awe, as it would do all through the night.

They were still lying on the bed holding each other the next morning when the phone rang next to the bed.

"Colby," Dash had barked. "Yes. Damn it, man, you don't need me for that. All right, all right, I said I'd come and I will." Dash cradled the phone with barely suppressed violence. "I have an appointment." He turned to look at her. "Another casino has come on the market. My business adviser assures me it's a good deal." Dash grimaced and hugged her close to him. "The last thing I want to think about is business, but I gave my word I would make this meeting. Will you wait for me here?"

Lotus felt shot with lightning. She had to go home today! She couldn't stay any longer! She had the file. "Dash, take me back to my room, please. I need a change of clothes." *And I need to say good-bye to you,* she added silently. She reached out and clung to him, her lips coursing his face and neck.

"Darling," Dash groaned. "I won't leave you."

"Yes. You must. Go to your meeting. I'll see you later."

Dash's face was expressionless as he studied her, his eyes seeming to X-ray her being. "I'll drop back to pick you up."

Lotus bit her lip, then nodded, her smile feeling painful as she stretched it across her mouth.

They rose and dressed, separating for moments only as each one took turns using the bathroom.

Sometimes Dash would stop and kiss her, startling her out of her painful reverie.

When they were driving back to Las Vegas, Dash kept hold of her hand, often kissing the palm, his teeth nibbling at the sensitive skin on her wrist.

Returning to her rented room, he came around to her side of the car and opened her door, leading her in the house and following her up the four flights of stairs to her tiny attic room, the ceiling slanted over the eaves. The dormer windows provided little sunlight.

"I'll be glad to get you out of here," Dash muttered as he ducked to keep from striking his head on the low ceiling.

"You'd better hurry. . . ." Lotus felt a sudden surge of tears as she embraced him.

"I'll see you later, darling." Dash kissed her long and lingeringly, then let his mouth trace her jawline and throat. "Take care," he told her huskily, then was gone.

Lotus didn't do anything until she had stood on tiptoe and pressed herself against her one window that would allow her to see the street. Yes, that was Dash's car pulling away.

In a daze, she phoned Petras and told him what she was doing. "So I can take a flight out today. . . ."

"Lotus, my God. We've been so worried. When you didn't come to dinner and didn't call . . ." Petras's voice cracked over the phone. "I almost went out of my mind."

"I'm sorry about the dinner and not calling," Lotus responded in a reedy voice. "I was detained."

"Martha and I were so worried about you. Are you all right?"

"Yes," she lied. She was dying, but how could she tell Petras that she was bleeding from a thousand cuts because she wouldn't be seeing the one love of her life again? She inhaled, trying to smother the groan that rose in her throat at the image of the gray existence she would have for the rest of her life. She would never marry! She could never pretend to feel the explosion of feeling for anyone else.

"Lotus, I never should have let you get involved in this. I can tell, even over the phone, that something is wrong. You have to get home as soon as possible. Lotus, listen to me. You get right to the airport. I'll get the first flight out for you. I'll book it under the name of L. Sinclair. I'll try to get you patched straight though, but I'll take anything, even a milk flight. You don't have much packing, do you?"

"No." Lotus smothered the sob that rose in her throat. She was only leaving behind her whole being. Dash had that and no matter what happened it was his.

"Lotus, are you really all right?" Petras's voice softened. "Why don't you come to the store? Martha is here and she can drive you to the airport. You need someone to talk to, I can tell." Urgency sharpened Petras's tone. "I'll send Martha back with you."

"No!" Lotus almost shouted. "No," she repeated, her voice lowered. "I'm all right. It's . . . it's just been a bit much."

"You aren't hurt, are you? Did anyone approach you?" Anxiety threaded his inquiry.

"No, I'm fine, really. I'm sorry I didn't get to

the house to visit with the children again." Lotus strived to speak normally.

"We'll be coming east for the holidays. Your mother writes Martha every week describing all the things she has planned for our visit."

Lotus's voice was shaking but she managed to laugh. "I know. She's planning a big get-together of all yours and Rob's friends from the service who are within a fifty-mile radius."

Petras laughed again, relief in his voice that she sounded relaxed. "Yes. And she has also planned a few trips for the children. I can't believe how good she is, Lotus."

"You shouldn't forget that she considers you and Martha her children, not just friends, ergo your children are her grandchildren."

"Yes, I know that."

"I really should go . . . get my things ready."

"Yes. Be careful, little sister."

"Yes." She knew she had to get off the line or she'd burst into tears. "I have to pack. Thank you for everything, Petras. I'll see you and Martha when you come to Rochester at Christmas."

"Right. Listen, sweetie, take care, will you?" Petras sounded uneasy.

"I will. Thanks. Good-bye. And, Petras, I'm fine, really I am."

She hung up and began to pack the few things she'd brought with her. Then she paid Mrs. Weltz, the owner of the house, who allowed her to use the house phone to call a taxi.

"It was nice meeting you, dearie. Where should I forward your mail if any comes?"

"Ah . . . I don't think there will be any mail," Lotus hedged.

"Seems funny you don't want me to forward things," Mrs. Weltz probed.

"Well, you see, I didn't have anyone write to me here." Lotus turned away from the woman when the taxi service answered their phone. "Yes, I'll be waiting outside the house," Lotus told the dispatcher.

Mrs. Weltz followed her out onto the rickety porch. "Won't some of your friends here want to know where you've gone?"

"No."

"Seems strange to me," Mrs. Weltz muttered, walking with Lotus to the curb, her arms folded across her ample breasts. "You ain't in trouble with the law, are you?"

"I am not." Lotus frowned at the sharp-eyed Mrs. Weltz.

"You can't be too careful in my business," Mrs. Weltz explained. "There are a lot of folks who try to chisel helpless ladies like me."

Lotus stared at the large woman at her side, who probably weighed on the sunny side of one hundred and ninety pounds, and nodded.

"You run a clean, decent house and there's them that would spoil it for you," Mrs. Weltz expounded, in no hurry to leave Lotus.

Lotus glanced quickly at the sagging house behind them, then at Mrs. Weltz.

"Cab won't be here for a time yet." Mrs. Weltz glinted at her. "Sure you don't want to tell me where I can reach you?"

Yes, I'm sure." Lotus heaved a sigh of relief when she saw the taxi turn the corner and slow down. She waved.

"It seems to me that by the time you get where

you're going on the bus, you might have mail that could be there to meet you if you had a forwarding address," Mrs. Weltz pursued doggedly. "You are going on the bus, ain't you?"

"No, I'm taking a plane home—back East." Lotus scrambled into the taxi and shut the door.

Mrs. Weltz was still talking when the cab pulled away from the curb.

She traveled to the airport in a gray haze, going through the terminal without really being aware of her surroundings. "Do you have a reservation for Sinclair? L. Sinclair?" she asked the ticket agent.

"Yes, but there will be stopovers and you'll have to change planes in Chicago," the woman informed her.

"Are you sure there's nothing else?" Lotus had the feeling she should only take an express to the moon, not just a plane to Rochester, New York.

"I'll check, miss, but I'm sure that your reservation is the best we can offer." The woman pressed assorted buttons on her computer, studied the answers, then pushed a few more and studied again. "I'm sorry, miss. You must make a stop at O'Hare."

Lotus nodded.

"Have you any luggage?"

"Just my duffel bag. I'll carry it on."

"Have a good trip, Miss Sinclair."

"Thanks," Lotus answered dully.

Clutching her ticket in one hand, her oversized duffel bag over her other shoulder, she looked around the crowded waiting room, and took a corner seat, which was empty.

She read and reread the typewritten instructions on her ticket. Flight 306 would be leaving

Las Vegas at . . . Not able to cope with arrivals and departures her mind wandered away from the printed page. At the moment it was a monumental undertaking just breathing, in and out, over and over again. She tried telling herself that she hated Dash, the gambler, the unknown embezzler who had damaged her family. She tried dredging up some of the zeal that had her burgling Dash's safe, coming out to Las Vegas and getting two jobs to do it, but all she felt was a huge loss and a burdensome emptiness that she couldn't fill.

Lotus was half asleep when a raucous voice announced that passengers on Flight 306 bound for Chicago's O'Hare Airport could board the plane.

Sighing apathetically, Lotus gripped her ticket and duffel bag and followed after a man whose carry-on luggage banged against his leg at every step. She tried to smile at the flight attendant who tore off part of her ticket.

"I'm afraid you'll have to put your duffel bag in the overhead or under your seat. The closet is full." The blond flight attendant smiled at Lotus.

"Fine. I'll put it in the overhead." Lotus was wondering how she would swing up the heavy duffel bag as she passed through first class and made her way to the window seat to which she'd been assigned. Out of breath, she managed with the help of an older man across the aisle to get her duffel bag into the overhead.

She scarcely noticed when the powerful machine scampered down the runway, then lifted off in smooth ascent. She closed her eyes, grateful that there were no passengers in the two seats next to her. She didn't just want to sleep; instead, she wanted to fall down a deep hole and never surface.

Lotus was halfway between sleep and consciousness when she heard the rattle of the drink cart being maneuvered down the aisle of the airplane. Yawning, she turned to tell the flight attendant that she didn't want anything to eat or drink. It was then she noticed that the curtain that had been pulled between the first class section and the second class section opened. She blinked her eyes, quite sure that she was sleeping and that she was in the middle of a nightmare. Dash Colby was standing there, his eyes fixed on her as though he had known where she was sitting. She closed her eyes and opened them again. He was still there! And he was coming toward her. She couldn't seem to take her eyes off him as he waited for the flight attendant who was next to Lotus's seat now.

"What lunch would you prefer, beef or chicken?" the flight attendant asked Lotus.

"Neither." Lotus pushed the words through spastic lips. "Not hungry." Her stomach churned.

"Something to drink then?"

Lotus shook her head, not able to trust her voice to say anymore. She felt herself stiffen as the cart went by and Dash swung into the middle seat close to her. "What are you doing here?" she asked, stunned.

"What are *you* doing here?" he inquired silkily.

"You can't threaten me," Lotus gasped, feeling the menace coming off him choking her like smoke.

"I asked a simple question." Dash ran one finger up her arm. "I thought we were supposed to meet later at the casino."

"Things change." Lotus gulped.

"Don't they?" The velvet hardness in his voice made every fine hair on her body stand erect. "I thought you acted a little nervous, my dove, so I called when I reached my meeting to see how you were feeling. The good Mrs. Weltz informed me that you had moved out and were flying back East." He took hold of her hand and put her baby finger into his mouth, his teeth snapping down on it. "Persons at the meeting thought I'd gone crazy when I exploded at the conference table after talking on the phone to your landlady." His sweet voice was like a fine-honed, double-edged blade. "I called Hans and had him arrange my flight while I drove to the airport, breaking every speeding law."

Lotus jumped in her seat, trying to jerk her hand free, but he wouldn't let her. "I told you my home is in the East," she said.

"So you did, but you didn't tell me you were going home today. I hope you haven't cost me a multimillion-dollar deal on the club I was trying to buy."

"You shouldn't have come," Lotus muttered, finding it hard to inhale.

"You shouldn't have left me. Tell me why you did."

"No," was all Lotus managed to say.

"Oh, but you will. I'll insist on that."

"You can't threaten me."

"So you've told me. Do you often repeat yourself?" he asked her with clinical interest.

"I don't want you on this plane."

"Do you own it?" Dash settled back in his seat, his eyes glittering. Then he smiled at the puzzled flight attendant when she approached them. "I'm sitting back here for the time being, trying to convince my friend to join me in first class." He explained to the curvaceous redhead who leaned toward them

"Oh, you should, miss. Mr. Colby has two seats in first class."

"No, thank you." Lotus tried to smile, but her lips felt like cement. She could kill him for finding her! And how did he know how to find her? She was just beginning to deal with the sense of loss she had felt at leaving him. Now he was here! Was he here to arrest her? Was this his way of entrapping her? All her paranoia resurfaced in one balloon of pain and uncertainty.

"Suit yourself." The flight attendant flashed a big smile at Dash, then wandered up the aisle.

"You can't be traveling on this plane all the way to Rochester." Lotus enunicated each word, trying to control the quaver in her voice.

"No. We change planes at O'Hare," Dash said pleasantly.

"Don't sit next to me. . . ." Lotus cleared her throat, hearing her voice rise. She caught the curious glance of the man across the aisle and spoke in a whisper. "This seat belongs to . . ."

"Me. I had my security people track you down. The L. Sinclair threw them for a moment, but not for long. They're very efficient. It didn't take them long to track down a very slim, attractive Oriental . . ."

"I'm as Yankee as you are," Lotus snapped.

". . . Looking woman who moved like a dream. They had you pegged in minutes."

"Oh? What do you have? A private F.B.I.?"

"Something like that. I couldn't run casinos and

not have a thorough security system. That would be stupid. And I'm not stupid."

"You are if you think that I'm going to allow you into my life," Lotus snapped, turning her head to look at him for the first time.

Dash faced her, his lazy smile not masking the silver fury that had turned his eyes to lava. "Too late. I'm already in your life. Would you like me to refresh your memory? We could start with the tiny, sweet mole you have on your backside, darling."

"Stop . . . sadist . . ." she hissed, her glance sliding away from him and hitting the man across the aisle who was looking at them.

"Settle down, Lotus. I'm going to nap." Dash slouched in his seat, his long leg hooked over the arm of the aisle seat. "Damn short seats here."

"Then go back to first class. Your seats are there."

"These two are mine also." His eyes closed.

"You bought four seats on an airplane? That's disgusting." Lotus exhaled brimstone.

His eyelids fluttered up, a pained look on his face. "I thought Orientals were inscrutable, silent types. How is it that I never noticed how you chatter?"

"I am an inscrutable, silent Oriental when I'm with normal people, not . . . not plutocrats . . ." Lotus sputtered, wondering for a moment if she would ever be back on even keel. In a few short days, Dash Colby had reduced her cool, calm demeanor to that of a gibbering idiot. She could kill him!

He squinted at her. "Are you relaxed now? I'd like to rest."

Lotus fulminated at him in silence wishing she could blacken those blue eyes of his as she watched them flutter shut. How could he sleep when she was so upset? Then she hunched her shoulder and stared out at the cloud blanket that seemed to sit beneath the plane. She didn't even realize she was sleepy until her eyes closed.

"Lotus, Lotus, wake up, we're landing in O'Hare. . . ." Dash pressed his mouth to her ear, letting his lips rove over the shell-like surface. Even her ears were perfect! She was a doll! But he was going to show her that she couldn't jerk him around like this! Leading him on a merry chase to the East when he had a deal pending in Las Vegas! He watched her blink her eyes awake. Then he leaned over and took her mouth with his when she tried to smother a yawn. "*Ummm,* nice. You yawned into my mouth." He muttered, watching her angry eyes shoot around them to see if anyone was looking at them. "Pay no attention to what people think."

"I happen to come from a respectable family," Lotus seethed as he pulled her from her seat to the aisle, then reached up into the overhead and took down her duffel bag.

"Let's go, darling." He urged her in front of him. When it looked like she would balk, he gestured to the people behind them. "Do you want to hold them up?"

"Ah . . . no." Lotus reached for her duffel bag, but decided not to argue when he shook his head. "Where is your luggage?" she asked him as they walked along the portable corridor to the terminal.

"Haven't any." He ushered her out into the teeming human condition that was O'Hare Airport.

Lotus was struggling to get her ticket out of her purse. "Are you sure you're going to the right gate? Ah, there's an attendant, we'll ask him. . . ." Lotus felt herself pulled back. Then her mouth dropped open as a golf cart vehicle pulled up to them, and Dash lifted her into the seat, then crowded in beside her. "But we don't need this," she hissed at Dash, then threw the driver a shaky smile when he stared at her. "Is it far to the . . . ?" Lotus began.

"Just get us to the area where we should catch our flight. You've been given your orders, haven't you?" Dash interrupted, gesturing for the man to get moving.

"Yes, sir."

"This is ridiculous." Lotus tried to wriggle away from Dash but he kept her tight to his side. "We're leaving the terminal! Why are we doing that?" Suspicion filled her mind. "You are not taking me back to Las Vegas." She threw herself sideways trying to get away.

"For God's sake, Lotus, hold still. Do you want to tip the cart? I am not taking you back to Las Vegas. I am taking you to New York, then we'll go to Rochester."

"I don't want to go to New York."

"I just have to pick up some papers and make some calls. We'll be leaving for Rochester as soon as I do that."

"I don't want you with me. I have a single ticket. My brothers are picking me up . . ." she babbled.

"We'll call them from my apartment and tell them we'll be a little late. It won't be more than two or three hours," he declared.

"Kidnapping!" Lotus shouted.

"Stop that." Dash leaned over and unthreaded her white knuckled hands. "Nothing bad is going to happen to you." His voice was soft. "Even though I felt like killing you at first."

"I'm not reassured," Lotus ventured watching the faces of people flashing past them, curiosity on their faces as they looked at them.

The long ride seemed to weave in and out of corridors and around corners. By the time the man reached his destination Lotus was lost.

Dash helped her out of the cart and threw a bill at the man.

"That would feed me for a week," Lotus muttered, pulling at his hand on her arm.

"Would it, darling?" Dash answered her absently as they went along a narrower hall, then out a door, where plane engines were revving up.

"It's so noisy . . . and windy. Why are we here?" Lotus raised her voice as Dash bent his head to listen.

He pointed downward to a sleek Lear jet on the field. Then preceded her down the steep steps to the tarmac, his hand reaching up to guide her behind him. "That's our plane."

Lotus dug in her heels and shook her head. "Can't be!" she shouted, fumbling for her ticket again. "I'm sure Petras wouldn't book me on a little plane. I don't fly on little planes," she tried to explain as Dash kept a tight hold on her and urged her forward. "I like the bigger ones better," she shouted. Was he really kidnapping her? She tried to break free. He wasn't the type to use torture even if he did know about the file, was he? *Oh, Lord,* she moaned to herself. *What's going to happen?*

"Not to worry, darling. Come on." Dash watched

the play of emotions over her face as she hesitated on the last step. It was like a hand squeezing his heart to see panic and fear war with determination. Her face was like a book! He could read every expression. When her eyes flitted to him again, he pulled her close to him and spoke against her ear to blot out the cacophony around them. "I will never hurt you, no matter what else happens between us."

"Then let me go." Lotus mouthed the words, her insides churning with delight and horror because he was with her.

He shook his head as he leaned back from her. Then, with his arm around her small waist, he led her to the plane.

Lotus tried to hear what he said to the man in gray coveralls who spoke to him, but most of Dash's words were carried away by the gusts of wind that buffeted them, or they were drowned in the noise of the engines. Lotus was glad Dash was holding her, but at the same time she had the feeling she should be running down the airstrip after the Japan Airlines plane that was just taxiing for takeoff on the other side of the field.

"Hurry, darling. Daydream later." Dash laughed down at her, seeing the bemused look on her face. She was plotting something, but it wouldn't do her any good. She wasn't getting away from him! Annoyed with himself at the emptiness he had felt when her landlady had told him she was packed and gone from her room, he resented the unfamiliar possessiveness he felt about her.

He kept his hands at her waist as he helped her up the steep steel steps that led into the plane, then he followed her and signaled that the hatch be shut. "Do you like it?" He watched her stare around the plush interior, her mouth slightly parted.

"I've never been inside an airplane that has paneling and a living room with tables and chairs." Lotus's smile trembled across her face. "Do I get to meet the pilot too?"

"You're looking at him, darling." Dash took her hand, ignoring her gasp and led her to the cockpit. "Buckle in, love." When she paused to stare at the instrument panel, he pushed her gently into the copilot's seat and buckled her himself.

Then he sat down, twisted the handle over his head, affixed the headphones, and contacted the tower. He smiled at her while he waited for instructions, leaning over to squeeze her knee. "Relax, angel. I wouldn't let anything happen to you. I've been flying for years and I even checked out on the big planes."

"Better for me to take one of those," Lotus muttered, adjusting the headset, her stomach fluttering. Then she was silent as a voice crackled over the headphones. She only caught every other word, but Dash seemed to have no trouble in understanding what was said.

They were moving! Lotus sucked in an excited breath as she watched the nose of the plane steer along the white line, then follow a marker to get in line behind a much larger commercial jet.

"It's not too backed up, for O'Hare, so we'll be in the air before you know it," Dash assured her.

"Yes," Lotus hoped, trepidation giving way to excitement as they taxied out onto the takeoff area. "We're next."

"Yes." Dash laughed, not able to believe the joy

that filled him because she was excited about the takeoff. "Here we go." Dash forgot she was beside him for a moment as he pushed in the throttle and felt the sleek machine quiver with power.

They scampered down the runway, the engines roaring to lift off in a fury of grace and speed.

"My goodness, we almost went straight up," Lotus said and laughed. "That was wonderful." It was crazy! She was with Dash, a man who could cause her and her family a great deal of trouble, but she had never been happier.

"I'll teach you how to fly, my dove. You'd be a very good pilot, I'm sure. You are a very steady lady."

Lotus couldn't hold back her grin as they climbed through the cloud level, Dash making some notations on a pad, then barking once into the headphone.

"Are we on course now?" she asked. Her anger and irritation with him were fast dissipating. She couldn't quell the happiness that being with him brought.

"Pretty much," he said. We'll be changing our heading a few times, but we're on course, copilot."

Lotus laughed out loud, then stared at him as his mouth opened a little. "What is it?" she asked. "You look surprised."

"You have a very sweet laugh. It runs up and down my spine like your fingers did last night, love."

"Now, listen"—Lotus struggled to keep the blood from filling her face—"if you're trying to embarrass me . . ."

"I'm not. I don't want you to be uncomfortable in any way, but you might as well get used to the idea of being with me . . . because that's the way it's going to be."

"Last night . . ." Lotus cleared her throat.

"Was wonderful and it will be repeated often, before and after you marry me," Dash said.

"You don't force people to marry you anymore. That went out with the tyrannosaurus Rex," Lotus sputtered.

"There will be no rough stuff, China Doll, but you will marry me. . . ."

"You don't know me. I don't know you." Lotus cast around in her mind for some way to tell him what she had done. There was no easy way. "I've done some things I'm not proud of—"

"So have I," Dash interrupted.

"Let me finish," Lotus said, wondering just how angry he would get with her. He wouldn't throw her out of the plane! Or would he? "I broke into your office," she blurted.

Dash looked her way. He inhaled. "So! You did do it," he exhaled. "I told my security people they were crazy, but they pinpointed you. Hans told me the same thing."

"He doesn't like me," Lotus whispered.

"He doesn't trust women. He thinks they're trouble." Dash ran a hand through his hair. "I'm inclined to agree with him."

"Now you had better let me go. You could turn around and take me back to O'Hare," Lotus suggested.

"Why the hell did you break into my office, and who taught you to use a burglar's tool, then wipe off the file?" Dash snarled.

"Ah, I can't tell you," Lotus hedged.

"Why not?" Dash quizzed, making her shiver. "Stop that. I damn well told you that you had nothing to fear from me."

"You're giving a very good imitation of King Kong right at the moment," Lotus shot back, inhaling a shaky breath.

"Well, what the hell did you think I'd do after you tell me a thing like that? It's a shock!" It frosted him that he was so shaken. She seemed so perfect! He hated finding out that she could be underhanded. "Tell me."

"No. I don't think so. Some of the things are really no business of yours . . . and . . . and I have to find out something by myself. . . ."

"Lotus!" he roared, making her cringe against her seat belt. "Tell me."

"I can't!" she shouted back, feeling tears sting her eyes.

He shot a look at her, then reached out and grasped one of her clenched fists. "Is it money you want? I have plenty . . ."

"No," she fired back at him, stung that he could think she was after his money. "No, not one penny," she gulped, trying to wrest her hand free of him to no avail.

He stared at her, checking the controls all the while. "Then let me tell you what my security people have surmised." He looked over at her, snapping his teeth together when she became white. "That, one, you're a compulsive gambler, looking for money. Two, that you're a spy from another gambling conglomerate. Wait, let me finish." He put his hand over on her knee again. "Three, that you have a record with us"—he paused only a millisecond when he felt her flinch under his fingers—"and fourth, that you have some weird idea of getting your hands on a system we might have."

"No, no, nothing like that," she told him looking out the window. *Never, never will I tell you, Dash. It's my family, my uncle who is on the block, and I won't do anything to hurt him. Besides, you will still want to collect on the gambling debt that bears my uncle's name. . . .* She bit her lip and reached down without thinking to pat the carryall at her side.

Dash was watching her face out of the corner of his eyes, his hands flicking over the instrument in automatic check. He saw her hand go down and pat the bag in a protective way. "Would you like to go back and lie down for a while?"

She jumped and stared at him for a moment, the hard planes of his face seeming to reach out for her. "Ah, no, I like being up here."

For long minutes they flew in silence, the throbbing of the engines mixing with the guitar cadence coming from the stereo system. When Dash pressed a switch, unbuckled himself, and rose to his feet, Lotus looked at him in alarm. "Where are you going?"

"Just to use the bathroom. Not to worry. It's on automatic pilot and we're in a light traffic area. I'll bring us some food when I return."

Lotus nodded, her smile fleeting, her gaze returning to the vista out in front of the plane.

Dash watched her for a few minutes, then went to the aft cabin, pausing there and watching the doorway he had just closed between the cockpit and the cabin. Then he pressed a button and the desk opened to a console that included a phone. He dialed and waited. "Yeah. It's me. How did it go? So hold them. I'll call you from New York, and we can arrange to have a phone meeting on the computer." He looked over his shoulder at the cockpit door again. "Have you found anything out about an L. Sinclair. Right. Yeah." He took a deep breath, then drummed his fingers on the console. "Don't read me the entire file, just run the facts by me." Dash listened for a few minutes. "Does he have a daughter? No. Wrong name. All right, keep digging. Save your breath, Hans, and do what I told you. Right. I'll call from the apartment." Dash replaced the receiver, then pressed the switch to hide the console once more in the desk. He stood there staring at the paneled wall, feeling his face crease in concentration. *Damn you, Lotus. You're putting me through an obstacle course, baby, but I will find out what's going on.*

He walked back toward the cockpit, coming to the small but well-stocked galley. He put two ham and cheese sandwiches in the microwave, then pushed the coffee button and took two cartons of milk and two apples out of the small refrigerator. He pushed open the door and let it close behind him. He saw the relief flash across her face when she saw him. "Miss me?"

"Maybe. I'm not much of a pilot," she said. She should be furious with him, yet she felt safe and comforted because he was beside her. *No doubt he'll turn me over to the authorities in New York and I'll need a lawyer,* she thought. She looked over at him as he sat down, fastened his seat belt, adjusted the headset, then took the plane off automatic. The slight dip of the engine didn't bother her. She felt secure with Dash. Why couldn't I have loved anyone else like this? Why didn't I love Jeremy like this? Thinking of him made her decision to tell him that they couldn't date anymore even more definite. She didn't want to take up his time and spoil his chance for a life with someone who would love him.

"What are you thinking?" Dash rattled her out of her reverie with his harsh voice. "Is it the boyfriend? Forget him. You're not going to marry him."

"You don't dictate my life," Lotus fumed.

"You won't marry him, Lotus. I won't let you."

"What I do or don't do is no concern of yours," she said and ground her teeth.

"Oh, but it is." He handed her an apple and a carton of milk. "Eat your apple. Then you go and take our hot sandwiches out of the microwave."

"I'll see how I feel." She bit into the crisp apple, savoring the juiciness. When she was finished, she wiped her hands on the napkin Dash had provided. "My hands are sticky. Where is the bathroom?"

"Straight back," he told her, getting on the radio and speaking into it.

Taking her tote bag with her, Lotus went back to the aft cabin. She felt guilty about not telling Dash what she had with her, but when she remembered her uncle, it strengthened her resolve. She would discover who masqueraded as Uncle Silas no matter what it took! Even if Dash prosecuted her, it wouldn't stop her!

On her return she removed the sandwiches from the microwave, put them on a tray with coffee, and carried it to the cockpit.

After they finished the hot sandwiches and coffee, Dash informed her that it was getting close to approach time and that they had been cleared for landing by the tower at LaGuardia Airport.

Coming down in a Lear jet was a heart-stopping thrill for Lotus, and she wished for a fleeting moment that she could indeed take flying lessons from Dash.

They landed with scarcely a bump, then taxied to a nearby hanger where men rushed forward to stand at the foot of the ladder when it was lowered.

"Good afternoon, Mr. Colby. You'll have to hurry, sir, the helicopter is on the pad and warming up. It's waiting for you."

"Thanks, Harry. We're on our way. Service her, will you? I'll be flying to Rochester tomorrow."

"Yes, sir," Harry told Dash, then gestured to a man who had a golf cart waiting. They were whisked around corners and past buildings, then out and across the field to another area.

Lotus stared around her bemused. Though it wasn't quite as busy as O'Hare, LaGuardia was still a madhouse of activity.

Dash kept his arm around her the entire trip, keeping her close to his side. He felt her hesitation when she saw the powerful rotors whirring as the helicopter was made ready for takeoff. "Not to worry, love. I'm here. Come on, we're a little late." Dash lifted her into the helicopter, amazed at her lightness. She was such a little tiger, she should weigh about two hundred pounds, he thought, letting his hand feather over her small backside, chuckling when he felt her stiffen.

Lotus felt feverish for a moment after Dash had touched her. She glared at him, barely taking note of the three other persons sitting in the machine. Gasping, she felt the roar of takeoff. Instinctively, she pressed back against Dash. He put both arms around her, his mouth close to her ear.

"Relax, love. You're going to have all of Manhattan under your feet. It's a wonderful city. And tonight after you've rested we're going to do the town. Would you like that?"

Lotus knew she should tell him that she would stay in her room until they left for Rochester tomorrow. Wasn't he the enemy? He might even try to put her in prison. "Yes. I would like to see New York at night."

"Have you ever been to New York?"

"Once, when I was four years old."

"Ah, well, then you have a treat in store. I think we can both use the recreation."

The ride was a delight. She saw the awesome glass and steel caves and mountains of Manhattan. "It's wonderful. The buildings shine in the sunlight."

"New York is on her best behavior for you. It's only a few hours until dark so you will see the beginnings of the sunset," Dash told her, his long arm holding her, the other pointing out the sights.

"The Statue of Liberty! What are they doing to her?"

"That scaffolding is part of the refurbishing job that will be done on her so that she will look like her old self again."

"I think she's beautiful now," Lotus breathed.

"So are you." Dash gently bit her ear.

Lotus sucked in a breath, looking around her, but the other passengers seemed to be busy, working out of briefcases or looking out their own windows.

"Tonight, we'll party, China Doll."

"Yes." *I want to keep him for just a little while,* she thought, begging whatever Fates were listening to heed her.

When the helicopter made its landing on the building without a hitch, it didn't take them long to get out. Then they took a swift elevator to the ground floor, where Dash whisked her to the street. His piercing whistle and upraised finger startled her. A taxi cruised to the curb, the squeal of brakes making Lotus jump backwards. Dash put her into the cab and followed her chuckling. "Now you are in for the thrilling part of the trip, love, a taxi ride in New York."

Lotus felt her head snap back as they jetted into the mainstream for traffic. "*Eeek!* He's going to hit that . . . no, watch out for . . ." Lotus choked, as their driver wove in and out of vehicles, his hand never once leaving the horn. She pushed her face into Dash's chest when he put his arms around her. "Tell me when we arrive," she mumbled into his shirt front. "Don't tell me if we get into an accident." She felt as though all of her sensible self had just flown out the window.

"Crazy lady," he whispered into her hair. "I've never enjoyed a cab ride so much."

"Masochist," Lotus mumbled, opening one eye, then closing it hurriedly. "What is the name of our hotel?" Her muffled voice was barely audible.

"I thought I told you I had an apartment in Manhattan, not too far from the Metropolitan Museum. If you like we can tour that. . . ."

Lotus lifted her head a fraction. "I must get home. As it is, I should call my brothers as soon as possible." She lifted her left hand and looked at her watch. "They'll be leaving to pick me up at the airport soon."

"We'll call as soon as we get in the apartment," Dash assured her, kissing her forehead. *And tonight, my elusive darling, I am going to try to get you to open up to me. Something is ripping you up and I'm going to find out what it is.* "Ah, here we are." Dash paid the driver and pushed open the door.

The sand-colored building with ornate carving in concrete at every window had a beige canopy over the entrance with a doorman in attendance. The small wrought-iron balconies jutted out over the avenue. Lotus knew without asking that it was an exclusive address. She hesitated, watching Dash as he pocketed his wallet, then looked at her. "Nice place."

"Yes." Dash was noncommittal. He sensed her discomfort, though she didn't seem to be impressed with his place. "I'm on the top floor."

Lotus looked up the front of the building. She could see a terrace at the top. "I see."

Dash took her arm and guided her to the door, now held open by the man who doffed his cap to them. "Good afternoon, Williams," Dash greeted him.

"Good afternoon, Mr. Colby. Miss." He smiled at Lotus who returned the smile.

"This is Miss Wes . . . Miss Sinclair. She may be coming back and forth to my suite."

"Yes, sir."

Dash led her through the small lobby decorated in ecru and beige, their feet sinking into the plush carpeting. Once he had her in the elevator, he noticed that she wasn't looking at him. When he tried to catch her gaze, it would slide away from him. "Is there something about my building that you don't like?"

"Do you own the building?"

Dash straightened away from the wall, the hair on his arms raising. Why did he have the sensation that his whole future rested on his answer?

Why does my little doll have an aversion to money? "Yes, I own it. Perhaps I should say that my family owns it, and that I share ownership with them."

"Are they in gambling too?"

"I prefer the word speculation," Dash told her, hard amusement in his voice.

"Whatever." Lotus felt a resurgence of the anger she had felt when she had first gone to Las Vegas. Her uncle had been victimized because someone was caught in the web of gambling. When she looked around her, she saw an opulence built by the vice. He and his family or conglomerate—whatever they called themselves—had built an empire on the backs of people who were too weak to control a bad habit . . . gambling. Even now her wonderful uncle was suffering because one of those weak persons had embezzled funds from Dash's organization and used her uncle's name.

"Come out of that dream world you're in. We've arrived. Besides, it doesn't look like a very happy dream world."

"It isn't." Lotus preceded him from the elevator into a small foyer with two doors. "You only have one neighbor?"

"Both doors are mine, love," Dash told her, feeling uneasy when he sensed her stiffening *What the hell was going on in that convoluted mind of hers?* He was losing more of her with each step they took into his home.

He pushed open the door, carrying her duffel bag on his shoulder and gestured with his head for her to precede him.

Lotus walked into the spacious two-story foyer with the curving stairway hugging one rounded wall and looked around her. "Is that silk on the walls?" she whispered.

"Yes." He was curt. Then he dropped her things on the floor and walked to her, gripping her upper arms. "Tell me what's going on? You're getting colder and colder toward me. Tell me."

Lotus looked up at him, wanting to tell him to get lost, go to hell, let her go. "Your money came to you on the backs of shattered people and their shattered dreams." She waved her hand around the champagne-colored, round foyer. "It's a sultan's palace constructed with flesh and blood. Do you honestly expect me to admire it . . . or you?"

Dash stepped back, feeling the blood drain from him. "I'm considered to be an honest businessman."

"By whom? The mob?" It was her turn to step back when she saw the hurricane of emotions in his face.

"I don't work with the mob . . . or any underworld persons," he told her, the words like nails driven into wood, amazed at the hurt feelings that filled him at her words.

Lotus felt stabbed when she saw surprise flash across his face; then his features closed like a book, and he looked down at her as though waiting to see what else she would say to him. "I didn't . . . didn't mean to hurt you." She meant every word. She felt tears on her cheek and put her hand there. "I never cry." Stunned, she breathed the words. "I'll leave." She went to her duffel bag on the floor. Before she could reach down for it, Dash's hands were at her waist, turning her toward him, lifting her into his arms.

"Don't go." He kissed her cheek, letting his mouth

travel the clean line of her jaw. "We have a long way to go with each other, and I think the road's going to be rough, but I don't want you to leave me. Please."

Lotus took in a shuddering breath, leaning against him, her eyes closed, her feet dangling a half a foot off the floor. "I don't want to leave you," she confessed, feeling a ton of weight lift from her emotions.

CHAPTER FOUR

The few hours left until evening became increasingly happy ones to Lotus. She felt bright, helium light as Dash led her from room to room in the ten-room duplex apartment. They were close. Even when they weren't touching each other, she had the feeling that they were connected. They had said no more about the gambling. Dash had not asked her the reason for her feelings. She had delved no more into his money-making, and though the questions remained between them, it was as though a decision had been reached. For the time being they would shelve the problems between them.

"And where is my room?" Lotus asked him, as she faced him across the large master bedroom with the mammoth square bed between them. She saw his eyes go over the bed, then raise to her face. She could feel the heat in his face as he continued to watch her. "You're not an Oriental . . ." she told him, feeling out of breath, ". . . but you are pretty inscrutable yourself."

Dash swallowed, feeling the corners of his mouth lift. "You know where I want you to stay. It's up to you. It will always be up to you. For the rest of our lives, if that's what you want, where you sleep, my sweet, will be up to you, but I won't want you to sleep alone . . . without me."

That had been a long speech for Dash and one which had rocked her to her toe nails. "Well, I'll look . . . at the other rooms . . . and make up my mind." She watched him, not even aware that she had been holding her breath until he nodded, and she exhaled a gust of air.

He held out his hand to her. "Let's look at the others, then, shall we?"

Lotus watched him come around the bed toward her, her hand coming up and fitting with his. "Let's." She felt warm and comfortable as she walked with him out of the bedroom, down a long hall of the suite to a wider corridor that led to another section of the apartment.

Dash held her small hand in his, feeling his pulse accelerate each time her flesh pressed to his. He felt like an adolescent with her! She aroused him just by holding his hand. He barely took note of the rooms they passed in and out of, his whole being on alert, waiting to hear her say that she was staying in the Rose Room or the Sapphire Room or . . .

She stopped in front of him at the top of the curving staircase that would take them down to the foyer. "All in all, I would judge your bedroom, with its sitting room, dressing room, oversized shower, hot tub et al. to be the best room, so I'll stay there." She could feel her lips part in surprise as red slashed his face, the bones pushing out the flesh as though they would come through the skin, his mouth moving harshly against his teeth.

"Will you now?" His voice was soft as he leaned down to her and clasped his hands under her buttocks and lifted her up his body.

"Yes." Lotus felt reckless as she reached one finger to trace his eyebrows and down his nose. "What do you think of that?"

"I approve . . . just because the suite has a hot tub, an oversized shower, a sitting room, and a dressing room," Dash said, imitating her and struggling to keep his blood pressure from going through the top of his head.

"Naturally," Lotus said and smiled, then leaned forward two inches and placed her mouth on his. "Have I told you that your lips surprise me?"

"No," Dash mumbled.

"They do. You really have a very tough mouth, but your lips are silky. I like that," Lotus told him, placing her mouth on his again, feeling his move against hers. "Nice."

"Thank you," he said and groaned. "I want to please you." His arms tightened on her, his one hand still remaining under her backside, his other hand roving from her shoulder to her coccyx.

"Do I please you?" It shocked Lotus that she would ever be coy. It was not her nature. She had always been straightforward and had shunned artifice. Even when she had been a little girl, she had bluntly told her mother that she wouldn't wear ruffles, that she preferred a T-shirt and baseball hat. Though her mother had bitten her lip over this, Lotus was allowed to play baseball and basketball with her brothers and bike all over town in jeans. With Dash she wanted to bat her eyelashes, slather her body with perfume, and dance an exotic dance of the East just for him!

"Very much, my sweet." He carried her along the hall and made the turn into the smaller corridor that led to his suite.

Lotus sighed and settled her head on his shoulder. A thought struck her and she glanced at her watch. "Lord, I forgot to call my brothers." She wriggled against Dash. "Put me down. I have to call at once. They might have left already."

Once on the floor, she ran pell-mell into his suite and sat down at a desk in the sitting room, dialing with shaking hands. Damn Dash Colby! He had a terrible effect on her nervous system! She never used to forget to do the things she was supposed to do! "Rob! Is that you? Oh, thank goodness, I caught you. Don't go to the airport. Well, because I won't be there. I'm in New York City, staying with a friend. I'll be home tomorrow. No. Of course I'm fine. I'll explain when I get there. Give my love to mother and father and everyone. How is Uncle doing? Really? No better? I'll be there tomorrow at . . ." She looked around at Dash, reading his lips as he mouthed the words. ". . . Four o'clock . . ." She read more of what Dash was trying to tell her when he pressed her arm. "Don't bother to pick us . . . Yes, I'm bringing a friend. I'll tell you about it when I get there. We'll be at the house around five or so."

She hung up and looked at Dash as he stood in front of her. "I'm sorry . . . I . . . really didn't want to spoil our mood, but . . ."

"Let's take a shower, shall we?"

"Together?"

"You said that I had an oversized shower."

Lotus laughed out loud. "So I did. Let's take a

hot tub first. I like those things . . . even though when I use the one at home I exercise first."

"You have one in your home?"

"No. My family belongs to a downtown athletic club called the Metro Y. We all work out there, even mother." Lotus grinned at him, then her smile faded when he led her into the bathroom and began peeling his clothes from his body. When he saw her stare, he paused.

"Mustn't feel shy, darling."

"I know, but I feel a bit strange. I haven't been doing this as long as you . . . sleeping with people, I mean."

Dash closed his eyes, then opened them. "That was a zinger, I believe."

Lotus opened her mouth to deny it, then she nodded. "I guess it was. I'm a little annoyed that you should have had so many women, yet I also considered myself a very up-to-the-minute, modern lady until I met you too." She shrugged. "Explain it to me. I don't understand my feelings."

"Well . . ." Dash lowered his arm, tossing his shirt toward the clothes tree and missing. "I don't have warm feelings for your friend, Jeremy, either."

"Don't worry about him." Lotus retrieved the shirt and put it in the clothes chute on one wall of the bathroom. She tried to peek down the narrow opening. "How long before your clothes come back clean?"

"One day." He pulled her away from the chute. "Now about how we feel about other persons being in our lives . . . don't you think we should concentrate on each other until we get our feelings sorted, then we can handle the extraneous?" He unbuttoned her blouse, watching her every moment. "If

I make you uncomfortable, stop me, love. You will soon learn that you are in control of our life together."

Lotus smiled up at him, seeing the uncertainty on his face. All at once she felt no uneasiness. "Keep going."

Dash felt his hand tremor when he lifted her blouse away from her body. "Your skin is like the lotus flower of your name, so creamy white, yet somehow it fits with your looks . . ." He was muttering and fully aware of it, but he couldn't seem to help himself. ". . . Yet, it's not incongruous with your Eastern features." He shook his head in awe. "In fact, your skin is perfect for your blue-black silky hair and almond-shaped green eyes. You are an incredibly beautiful hybrid, my darling."

"You're repeating yourself." Lotus chuckled. "That's what my brothers call me . . . the Sinclair hybrid."

Yet she had called herself Weston. Dash's mind churned with it. Why had she hidden herself from him? Bit by bit, China Doll, the outer layer will be peeled away. He would discover all her secrets. "Do they, my lotus?" Dash discarded her blouse, then the skirt and panty hose she had been wearing. When she was standing in front of him wearing only a pair of briefs, he scowled at her. "I don't like the thought of you traveling from New York to Las Vegas without a bra."

"That remark's from left field, isn't it?" Lotus stared at him, feeling her lips parting in surprise. "You must have realized by now that I wasn't wearing a bra on my trip east with you . . ." Lotus began.

"You were with me. That's different." Dash's

frown deepened when she tried to mask her amusement behind her hand. When she laughed out loud, he could feel his expression softening. "You trill like a bird, precious." He faced her, feeling his body harden in response to her beauty, watching her eyes scan him then fix on his face again. "I cannot hide how I feel about you, love. I don't want to hide it."

"Hot tub," Lotus suggested, then closed her eyes as she felt him pull her closer again, then touch a wall switch.

In minutes water frothed steamily around him as Dash led her down the three steps into the good-sized tub that could have held at least two more persons.

Lotus gasped and laughed as the hot water swirled around them. "It's nice, isn't it?"

"Yes," Dash told her. Anything was wonderful, doing it with her. He lifted her over his body, letting her slippery silkiness slide up and down his form until he thought he might go mad. "We have to get out of here soon, darling. . . ."

"Why?" Lotus turned over until she was on her tummy on top of him. "I like it here." She slithered downward, feeling the hardness of him probing her lower body. She fitted herself to him, hearing him groan. When she heard other moans, she knew they were her own. "Dash . . ." she gasped, feeling the rhythm that he was beginning deep inside her.

"Yes, my treasure, I'm with you, all the way."

Her last, fleeting thought was that it would be hell to say good-bye to him now, and that it would be well nigh impossible. Then she was soaring with him, out, out, beyond all limits until the galaxy exploded between them. Lotus clung to him as they descended from the star plane to earth again. It took moments for her to realize that they were still joined and that Dash was watching her, his hooded stare mesmerizing her. "Are . . . are we going to stay like this forever?"

"I think we might." His words were soft and slightly slurred. *Lord, does she know what she does to me?* He had thought maybe the first time together was a glorious fluke, a full moon phenomenon. Not so. A lotus blossom with the green eyes and pink pearl skin had moved into his life and possessed it. *What would you do if you knew that, China Doll?* His mind raced with the question.

"What are you thinking?" Lotus smothered a yawn behind her hand.

"About you. Sleepy?" He could feel his body beginning to react to her again. Once more he was amazed. He had always been a very sexy man, but he never had the quick responses he was having now. "Too sleepy?" he crooned, undulating his body, the warm water sloshing around them.

Her eyes flew wide and she stared at him. "So soon?"

Dash nodded, restraining himself in case she wasn't willing.

"Nice." She wriggled against him, feeling the gentle spear of his body. "I didn't know that it could happen like this."

"Neither did I," Dash told her ruefully, hugging her when she giggled.

The love cadence rolled over them again, slower, with great savor as each of them exerted themselves for the other. The passionate joy of giving consumed them.

Lotus wanted him to be lost to others in that moment, so that the long line of other women who had marched through his life would be forgotten. She felt her hands curl into his shoulders as the arrows of hair on his chest abraded her breasts with loving persuasion. Her body tingled in awareness as he swung her around to cradle her in his arms, suspending her on his body as he lifted her higher to take her foot, kissing each toe.

"You taste good, love." Dash felt his blood heat to a higher temperature than the water as his lips sucked and pressed along her calf to behind her knee.

"This is fun." Lotus gulped, her body bumping gently against the sides as Dash forayed up her leg. When he ducked his head under the water, and she could feel his mouth intruding so intimately, she felt as though she must be fibrillating.

All at once he left her for a moment and surged to his feet, lifting her with him and out of the tub. In minutes he had her body lathered in scented oil. "Must protect your skin," he muttered to her in lazy heat.

"Heavens, yes." Lotus agreed. "But I'd much rather continue what we were doing."

"And we shall, my love," he assured her as he dried her with warm towels, then swung her up into his arms. "We shall." He kissed her mouth as he carried her through to the bedroom, placing her gently on the king-sized bed, then following her down, peeling the towels away with loving concentration. "Now where we're we? Ah, yes, now I remember." His face slid down her body, kissing each pore on his journey. He lifted her hips and began a sensual search of her body with his mouth, feeling her body jerk and arch as he probed her.

"Dash, I . . ." Lotus forgot what she was going to say to him.

Dash reacted to her clutching hands and took her fully with his body, the climax reached together in an explosion of light and gentleness. They slept, their arms around each other, their breathing deep and satisfied.

When Lotus woke she was alone. She shifted her body and felt an unfamiliar aching soreness. She remembered, feeling her body turn to fire and ice. Dash! She leaned back and stretched, blinking her eyes at the slanting rays of afternoon sun.

"Hey, sleepyhead, get up." Dash spoke from the bathroom doorway, a towel wrapped around his waist. "We don't have much time to shop, and I want to take you to Henri Bendel's."

Lotus jackknifed to a sitting position. "I'm not letting you buy things for me." She felt a smothering hurt that he could think that she would let him. She pulled the silken sheet up to her chin.

He was across the room in long strides and down on the bed beside her. "I'm not trying to denigrate what we have, darling. I wouldn't do that. I just thought you would like to shop in New York. I know you haven't been here for years . . . and never as an adult. I'll pay the bills, then you can give me the money when you get back to Rochester and your job."

Lotus pressed her hands against his chest when he would have hugged her to him. "I will pay you back, you know, so I don't want to go to expensive places. Take me somewhere inexpensive."

Dash grinned at her. "If we have time." He kissed her nose, then pulled her from the bed to her feet. "Come on, lady, let's move."

She scampered past him, gasping when she felt him pat her backside. She threw cold water in her face and freshened her body with a washcloth. Then she remembered that she hadn't brought her underthings with her. She gaped down at the silk briefs and chemise on the vanity top, the note next to them telling her that Dash had ordered these over the phone for her. He hoped they fitted.

For two heartbeats she toyed with the idea of not wearing them, but the silk lacy underthings magnetized her. She hopped into them and went out to the bedroom. Dash was there, placing her skirt and blouse on the bed.

He turned around and smiled at her. "I took these out of your duffel bag and ironed them for you. Will they do?"

"You ironed them?" Lotus said disbelievingly. He looked in her duffel bag! Had he seen the file there? She stared at him, but could discern no anger. She felt perspiration coat the palms of her hands as she relaxed.

"Of course I ironed them. I worked my way around the world after attending the university, and one of my jobs was as a valet at a hotel in Singapore."

"Truly?" Lotus pulled on the denim skirt, wondering fleetingly why she wasn't embarrassed about dressing in front of Dash.

Dash nodded, then pushed her gently into a

chair and fitted her shoes to her feet. "I find that I enjoy being your valet very much. Consider hiring me full-time?"

"I'll think about it." She looked away from the hot amusement in his blue eyes.

Dash put his arm around her as they went down the stairs to the main floor of the apartment, insisting that she eat an apple and drink a glass of milk before they left. Lotus muttered to herself all the while she raced back upstairs, brushed her teeth, and rushed back down again.

They took the elevator to the street, where a cab was waiting for them outside to whisk them on another hair-raising trip in Manhattan. The short ride ended in front of the discreet establishment with the name Henri Bendel on the front.

Lotus gawked but she couldn't help it. The store was so elegant. They took the escalator to the designer section of the store.

"Don't worry, we'll come again. Then you'll have time to see everything."

The saleslady glided up to them, her well-trained eyes running over Dash, her thin-lipped smile widening slightly. "Can I help you?"

"Yes, I want to see something for her." Dash kept his arm around Lotus.

"A specific color?"

"Blue," Lotus answered.

"Coral or a medium green perhaps," Dash said at the same time.

Lotus looked at him. "Blue is my favorite color."

He kissed her nose. "I like it myself, but I want to see how you look in . . . ah, that's nice . . ."He nodded to the woman as she and two of her assistants spread some dresses and suits in front of them. "Try the satin suit, darling." Dash indicated the salmon-colored Chanel suit one of the women was carrying.

Lotus tried on the suit, glad that she had succumbed to the temptation of the fine lingerie and worn it as one of the attendants helped her off with her clothes. She wished that her panty hose didn't have a run in one leg, but that was life.

"Ah, that is attractive on you," the saleswoman said as she stepped back and Lotus stared at herself in the mirror.

Her long, straight, black hair seemed to gleam with an ebony fire it had absorbed from the dull gleam of the salmon-colored satin, her pale skin had even deeper pink tones, and her green eyes flashed emerald. "It is pretty," Lotus faltered, trying to feel for the price tag on the suit.

The saleswoman watched her for a moment, then pulled back the curtain and gestured for Lotus to precede her. "I am sure that Mr. Colby would like to see this on you."

How did she know his name? Suspicion warred within her. Of course, salespersons would know him, she argued with herself, not feeling one bit mollified. She squashed feelings of jealousy when visions of Dash arm in arm with gorgeous creatures crossed her mind.

Dash rose from the beige-colored silk chair where he'd been sitting. "Darling, that's beautiful on you. We'll take this one, and we'll get some shoes for you, love."

"What's the price?" Lotus hissed at him.

"Very affordable," Dash told her, smiling.

"For whom?" she persisted, plucking at his sleeve.

"Not to worry." He gave his credit card to the

saleswoman and Lotus went to change back into her clothes. When she came out, Dash had the dress box under his arm and he led her to the shoe salon.

A small army of personnel appeared from nowhere and soon had boxes strewn everywhere for Dash's scrutiny.

"Would you believe they would have just the right color to match your suit? Right size too." Dash looked smug after they had made their choice.

Lotus computed the length of time it would take her to pay off the shoes and grimaced. "I will be paying you back for years," she grumbled even as she admired the coral slings that emphasized her trim ankles and calves.

"Purse." Dash aimed himself and Lotus toward the counter of bags that the salesperson assured him would hold a matching clutch bag. "Don't worry, I have no intention of charging you interest."

"I am still paying off some of my school loans, buster," Lotus said grimly.

"Do you think that there would be hose in this color?" Dash ignored her and quizzed the shoe saleswoman who immediate gestured to an attendant, who looked at the color of the suit in the box and nodded.

"This is ridiculous. I was brought up in a very conservative family. We don't run up big bills unless it's for something worthwhile like education or helping the poor. . . ." Lotus huffed after him as he thanked the woman for the pale coral stockings that she had handed him, then with his parcels he strode toward the escalator.

"Good principle," Dash assured her as he took

her arm and escorted her out the door down Fifth Avenue to Van Cleef & Arpels.

Lotus dug in her heels. "Oh, no, you don't. I would have to take out a loan and use my parents' home as collateral. No way."

"Don't be silly." Dash half lifted her into the elegant shop of Van Cleef and Arpels.

"Let's leave," she whispered, pleading with Dash as a man who looked more like a funeral director than a salesman approached them.

"Mr. Colby. How are you, sir?"

"Good God, you know the help in a jewelry store? That's disgusting," Lotus muttered through her teeth as the dark-suited man inclined his head toward her, then ushered them to stools placed in front of an enclosed case. "This is insane. I could go to jail. I want to go home."

"Tomlinson, the last time I was in here, you showed me a fine collection of coral jewelry. Do you still have it?"

"I think so, sir," he said and disappeared into another room.

Lotus looked left and right. She saw a man go to the front door and activate the lock. She rose to her feet. "Closing time. We have to go." She pulled at Dash's arm. "Don't want to get locked in."

"Sit down, Lotus. Everything is fine." Dash urged her to take her seat again.

"I don't like it here. It smells so rich. He'll see right through me. People can tell if you have student loans, you know."

"How?" Dash arched one dark brow.

"Infrared lamps?" Lotus begged.

"Ah, here's Tomlinson. Do you have it?"

"He doesn't have it." Lotus rose to her feet again, only to be pushed back into place by Dash.

"Look at these. Won't they be perfect with your suit?" Dash lifted the Daliesque slash of coral that would fit along the outer edge of her pierced ears.

"Wrong color," Lotus bleated, throwing anxious glances at the phlegmatic Tomlinson.

"They're perfect. We'll take the earrings and the pin."

"Not both," Lotus said from the side of her mouth, trying to smile at the expressionless Tomlinson at the same time.

"And I think the pendant is beautiful." Dash pushed the silk-lined velvet-covered box at Tomlinson and nodded.

Open-mouthed, Lotus watched the man wrap the box in silver paper. "I will be in debt until I'm ninety-two . . . if I'm not thrown into debtor's prison before then," she muttered.

"They don't have debtor's prisons anymore." Dash soothed her as he took the small bag from Tomlinson and led her toward the door.

"Do too," Lotus mumbled, glaring at him when he signaled for another taxi and helped her inside.

"You'll love wearing the jewelry with your suit." Dash took her flaccid hand between his two, lifting it to his lips to kiss the palm.

"I'll bet you were at the official counter when the aristocrats were led to the quillotine," Lotus said through clenched teeth, frustrated by her inability to fight his persuasiveness.

"Darling, that would make me so old."

"You are in your third life, I'd bet my next check on it," Lotus said darkly, wishing her pulse would settle down, wishing she didn't love what he was doing to her.

"You'd lose."

She turned to look at him. "You don't know me, or what I want to do with my life."

Dash felt alert, his skin prickling in warning. "What don't I know, Lotus?"

"My family will hate you. They'll want to draw and quarter you," Lotus wailed, even as she snuggled close to him as he pulled her into his arms.

"Why?" Dash whispered.

"Because." Lotus sobbed.

"Tell me, Lotus."

She wiped her cheeks. "I don't know where my courage has gone. I never used to cry about anything. I didn't even flinch when my brothers poked me in the arm . . . not that they did it much." She gulped. "They love me . . . and I love them. And I love my cousins and my aunt . . . and uncle . . ." Her voice trailed.

Dash held his breath, deciding to nudge her himself. "There was a Sinclair in my files. Hans and the rest of my security people seemed to think the file had been disturbed." He paused as he saw how white she became. He felt his jaw ache as he clamped his teeth together.

"Hey, buddy, this is your destination. Gettin' out?" The weary cab driver looked over his shoulder and indicated the pay box.

"Right." Dash pushed some bills into the box and told the driver to keep the change. Then he pulled Lotus out of the cab with him. "Stop looking like that. Nothing is going to happen to you." Dash leaned over her as he led her into the lobby of the building.

"My uncle," Lotus breathed as they stepped into the elevator and were whisked to their floor.

"Will you tell me about it now?"

Lotus hesitated, then nodded. "I will tell you all I can."

"Fair enough." Dash decided in that moment that he was going to wipe away that strained look on her face no matter what it took.

He led her into the apartment and up the stairs to the bedroom where he threw their bundles down on the bed. "Now, do you want to sit down here and talk to me?"

"Why don't we dress first?" Lotus struggled to keep the tremor from her voice.

She is really uptight about this, Dash thought, watching her walk toward the bathroom, then retrace her steps to pick up her duffel bag and hug it to her.

She stopped before she entered the room. "I don't think I want you looking at me when I tell you." She went into the bathroom and closed the door. She pressed her face against the wood of the door, drawing in deep breaths. Why should she feel guilty and afraid? He's the gambler. It was in his gambling casinos that the man who besmirched her uncle's name played. How could she have approached Dash and told him what she was planning to do? He would have had her thrown out of the place or arrested. She looked at her duffel bag, then lifted the file out of her bag. She hated it! Now when she showed it to Dash, he would hate her.

Dash stood there in the outer room, listening to the muffled sounds of her movements in the bathroom, his hands jammed into the pockets of his suit coat. He had pushed her to the wall, forced the issue. She could end up despising him. He took a deep breath. "Whatever it is, darling, we will be staying together. Don't doubt that." He spoke to the closed door, then he peeled off his suit coat and shirt and flung them at a chair. He stalked down the corridor to the other bathroom that belonged to the suite. He shaved, alternately cursing his image and telling it he was right. He washed quickly and left, retracing his steps toward the other bathroom. He inhaled a deep breath and pushed the door open.

Lotus was sitting in front of the vanity in the bathroom doing her nails when Dash entered, a towel around his waist. "Hi."

"Hi."

She pushed at the folder on the vanity. "That is a copy of the file in your office. I took the file, had it copied, then returned it."

"Why?" He spoke low, not wanting to interrupt the jerky statements she was making.

"Because the file says that my uncle ran up huge bills in your casinos both in Las Vegas and in Atlantic City. It isn't true." Her eyes flew to his face. "He isn't a gambler, and even if he were, he would never take funds from the family company."

Dash sighed. "I have heard the same story many times before, Lotus."

"This time it's true. Uncle loved Sinclairs. He would never do anything to harm the business. He and my father have expanded the company so much. They have put their blood and backs into it, so have my brothers and my cousins. No one in our family would do such a thing."

"I see," Dash said quietly. He took the file from the vanity, turned, and left the room. He sat in one of the chairs, his eyes speed-reading the information in front of him, aware that she had come into the room and stood at his side. When he was through, he handed the file back to her and rose to his feet. "If what you say is true, then the file is a lie and someone has embezzled funds from your family's company."

Lotus's eyes widened. "You accept what I say?" Relief and a flood of love filled her. She felt blinded by Dash for a moment.

"I accept that you would tell the truth to the best of your ability. That means that someone else is lying. So . . . we'll find out who that is."

"*We.*" Lotus's voice trembled.

"We, my darling. We are going to settle this together. Then after we settle it, I'm going to take you to Boston to meet my family."

"I like Boston," Lotus ventured, feeling a small wriggle of relief deep inside. Perhaps they could settle things! No, she wouldn't get her hopes up! "Do you live near Quincy Market?"

"Ah, we own some land around there." Dash smiled at her, delighting in seeing some of the tension dissipate in her face.

"Oh, is your family in fishing?" Lotus knew that the Charles River wasn't that far from the market.

"Ah, yes, we have been in fishing."

Lotus nodded. "Fishermen."

"Now maybe we should study this file more closely. We might pick up a glimmer of who the culprit could be," Dash told her, taking her arm and sitting her on the chair while he took the hassock in front of her.

"All right." She felt almost euphoric. He believed in her! He wanted to help her! Could he be fooling her? She brushed away such a stupid thought. She loved Dash.

"Then after we look at it, will you tell me how you got into my office, and even more important how you learned to use a burglar's tool?"

Lotus laughed. "It wasn't that difficult, but I won't tell you how I got Hans away from the door because then you might fire my friend."

"Richard?"

Lotus gasped. "How did you know?"

"You were seen talking to Richard. And he won't be fired, but I am putting him in another casino away from Hans. There would be ill feeling if he stayed at Cicero's."

Lotus stood, rocking the overstuffed chair, seeing Dash rise from the hassock. She reached up to him. "Dash. Thank you." She kissed his chin.

Dash held her when she would have moved back from him. "He has his job because he's your friend, my darling." His mouth took hers in a plundering kiss that had her dizzy.

They sat down again, but this time Lotus was in his lap. They pored over the file twice, but Lotus couldn't find anything pertinent. Dash didn't say anything. She assumed he had come to the same conclusion.

He rose with her in his arms. "I think it's time to relax a little." He kissed her nose as he stood her on her feet. "Now get dressed." He took the file with him and left the room.

Later, as Lotus dressed in the beautiful salmon-colored satin evening suit, with matching shoes and bag, she studied herself in the mirror as she donned the jewelry. *I don't know him. I never know what he's thinking, but he doesn't frighten me. I don't feel threatened. But what kind of man is Dash Colby?*

She was turning in front of the full-length mirror in the bedroom when Dash entered from the hall. "How do I look?"

"Wonderful."

Lotus saw the heat in his eyes and she felt like preening. She lifted her chin, sucked in her tummy, and inhaled.

"Darling, you are lethal enough already. Don't try to arm yourself any more than you are. You're shooting me down as it is." His body reacted to her at once. He grinned at her ruefully when he saw her eyes drop down to the revealing bulge in his trousers. "We'll have to hope my jacket camouflages your effect on me, angel. I can't seem to control what you do to me." He slipped into the jacket he had been holding over his shoulder with one finger. "Do I look covered enough?"

Lotus let her eyes rove over him as he stood before her in the gray silk evening suit, the fine silver threads the same shade as his gray-blue eyes and making the silver lights in his hair gleam. "You're gorgeous," she told him.

He felt the blood cascading through his veins at her words, his heart thumping painfully in his chest. He struggled to control his ragged breathing. "You do have a way with words, angel."

"Hasn't anyone ever told you that you're gorgeous?" Lotus chuckled feeling like Wonder Woman all at once, feeling such a rush of love and gratitude for him. He had accepted that her uncle was innocent! He was already committed to finding out who the real criminal was! She felt humble and proud that she was with Dash. What an awesome fate had led her to him!

"Maybe. I don't know. Even if they did, it sure never mattered as much as it does now," he drawled, the lazy heat of his smile reaching out for her. "Shall we go?"

"Yes." Lotus felt helium light as she glided toward him.

"Will I muss your lip gloss if I kiss you?"

Lotus lifted her head. "Kiss proof."

Dash's mouth covered hers in a deep, searching kiss. He had to push back from her, his breathing ragged. "Darling, we have to go."

The taxi ride along Fifth Avenue was a blur to Lotus because Dash held her, but when she saw that they were pulling up in front of the Plaza Hotel, she gasped. "I've always wanted to dine here."

"You'll like the Edwardian Room." Dash watched her, passion and amusement filling him as her head swiveled every which way as they entered the side door and walked along the short corridor to the Edwardian Room.

"I like piano," Lotus said when the maitre d' led them to a cozy table in the corner so that one view was toward Central Park, the other toward the square across from Bergdorf Goodman. She stared at the graceful brunette playing the instrument, her hands flying over the keys as she played a Gershwin tune. "She's quite good, isn't she?"

"New Yorkers are very sophisticated even to the cab drivers, bus drivers, maids, you name it. They demand the best . . . and they get it in New York. There is very little second best here." Dash smiled at her, then nodded to the wine steward to bring

Dom Pérignon, ordering prawns Pernod at the same time. "I know you like seafood."

Lotus smiled and nodded, wondering at herself. If her brothers had ordered without asking her, she would have railed at them, but she let Dash do it without a murmur.

He leaned toward her. "I won't do it again. I know you're independent, but I wanted you to taste this dish. It's very special."

"You read my mind?"

"I could see it bothered you that I had ordered for both of us."

"It should have bothered me. I don't know why it didn't," Lotus told him frankly. "You have a strange effect on me."

"God! Tell me about strange effects." Dash hovered over her while they drank the champagne and ate.

The only person who claimed their attention was the pianist and then only when she played a love ballad.

From the Plaza they went to Regine's where they danced.

It stunned Lotus at how easily Dash moved through each motion of the slow or fast dancing. He was liquid movement. "Thank you for being you," she murmured to him, bending her head back to look at him, chuckling when she saw the bemused expression on his face.

He shook his head. "I won't bother to ask what's going through your head now." His voice was thick as he bent over her.

When at last they took a cab home, Dash held her and kissed her. Even in the elevator that took them to the apartment he embraced her. Lotus knew she would have been angry with him had he not taken her right to bed and made love to her all night.

The sun was coming up slowly when she remembered that there was much more to discuss about the Sinclair file. How would they go abut searching for the person who had masqueraded as her uncle?

CHAPTER FIVE

Lotus's body ached when she awoke, but she felt as though she were seeing life anew. Yet, her limbs felt heavy. Her body seemed to have a density to it that it had never had. She was very much in love.

"Hello." Dash rolled her over on top of him.

"Hello," Lotus breathed, loving the way her hair curtained them from the world.

"I've put the coffee on and I came back to this room to waken you, but when I saw your little backside, I had to get back in bed."

"Did you?" Lotus felt tingly. Then she remembered, masking a yawn behind her hand. "Should we talk more about the file?"

"So talk, darling."

"Right here. Shouldn't we get up? I should dress."

"Here is fine."

Lotus stared down at him, not wanting the world they had built between them to crack and crumble. She sighed. "It's not a long story."

"Go on."

"I didn't break into your office. As you know, Richard took Hans's attention away so that I could slip in the door. I did break into your safe. I'll show you the tool. I told you a little about my uncle last night and how ill he is. I did it to clear his name of running up gambling debts at your casino and skimming money from our company to pay for them."

"Go on."

"He couldn't do such a thing. He's incapable of being anything but forthright. That's why I wanted the file. I don't know who signed his name but it wasn't my uncle."

"Who do you think did this?" Dash probed in quiet tones.

"I don't know."

"You can't think of anyone?"

"No. It must have been a stranger. Someone who has access to the company . . ."

"That doesn't make sense, love. How could a stranger juggle the books? What type of accounting department does the company have?"

"The company is called Sinclairs, after our family. My great-grandfather was a friend of George Eastman, the founder of Kodak," Lotus said, repeating the proud maxim of the family in a distracted way. She gulped a shaky breath. "It has to be a stranger, Dash. Most of the employees at Sinclairs, in every department, have been there for years. Loyalty is a built-in commodity."

"Gambling can get out of control, like drinking or drugs get out of control. There are no friends, just the game, the thrill, the roll of the dice. An addicted person will do almost anything to satisfy the craving." He stroked her. "And then there is the person who has a larcenous soul. They all don't come with a mask and gun, Lotus. Some of them wear business suits and carry briefcases, but they systematically rob the companies or persons they work for year after year. How many times have you read about a lawyer or business manager dipping into another's income? Thievery has many faces, some of them sophisticated."

Lotus studied him. "I guess I know you're right, but it's very hard to accept that someone like that works at Sinclairs."

Dash kissed her throat, his hand going over her like a sensuous feather. "Maybe I'm way off the target, sweetheart."

"And maybe you're not." She sighed. She smiled at him, feeling her lips tremor. "If we are to keep talking, you'll have to stop rubbing my backside. My concentration is slipping."

Dash chuckled throatily. "Tell me about it."

Lotus let her head sink on his chest. "Let me finish. This isn't easy."

"All right." Dash's breath lifted the fine hair on her brow. "Go on with your story."

Lotus's insides felt raw as she recalled those days just after the discovery was made by an outside auditing firm that had always come in and done the books twice a year. "When the officers of Denton, Denton and Fix came to my father's and uncle's offices that day, I was there, working, as I usually did whenever there was a break in my studies. . . ."

"This is when you were in the master's program at the university?"

"At Rochester Institute of Technology, actually. They have a fine Graphic Arts department."

"And you wanted to be a photographer?"

"Yes. I have always wanted to be a photographic

journalist, especially an overseas correspondent, but I have been sidetracked a few times."

"You're beautiful enough to be in front of the camera as a model, not behind it as a photographer."

"I did do a little modeling but I like the camera work best."

"Did you model in Rochester?" Dash felt a choking constriction in his throat and chest. Jealousy! He'd never experienced such an emotion before meeting Lotus.

"Some, but not much."

Dash had a vivid vision of her doing lingerie modeling and flinched. "We're getting away from the subject. You were telling me about the accounting firm confronting your uncle and father."

"Yes. They told them the attempts to juggle the books were done by someone knowledgeable in accounting and that the handwriting was familiar to them. . . ." Lotus gulped and pressed her face into Dash's chest. "It was uncle's handwriting, and he had signed the pages, but he swore he didn't do it." She jerked her head up. "And we all believe him . . . but, it came out in the papers anyway." Tears rolled down her cheeks. "God! I never cry!" She gasped. "He turned into a ghost overnight."

Dash rolled her on her side next to him, reaching down to lick the tears from her cheeks. "Darling, don't."

"He's such a good man. His face went from sunny health to gray. He stopped smiling. He wouldn't look at anyone. Then he had the stroke." Lotus sobbed.

"Damn it. I'll find out who did this. And as for the debts, darling, they're canceled."

Lotus dried her face with her hand. "No. My family always pays its debts. We'll pay this one."

Dash looked down at her, her tear-filled eyes having an emerald luster, her pink-white skin flushed as she struggled with her agitation. Her blue-black hair was in damp strands across her face as his fingers gently lifted it away from her skin. "You are so very beautiful, my China doll."

"Thank you." Lotus tried to smile at him.

Dash grasped her close to him, his face in her hair. "God, darling, I won't let anything make you cry."

Lotus lifted her arms and twined them round his neck. "I don't think I'm going to get breakfast." She gave him a watery smile.

"Not at this moment, no." Dash growled into her ear, his mouth sliding down her frame, touching every pore and pulse point on her body.

Again the life force filled them and exploded in kaleidoscope around them, showering them with electric bliss of sensual love.

"Oh, I do like that," Lotus simpered, blowing in his ear.

"You are a little devil," Dash whispered, patting her behind. "Now get yourself out of this bed, woman, or we'll never fly to Rochester."

"I forgot." Lotus shot to a sitting position.

Dash grinned at her as he rose to his feet, pulling her with him. "Think nothing of it, angel. I've forgotten a multimillion dollar deal . . . and it doesn't bother me," he finished, amazed at what he had just said. It was true! It didn't bother him that he'd put a mega-bucks deal in jeopardy just to be with Lotus.

They showered, Dash telling her ruefully that he had better take his shower in the extra bathroom of the suite. "I couldn't take a shower with you . . . and not caress you, China Doll."

Lotus was appalled at the sense of loss she felt when he left her. "Pull yourself together, girl," she chided herself while scrubbing her head. "He isn't your lifelong companion. You'll lose him to someone, or something else in the not too distant future, so bite the bullet, kid," she muttered to herself as she toweled her body dry.

When she returned to the bedroom wearing only bikini briefs and lacy bra, she started to repack the few things she had taken from her duffel bag, putting everything on the bed she had just made and carefully folding them. She was still bent over, putting things into her duffel bag, when she heard the guttural sound behind her.

"God! I thought you wanted to get out of here today." Dash was braced against the doorjamb.

Lotus grinned and straightened, not pretending to misunderstand him. "I do. We have to leave in twenty minutes, according to the time I heard you mention when you called the airfield."

"Then stop walking around in that peach-colored stuff." He grumbled, glaring at her when she laughed. "Testing your powers, darling?"

"Don't be silly." Lotus chuckled.

"I'm not the one strolling around in micro lingerie," He snapped, his eyes roving her from head to feet.

"I'm standing still." She poked her tongue at him, grabbed at the blouse and cotton trousers she would be wearing, and sprinted for the bathroom.

"You're a siren, lady." Dash's words came through the door, making her laugh.

She stared at herself in the mirror, the high color in her face, the emerald glitter of her eyes. "You love teasing him. It does make you feel powerful." She nodded at her mirror image. "I want the wonderful feeling he gives me. I want to love him," she whispered to herself. Was she deluding herself? She stared at the eyes shining with happiness that stared back at her. Was she building a dream out of pink fluff that would blow away at the first puff of trouble? She tried to send concise sensible reasons for being cautious to her brain, but all she could think of was being with Dash today, tomorrow, and all the other days in the future.

In a flurry of left-behind things to be returned for, and a jacket that she had misplaced, Lotus was out of breath and red in the face as they went down in the elevator to the waiting cab. "How do you manage to keep cool?" she quizzed him resentfully, scowling at his calm demeanor.

"Good planning." He gave her a smug smile.

"Not true," she yelped, stung. "You aren't even carrying luggage."

"That's good planning," Dash explained as though talking to a kindergartner.

"Humph." Lotus turned her back on him when he chuckled, stalking ahead of him out of the elevator and across the short lobby to the outer door that was opened by the doorman.

"Good day, miss."

"Good day to you." Lotus smiled at him, then hurried into the waiting cab.

The ride to LaGuardia Airport was as shattering to Lotus as the one they had taken from the helipad to the apartment, but this time they had to go through a tunnel. She could feel moisture bead on her body as the cab crawled forward into the enclosed area, then ground to a halt.

"What is it, darling? Aren't you feeling well?" Dash slid across the seat to take her in his arms. "Your face is perspiring." He could feel his teeth snap together as fear took him. Reason told him that she couldn't have contracted any disease, yet he could feel panic rising in him. "Did you eat something that didn't agree with you?" He forced calm into his voice.

"No," she whispered, turning her face to his chest. "I hate being shut in. Once, when I was small, I was playing with my brothers and cousins, and I hid in the fruit cellar in my uncle's basement. I couldn't get the door open, and I screamed and screamed . . ." Lotus gulped.

"And they wouldn't let you out?" Dash felt murderous.

"Oh, no, that wasn't it. The door was stuck and they didn't hear me. By the time they found me I was pretty shook up." She raised her head to give him a wobbly smile, then saw the cement block walls of the tunnel and buried her head again. "I'll be better once we leave here." Her muffled voice was barely audible to him as she pressed her face into his jacket.

"Darling," he groaned, keeping her close to him. "I should have arranged to take the helicopter." He pressed his face into the ebony silkiness of her hair, inhaling the special clean odor of her. "I do love the sweetness of you, love."

Lotus lifted her head, a slight tremor running through her body, then she fixed her eyes on his face. Much of her fear faded. "Silly man."

Dash could see the haunted look fading from her eyes. It made him feel such a surge of power that perhaps she wasn't afraid because he was with her. All his life he had looked down on machismo and men who adhered to it, and he always would, but all at once his masculine ego swelled. He wanted to protect her, stand between her and the world, be there for her, and take all the punches aimed at her. He wanted that more than anything in the world. "Nothing is going to hurt you."

Smiling at him, Lotus sighed with relief when they left the tunnel. She ran her finger down his nose. "And are you going to be my armor?"

"Yes."

Lotus felt shaken to her shoes. She stared into his eyes, trying to read behind the good-looking mask of his face. She saw strain there, but she couldn't really read him. Dash Colby was the orginal enigma, she thought. Nothing came through his skin from the inner person unless he chose to let it. Nothing penetrated unless it was his wish. How many persons ever got under his guard? she wondered. Yet, she didn't fear him. At the moment the only thing she really feared was losing him, not even her fear of being in an enclosed place was bigger than that. She wished she could summon all Dash's confidence that nothing would keep them apart.

"Not too many people get to me," Dash averred reading her mind. His lopsided grin widened when her lips parted in surprise. He touched her lips.

"You are Oriental, but you are not inscrutable. I thought I told you that."

"Yes. We decided that you're the inscrutable one," Lotus shot back, a little miffed that he could read her that way.

"Temper, temper." He chucked her under the chin, his grip tightening when she would have pulled away from him. "No, I don't want you out of my arms."

Lotus subsided, exhaling a deep breath. "I don't want to leave." No truer words were ever spoken, she thought. She didn't want to leave his arms, but she had a feeling the world could get in the way. She hated the thought of it.

"Stop building ghosts and relax," Dash said into her hair, happy to hold her and answer her desultory questions as they approached the airport.

The taxi driver had less of a problem with traffic once he left the highway to get onto the access road that led to the private plane hangars.

Lotus sat up as Dash released her as they pulled over to the curb. "My goodness, I never realized that so many people flew their own planes."

Dash laughed. "Yes, there are quite a few, but some of those planes are corporate jets too. Many companies feel that it's more convenient to maintain a jet for their staff than to fly them commercially. It is certainly more comfortable for them." Dash led the way, carrying her duffel bag, hurrying Lotus when she dawdled to stare out the window at a small plane taxiing up to the door of the terminal.

Dash held a door open for her with his shoulder, and she passed him to go out to the field. They hurried to the open door of a Lear jet standing by.

"Is someone else going to fly us this time?" Lotus noticed the name Coldris Limited, Inc. on the side of the plane just before they went up the steps into the craft.

Dash signaled to an attendant to close the door. Then he turned and nodded. "I thought you might prefer to have me conversing with you on the trip."

Lotus nodded, feeling shy with him all at once. "You mustn't look at me like that in front of my family. They might bring out the shotgun."

"Great idea," Dash drawled, walking over to her, and lifting her jacket from her shoulders. "Come on, darling, there's the bell. I want to strap you in." Dash led her to a round-backed chair with a large desk-cum-table in front of it.

"They look more like easy chairs than airplane seats." Lotus put her head back on the overstuffed cushion and watched him strap himself in next to her.

"The idea is to be comfortable." He lifted her hand and put her small finger into his mouth, sucking at the tip. "Are you?"

"Am I what?" Lotus said, feeling her blood heat to caldron temperature.

"Are you comfortable, darling?"

"Very," she replied, not even realizing that the Lear jet was rising in almost vertical ascent. "It's so private."

"Yes, indeed. Perhaps one day we'll take a trip to a little island I know in the Caribbean. What do you think?"

"I have to work." Lotus felt out of breath.

"So do I. You must be able to take some time off."

"I'll get one week's vacation this year."

"God. We should be able to do better than that." Dash looked at her, the bridge of his nose creased in disapproval.

"I am not a plutocrat." She lifted her chin.

"Are you censuring me, angel?"

Lotus held his look for long minutes, then she nodded, smiling. "I suppose. I don't know why I do that to you."

"I think you disapprove of my way of making a living."

Lotus was about to shake her head, then she bit her lip. "Maybe that's it. I never thought of myself as someone who disapproved of gambling, but my attitude must have changed because of my uncle. I don't know." She looked away from him, feeling her brow wrinkle.

"It won't keep us apart, China Doll."

She swiveled her head around to look at him. "Dash, it could just do that. I think we should be realistic."

"It won't because I won't let it."

"Dash, I don't think we should pretend that we could have a long-time relationship. . . ."

"And I think you should come right out and tell me if you are trying to dump me," he said, the bones in his face pushing through the flesh and skin.

Lotus stared at him. "How can you think that?"

"Because that's the way you're talking," he shot back.

"I don't mean to"—Lotus threw up her hands—"you see. We don't know each other well enough to really understand each other, and understanding is basic to any—"

"Don't say it," Dash interrupted her. "Whatever it takes, however many compromises, the changes, the retreats . . . I am prepared to do it."

Mouth agape, Lotus stared at him. "You are?"

"I am."

"Dash . . . my family . . ." Lotus took a deep breath. "They are the best people in the world, but they might not welcome you when they find out who you are."

"Don't tell them who I am. Introduce me as J. D. Colby. Call me J.D. They won't make the connection, especially if you tell them that I'm one of the Boston Colbys."

Lotus lifted her chin, looking down her nose. "Ah, yes, the fish people, don't you know? They have a marvelous fleet of boats, the longest of which is five feet."

"A little longer than that," Dash told her lazily.

"Not to mention the property on Cape Cod."

"Martha's Vineyard," Dash corrected her.

"That too." Lotus flapped her hand at him.

"And the house on Beacon Hill," Dash helped her.

Lotus paused, then shook her head. "I don't think we should say that. That's a bit much. Some-one is liable to say that they know someone on the hill and then where would we be?"

"Behind the eight ball?"

"Precisely."

"Then we'll just mention the fishing boats and delete Beacon Hill. Should we mention that I went to Harvard?"

"Fatal. My brothers would be bound to ask you what year and if you crewed or something." Lotus settled back in her chair letting her eyelids droop when she felt his hand massaging her back, his mouth at her temple.

"I don't suppose we could tell them I crewed and played football."

"Uh-uh." Lotus yawned. "Better to be vague about your schooling."

"Vague it is," Dash assured her. "Take a little nap. You had a late night."

"Yes. Some cad was in my bed," Lotus said and chuckled.

"I had a funny experience myself. Some sexy Eastern goddess attacked me. I tried to resist, but she overpowered me."

"Poor baby." Lotus snuggled under his chin, feeling so safe and warm.

When the plane began its descent for the city of Rochester a little better than an hour later, Dash hated to wake her. She felt so right in his arms. He wanted to keep her there. "She's mine, and I'll do whatever I have to do to keep her," he vowed just before shaking her gently awake.

"Did I fall asleep again? I'm terrible. I never used to nap like this." Lotus smiled sleepily when he laughed. "And don't get too conceited about your prowess in bed. . . ." Lotus gulped and cringed when an attendant stopped at their seat. She was sure he had heard her even though his impassive expression gave her no clue.

"Sir, we'll be taxiing up to the gate and there is a car waiting as you ordered."

"Thank you, Jimmy." Dash chuckled as Lotus continued to press against him even after the attendant turned away and went to the forward cabin.

Lotus wouldn't lift her head even after the two-bell signal, telling them that they could unbuckle their seat belts.

"Here, let me unhook you, darling."

"No, I am going to hide under the seat. I know he heard what I said to you."

"No matter. We're getting married."

Lotus's head shot up. "We don't know that . . . even if we are, I don't want people hearing me talk like that. My family would be shocked . . . well, maybe not shocked, but they would be surprised that I talk that way."

"Families are always shocked, stunned, surprised, whatever at what their progeny do. It's the name of the game. From what I hear it's always white-knuckle time raising a family," Dash told her, kissing her on the cheek.

A baby boy with laughing eyes who looked just like Dash was pictured in her mind. Lotus caught her breath, looking up at Dash as he stood, stretching. Then he reached out a hand to help her from her seat.

"Ready, darling?" Dash inclined his head as he looked at her.

Lotus's imagination took over again and she saw a tow-headed toddler with blue eyes like his father. He would be strong and determined, ready to ride a bike the day he learned to walk. She felt soft and warm inside as she pictured him. The bottoms of her feet tingled as she thought of feeding and caring for a baby who looked just like Dash. It was insane!

"Darling, you're daydreaming." He kissed her cheek, then patted her backside, urging her toward the door.

Lotus nodded, dreamily, barely taking notice as

they walked across the tarmac to the small terminal building across the field from the larger one used by commercial flight travelers. All at once she snapped alert. She was beginning to accept that it was a feasible thing to marry Dash! She tried to throw her brain into full stop, but she couldn't stop the rosy imagery. In minutes they were in a brand-new Mercedes sedan. "My goodness. Rental cars are marvelous, aren't they?"

"I hope you like this." Dash leaned on the wheel and looked at her after he started the car. "I just thought of something. This is your hometown. Perhaps you should drive."

"You would let me drive this?" Lotus grinned disbelievingly. Her brothers had fits when she drove their cars, and it took a great deal of pleading and coaxing to get them to relent.

Dash watched the play of emotions on her face. Then he opened his door and came around to her side of the car, opened it, and ushered her around to the driver's seat. He waited while she adjusted the seat to the right height to accommodate her shorter legs. "There." He kissed her, closed the driver's door, and went around the car to get into the passenger seat. "The more I think of it, the better it sounds. This way you can drive and show me the sights, and I can look at everything."

Waiting for him to give her instructions or admonishments, she felt a moment's nervousness. She looked over at him, her breath catching at the lazy intimacy of his smile.

"Well? Are we ready, darling?"

"Yes." Lotus breathed, engaging the clutch and pressing gently on the accelerator.

With a barely perceptible jerk the powerful car purred forward.

Lotus was delighted with the hum of the engines, the easy motion of the well-tuned mechanism under her hands. "It's a wonderful car."

"Do you like it, darling?" *I'm going to buy her one,* he decided. A Mercedes Sport would be more her style. The thought of buying such a car for her excited him more than anything had in a long time. Giving things to Lotus would be like getting a gift himself, he mused, watching her small strong hands grip and slide over the steering wheel. Even driving, she is the most graceful of women. She has a built-in beauty of motion. *God! I'm getting poetic about my China doll.*

"Are you ready to tell me to pull over? Is that why you're so quiet?"

"Wrong, China Doll. I was just thinking how gracefully you handle this automobile. You have great instincts."

Lotus felt herself swell with pride. "Thank you."

"Thank you for chauffeuring me," Dash told her then looked out his window. "Now tell me where we're going and what I should look for."

"We're going to the Strathallan, I think you said. That is one of our best hotels in the city." She threw him a quick grin. "I've never stayed there, but I've had a drink in Hattie's Lounge which is a fun place for cocktails in Camera Town."

"Is that what Rochester is called?"

"That plus a few other things, like the city of cold weather, city of the lilacs, and a few more." Lotus laughed.

"But you're proud of your hometown?"

"Oh, yes. I can't really recall living any other

place. I have a hazy recollection of Japan with my other parents, but nothing too concrete. I would like to travel back to Japan someday and see China too."

"I'll take you . . . to both countries." He grinned at her when her head swiveled momentarily his way. "Really. I mean it. We'll go there after we're married." Dash felt his chest expand with delight as he thought of Lotus Sinclair becoming Lotus Sinclair Colby.

"Really?" Lotus answered, halfway between believing and disbelieving, her hands tightening on the steering wheel.

Dash slid toward her, still slouched down on his spine. "I am not fooling about this. I intend to marry you. Do you intend to marry me?" He sucked in air and held it.

Lotus was silent for a minute, then a smile lifted her mouth. "I'm going to take the Fifth Amendment." She felt happy and sad all at once. Dash said he wanted to marry her. Yet Lotus knew they were poles apart. He had come from working people like hers, but he had risen above the strong New England work ethic that spawned him. He was far beyond that!

"So far you have not pointed out one sight that I should look at in your fair city," Dash whispered.

"What?" Lotus was jerked back to the moment. She took time to pull out into the center lane to pass, then she scooted back to her own lane. "Let's see. Oh, we've traveled farther than I thought. There's the Genesee River and to the south you can see the river campus of the university. That is the center of town straight ahead." She pulled the car into the turning lane. "We get off here. This isn't the shortest way to go, but I thought you might like to see the center of town." Lotus made a few turns, then they were in downtown. She wove in and out of traffic, finally getting to East Avenue. "This is a lovely street. The George Eastman House is located here and the homes are quite beautiful."

Dash put his hand on her knee and squeezed it. They turned down a street called Strathallan Park, and he looked closely at the discreet wooden sign in front of the modern building saying only STRATHALLAN. "Nice building," he commented as Lotus pulled into the circular driveway and an attendant from the parking livery opened the passenger door.

Dash came around to usher her out before the attendant could get there, glaring at the individual when he tried. He wasn't about to let anyone put his hands on Lotus! Fierce possessiveness was alien to him, but he recognized it. For most of his life he had been indifferent to maintaining a relationship. Now he found himself ready to take on a planet to keep Lotus. "Come along, darling. It shouldn't take long to settle things."

"But will they want to take you? You have no luggage," Lotus murmured from the side of her mouth as they approached the concierge in the small lobby.

Dash shrugged. "I should think so. Besides, Hans probably arranged to have some things sent here."

Lotus shuddered. "He doesn't like me."

"No, I don't think he does, but you must remember that to Hans, Cicero's is everything—home, wife, pastime. He has few other interests."

In moments they were being swept up to the floor where Dash's suite was located.

"Why don't you call your folks, and I'll shower and change? Then perhaps you could join me in the shower."

Lotus gave a breathless laugh. "We'd never get to my parents." She watched him chuckle then turn away. "Dash."

"Yes, love." He swiveled around to look at her.

"Do you think I'll be able to discover who forged my uncle's signature?"

"We'll find out together, China Doll."

"I hope we can."

"Believe it." He blew her a kiss and went through to the bathroom. "Lotus. Honey, come here a minute."

In the middle of dialing the phone when she heard him call to her, Lotus replaced the receiver and followed him.

"See," Dash said, and pointed to the open closet in the dressing room that held shirts, sports coats, and suits. He pulled out some built-in drawers.

"Socks and underwear," Lotus exclaimed. "You're a very spoiled man."

"Wrong. I have a very efficient staff." He walked toward her, his eyes glinting over her. "You are one pretty lady, China Doll."

"Dash." Lotus backed up. "We haven't got time. I haven't called my parents."

Dash reached out for her, lifting her toward him, impatience coursing through him at the thought that other people would be intruding between Lotus and him. He didn't like it! Even if it were her family! He sighed as he kissed her. "All right, you have to call your parents. Then join me in the shower." He saw the negative look on her face. He would be showering by himself. As she turned to leave the dressing room area of the suite, he patted her backside, rubbing his hand over the firm roundness of her. "I really do love to touch you, my sweet."

"You touch me all the time." Lotus grinned at him before she closed the door.

"Are you going to show me the lilacs?" Dash managed to say before she closed the door entirely.

"Of course." The door shut.

Dash thought of her as he stared at the very adequate shower area. It was a relief to him. Being a tall man, he felt very uncomfortable when he was forced to slouch in the shower.

Lotus looked at the closed door for a few minutes then she sighed, went to the phone and dialed her home. The trouble was that she wanted to join him in that shower in the worst way. "Hello. Yes, Mother, it's me, Lotus. Oh, no, nothing's wrong. I'm just fine. I'll be home in about an hour. I'm waiting here for—for J.D. to get changed. No, we're at the Strathallan. Yes, that's right. How is Uncle? He is! Oh, I'm so glad. Yes, I love you too. See you in a bit." Lotus replaced the receiver, then listened to the water of the shower. "Watch out, Dash Colby. Here I come." She was stripping off her clothes even as she walked to the bathroom, dropping them on a chair, taking care not to wrinkle the skirt and blouse that she would need to wear later.

Then she pushed open the door, smiling at the steam issuing forth from the shower. She took a deep breath, removed her underthings, opened the door, and stepped inside. "Hi."

"Hi." Dash's hands were still uplifted, scrubbing his head as he looked at her. "Nice outfit."

"I'm not wearing anything."

"Definitely haute couture, love." He reached out for her with soapy hands and pulled her closer to him. "Shall I make the water warmer?" His voice was thick all at once as he put his wet face down on her shoulder. "Darling, you are so beautiful."

"Thank you. You're cute too." Lotus felt her breathing skip out of rhythm as he stroked her.

"I'll love being cute if that's what you want."

"Oh, I want you all right," Lotus dared him.

"You've got me." He rinsed the soap from her body and lifted her out of the shower to swaddle her in a warm towel. "And you're going to have me more fully in just a few more minutes."

"Wonderful." Lotus let her head flop foreward on his shoulder as he carried her to the bedroom. "We'll be late."

"Not too late," Dash assured her as he laid her on the bed, then followed her down, casting aside the towel he'd wrapped around his own waist.

"Your bed will be damp tonight."

"I don't mind, love. There are clean sheets in the linen closet if I want to change them and the mattress will be dry," he muttered, not seeming to care as his eyes roved her from head to toe. "You are my China doll."

"Yes." Lotus reached up and pulled him down to her, kissing his mouth and clinging to him. She loved him! Oh, how she loved the man!

Dash felt his heart thudding against his ribs as she continued to caress him. Never had anyone moved into his life and taken it over as this tiny Oriental Yankee had done. The scope of her hold on him awed him, yet it didn't frighten him away. He had kept other women at arm's length easily.

He wanted to glue himself to Lotus. The power drew him like a magnet. He felt her body quiver under him and excitement swirled around them. "Darling, wait, don't touch me. I want to make it good for you."

"It's good now. I want you this minute," Lotus choked.

Soaring delight took them away. Dash felt helpless, but more potent than he had ever been. His muscles were flaccid but he felt as strong as Atlas. Nothing had ever made him feel more gentle or aggressive than this fragile, dark-haired, light-skinned woman.

Lotus sank back on the bed as the peak of their passion passed and she was sliding back to reality. "My goodness. That should be bottled and kept in the Smithsonian. I do like making love very much."

"But only with me." Dash felt a froth of jealousy sweep through him.

"But of course." She smiled up at him. Another thought intruded and Lotus frowned. "Dash, I don't want you to be angry if Jeremy is at the house. He often is."

"I'll still accompany you. I want to be with you."

"Oh, Lord, that's what I want too. I really want you with me." She reached up and touched his chin. "Jeremy isn't in love with me, just as I was never in love with him, but he is friends with my brothers and the rest of the family. I don't want him to be made uncomfortable in front of everyone, so I think we should wait for a more private time to talk to my parents."

Dash nodded.

Lotus looked at the wall clock and yelped,

"Goodness, I'll be late, and I told Mother that I would be there in an hour."

"We'll make it. Just put your tush in gear."

"Yours too, mister," Lotus said. As Dash walked by her, she slapped him on the bottom. "I do like that backside of yours."

Surprise flashed over his face and was gone. "Was it too macho when I patted you?"

"No, not coming from you, but I just thought I'd point out how that seems to a woman. From the man she loves and who loves her, it's great, but from just any man, it's an insult."

"Well, I love you, China Doll." He ran his hand through her hair.

"I love you too," Lotus said sadly. "But I'll bet you anything it won't work out."

"Believe it. It will." Dash hurried her into the bathroom, then disappeared.

They dressed in record time and were downstairs waiting for the rented car to be brought to the front door in less time than Lotus figured.

"I can't believe you're letting me drive," Lotus said as they tooled down the drive. "Did you see the attendant look at you when you helped me into the driver's seat?"

Dash shrugged. "I like the way you drive."

Once on the expressway, Lotus began to think of her homecoming. "I really like to come home. We live right on Lake Ontario and in the summer we swim and water ski, and we golf in a park close to us. We can walk there." Aware she was chattering, Lotus paused.

"I hope you won't feel too bad if we live some of our time away from here. My businesses are in

Las Vegas and Atlantic City and I have holdings elsewhere, so we won't always be here."

"Dash, don't talk as though we are getting married right away."

"We are."

"No. Let's table that kind of talk until I see how it goes with my uncle and family."

Dash said nothing for long seconds, then he lifted one shoulder. "We'll see." He picked up the folder she had copied from his files, scanning it. "I can tell you that the man who signed these IOU's is not on my personal staff. I know their handwriting. So if there was some hanky-panky with the books, it doesn't look as though it was at our end."

"No. It wouldn't make sense." She sighed. "I think you're right about it not being a stranger. It could be someone in Sinclairs' though, and that's what worries me. There are quite a few people in the accounting department."

"We'll find out one way or the other. I've told my staff to examine the books and the files and see if they come up with any pictures of the man who called himself Sinclair and signed the IOU's and sent us the checks to cover the transactions."

"Thank you." Lotus felt teary. Dash believed in her! Not once had he indicated that he felt that she could be wrong about her uncle.

CHAPTER SIX

Lotus's family overwhelmed her with greetings. It seemed that everyone had shown up to greet her. Even her cousins were there.

There were dogs barking and everyone was talking at once.

"I can't wait to see Uncle. Mother told me he was improving."

"Yes," her cousin Lee told her. "He came home three days ago and he seems better every day. That's why we're here. We talked your mother into having dinner with us. So we're taking the bouillabaisse to our house. Mom made the bread."

Lotus nodded and stepped back, pulling at Dash's hand. "Everybody, this is my friend, ah, J.D. Colby from . . ."

"Massachusetts," Dash finished, shaking hands with her smiling father whose wary eyes took in every detail of Dash. "My family is involved in fishing."

Her mother stepped forward with her hand outstretched. "You aren't related to Elspeth Cowles, who married one of the Colbys of Worcester, are you?"

"Elspeth's my aunt." Dash smiled.

Lotus watched her mother's eyebrows arch; then her mother frowned.

"I didn't know they were in fishing, exactly. I knew they had boats, but I thought they were on the stock exchange or something."

"Getting forgetful, Ginna." Her father kissed his wife's cheek.

"Hi, brat. How did you manage to keep out of trouble? By the way, Petras called and asked about you," her brother Robert said as he hugged her and gave her a smacking kiss.

"Did he ask why he wanted to know?" she asked, afraid that he might have told Rob she had been in Las Vegas.

"No, he just said he was thinking about you."

"Yeah. Everyone can sense when the brat is on her own," her brother Todd interjected, squeezing her.

"Don't tease her." Her father put his arm around Lotus. "How's my baby doing?" Her father gave her a big kiss, his eyes still assessing Dash.

"Good, Daddy. How are you?"

"Fine. Did ya have a good time? Did everything work out?"

"Uh, yes, thank you."

"You still have a few things to iron out, love," Dash interjected.

"Love?" Rob echoed, his eyes narrowing, his hands closing into fists. "Lotus, what's going on? Jeremy is going to join us at Uncle Silas's, and I think he expected to be your date."

"I don't think so," Dash said mildly.

Todd, the more reserved brother, looked from Lotus to Dash and back again. "Back off, Rob.

Our little sister is growing up. She doesn't need us to tell her how to behave."

"No, she doesn't," Dash agreed.

Lotus glared at him, then smiled at her older brother. "I do have something to discuss with Jeremy when I see him."

"Lotus . . ." Ginna Sinclair said worriedly.

Her husband shushed her. "Leave her be, Ginna. She's always had a good head. But I think there's something you're not telling me."

"Quite a few things, I think," Rob said darkly.

Her cousin, Lee, named after her own mother, Lela, put an arm around her. "Lotus knows what she's doing."

"I hope so," Lotus muttered, eliciting a chuckle from Dash.

"Will you be staying with us, Mr. Colby?" Mrs. Sinclair smiled at him.

"Thank you, but no, ma'am. I have a room downtown."

"Staying at the Strathallan is a little more than having a room," Rob interjected, his eyebrows almost meeting over the bridge of his nose.

"Robert," Mrs. Sinclair admonished. "Mr. Colby is our guest."

"Yes, Mother." Robert inclined his head, telling Dash to precede him into the living room of the old-fashioned high-ceilinged house that had been built by their grandfather before the Great Depression. Floor-to-ceiling leaded glass windows overlooked the expanse of Lake Ontario, and though not much could be seen in the dark, the moon and stars cast silver paths across the surface of the water.

Dash accepted a beer from Todd and stared out the window. "It's beautiful here."

Lotus turned eagerly and nodded. "Yes, it is. I love it."

Lee came up to them with a glass in her hand. "I brought you seltzer water and lime." She smiled up at Dash, her curly blond hair dancing around her pretty face. "You're the first man Lotus has ever brought home who hasn't lived in this area. . . ." She sipped her own seltzer water and lime. ". . . She has always had boyfriends, that's for sure." Lee stopped abruptly, her face pinking. "You'd probably like to be alone. Sorry."

Lotus hugged her cousin who was also her best friend. They had gone through grammar school and high school together, and though they had gone to different colleges, it hadn't changed the friendship between them. "Don't be silly."

Lee shot Dash a quick glance after he looked out the window again. "What do you think Jeremy will say about the competition?"

Lotus shrugged. "We dated very casually. I don't think he'll be too hurt." She frowned. "We've actually been pulling away from each other for a while now. He travels a great deal for the company, and he's so absorbed in his work."

"You and he were friends because of Rob and Todd anyway," Lee said, her lips pursed.

"You and Will have never cared for Jeremy too much . . ."

"We don't happen to think he's treated you that well, breaking dates at the last minute . . ." Lee stated.

"That was the job," Lotus answered automatically, using the excuse she had always used when Jeremy had forgotten dates. "It doesn't matter." And she knew it didn't.

"Are you going to marry the hunk from Massachusetts?"

Lotus laughed, bringing Dash's head around, his face creasing in smiling warmth when he looked down at her.

"What's funny, darling?"

"Darling! He calls you darling," Lee said from the side of her mouth. "God, that's beautiful. Does he have a twin?"

"Ah . . . J. D., do you have a twin?" Lotus checked herself in time, trying to remember not to call him Dash.

Dash turned around, Todd at his side. "No. I have three sisters and a younger brother. I do have cousins, just as you do, who are close to my age."

"Still scouting around, Lee?" Todd said, amusement in his voice.

"Stop being so smug, Toddie. Just because you have Kate Dilson barking at your heels doesn't mean you're an expert on the subject," Lee told her cousin, kissing him on the cheek when he reddened. "I'm going to get Aunt Ginna going." She skipped from the room.

"I like Kate." Lotus patted Todd's arm. "She has a great forehand."

"Ah, yes, tennis." Todd kissed her cheek. "Did you miss playing while you were away, brat? Rafting must have been rough. Is that where you two met?"

Lotus felt uncomfortable with the lie she was living, but she couldn't tell Todd about the file just yet. She wanted to get a sample of everyone's handwriting at Sinclair's. Then, when she had the person in the accounting department who was doing the doctoring of the books, she would involve the family, but until she had concrete knowledge of the person she didn't want to say anything to them.

"We're hoping to play tennis before we go to Boston to visit my family," Dash said, trying to get the subject away from where Lotus had been.

Lotus whirled to face Dash, opening her mouth to ask him when they had discussed that; when she saw the small shake of his head she said nothing. "I think I'll go and help Mother." Lotus stalked away, her mind whirling. He had some nerve saying she was going to Boston! As far as she knew he hadn't even called his family to ask if they would be welcome. Was this the fishing season? What if all his family and their children were out in boats?

Once in the kitchen, she began working with Lee and her mother, preparing the big cauldron of bouillabaisse that would be taken just a quarter of a mile down the road to her uncle's home.

When Lotus saw Lee carry some dishes out to the waiting truck that would cart the stuff down the road, she faced her mother. "Tell me the truth, Mother. Is Uncle Silas better?"

Ginna Sinclair looked at her daughter, then patted her cheek. "He's truly improving, love, and in just the last few days. We think he's getting his old fight back. We had a family meeting about the . . . the discrepancies in the books, and we've decided" —she smiled at her daughter—"and we felt sure you would have agreed since you are a stockholder, that we will pay back the loss in small increments just like a loan."

"Uncle Silas didn't do it, Mother." Lotus sounded anguished. "I think we can prove that."

"Darling, we couldn't subject your uncle to another painful investigation."

"But he's innocent."

Her mother patted arm. "We know that, child, but there's nothing we can do about it at the moment without endangering your uncle's health. I know you don't want to do that."

"No." Lotus inhaled. "Someone used Uncle Silas."

"We know that just as well as you do, dear, but we also feel that the family has to pay this debt, so we will. You agree, don't you?"

"Yes, but that doesn't clear Uncle Silas's name and we must do that."

Ginna Sinclair sighed and shook her head.

In minutes the rest of the things were loaded with the bouillabaisse in two big steel pans with tight covers.

Dash appeared at her side as she was about to go upstairs. "Showering again?"

Lotus felt herself redden. "No, but I am going to change into a cotton dress. It has warmed up."

"I always feel warm around you," he crooned, sending her hightailing up the stairs, his chuckle clinging to her like another skin.

When she came back down the stairs after reapplying her makeup, Dash was still in the foyer. He looked up at her from his vantage point at the oak newel post at the foot of the stairs. "Lovely. I like that cherry red color on you. It makes your hair glisten almost the color of a black patent leather belt."

"The jacket's linen," Lotus said, feeling shy with him. "I was going to wear cotton . . . but . . ." *What a foolish thing to say,* she chided herself. *As though he cares what material you wear! You are a such a fool with him, Lotus Sinclair!*

"It looks very cool." He lifted the black linen jacket from her arm and fitted it around her shoulders, noting that she was wearing higher heels. "Now you're up to my chin . . . almost," Dash said, leaning down to inhale the fragrance of her, the silken strands of her hair brushing his face.

"It's a nice evening for a walk. We'll take the path along the beach and you can see the water." She looked over her shoulder at him.

Dash took her hand in his, loving the feel of her. God, he wanted to make love to her right in the foyer of her house. "When I was talking to your brother, Todd, he mentioned your uncle."

"What did he say? Mother says he's better." Lotus tightened her fingers around his.

Dash lifted her hand to his lips, kissing each nail. "He made the remark that he felt edgy about getting a private investigator to handle your uncle's case. Two had turned him down." Dash grinned down at her. "He told me that he assumed I knew about the incident because if I was close to you, you would have told me. He said you are very close to all your family. I told him that I knew and wanted to help."

Lotus nodded. She stopped for a moment, facing him. "Do you really think we can change . . . I mean . . ."

Dash leaned over her. "If you're asking if I think we can find out who did this to your family, again I tell you that I think we can." He stared down at her anxious face. "We will settle this thing, darling. I promise you."

"Thank you."

They started to move forward slowly again.

"Have you always lived at home?" Dash voice sounded loud in the cool quiet of evening.

"When I was at college I had an apartment, but it was always good to be home. I like the water . . . swimming, water skiing."

"I like that too. When we get to my home, I'll take you out sailing."

She stopped, her foot sliding off the narrow walk into the deep sand that filled the wide beach leading to the water. She shook her foot, hanging onto his arm. "When did we say we were going to Boston?" Anxiety filled her. She didn't want to lose Dash. Yet she knew they were moving too fast. What if his family disliked her on sight?

"Don't you think you should meet my family before we marry?"

"We didn't say we were marrying," she tried to rally.

"You didn't. I did."

"But, Dash, I don't want to leave my family just now. I want to find out who did this to my uncle. . . ."

"I can tell you right now it wasn't your father or your brother, Todd. They—"

Lotus stamped her foot. "Of course it isn't my brother or my father! I never assumed that it was. The culprit is someone who works at Sinclair's. I'm sure of it." She was angry that he had even checked their writing.

"It doesn't hurt to cover all the bases, love."

Lotus shook her head. "It's foolish to suspect

my family." She tried to study the silver mask of his face in the moonlight, but it was closed to her. His eyes were warm but hooded. "I'll never really know you, will I? There are so many layers to you, so many depths."

"Ask me anything, darling. If I can't tell you, I will let you know why. Fair?"

"Yes. Have you ever been married?"

"Yes. I was divorced from my wife after six years of marriage. She obtained the divorce."

"Were you unfaithful to her?"

"I never slept with another woman until my wife asked me to leave our home. She told me that she was filing for divorce. One of the reasons given for the dissolution of the marriage was my infidelity, but I hadn't been unfaithful to her. I didn't care at that point what was said. I was glad to be out of it. We had made each other miserable."

"Does she live in Las Vegas?"

"No. She lives in Boston, and she's remarried twice since then. She still sees one of my sisters and once in a while my mother."

"I see."

"No, love, you don't see. I was never in love with anyone until I met you, but I never knew that until the moment I saw you standing in my office."

Lotus stood on tiptoe to kiss him and squealed with joy when he swept her high against his chest so that they were mouth to mouth. "I would like to meet your family."

"Good," he said against her lips. "First, we'll settle the problem here. Then you won't have it on your mind," he said simply.

All at once she knew with blinding clarity that

the "problem with her uncle" was almost settled. Dash would see to it!

They arrived at her uncle's home and were greeted by her uncle and aunt. Lotus hugged the two persons who had been like another set of parents to her.

"Darling, you look well." Uncle Silas's mouth twisted in a semblance of a smile.

"And so do you," Lotus said, relieved, giving her uncle a kiss. She introduced Dash to them, then they moved into the great room of the house where most of the people were gathered. Almost the first person Lotus saw was Jeremy. She felt a stab of guilt as she looked at him and saw the reproachful look he was giving her as he stood with Rob, her brother. "Dash, please forgive me, I have to speak to Jeremy. Alone."

Dash looked across the room, sizing up the dark-haired, tall but burly man who scowled at him. "All right, but I'll be close by."

"Don't be silly." She gave a choking laugh. "No one is going to hurt me."

"I'll be close," Dash told her, his face unsmiling. "If you were telling me good-bye, I would want to tear the town apart. So I'll stay near you."

"All right." Lotus left him. She saw that Todd had left his cousin, Will, and was approaching Dash. She walked over to Jeremy and Rob.

Rob nodded at her, then left them.

"I suppose I know what you're going to say, but it might be better if we went out on the terrace to talk. It's quieter," Jeremy said in his cool way.

"Fine." She passed him as he held the terrace door for her, then faced him as she tried to stay in the leeward corner of the porch. The northern breeze was brisk and had a bite to it in the early May evening. She took a deep breath. "We both know that we enjoyed each other's company, but we were never to love."

"Are you now?" Jeremy coughed.

"Yes," Lotus blurted out, then she sighed. "Oh, yes, I love him." She tried to smile at her friend. "If we dated for a thousand years, we would only be friends. We both know that."

"Rob says he comes from a wealthy Massachusetts family. That your mother knows the family."

Lotus gasped. "His family is in fishing. He has made his own money, and even if his family did have money, that wouldn't have influenced my decision."

"If you say so." Jeremy was still cool, but his eyes glittered. "I have no intention of leaving the company . . . at this time, Lotus."

"I wouldn't want you to do that." As they talked Lotus realized how apart in their thinking she and Jeremy really were. For a split second she wondered if Jeremy would have dated her had she not been a Sinclair. Then she pushed the thought away.

They rejoined the others and Dash was there. He put his hand out to Jeremy. "My name's J. D. Colby."

Jeremy's eyes flickered and narrowed. "I'm Jeremy Leeds. I've heard that name somewhere . . ."

"Dinner everyone." Lotus's mother came up to them and ushered them to the long great room at the front of the house that encompassed a large sitting room and a huge dining room together. While they dined, they could enjoy the cascade of moonlight and starlight that silvered the waters of Lake Ontario.

"The bouillabaisse is wonderful, Mrs. Sinclair," Dash said, and nodded to her mother; then he turned to Aunt Lela and smiled. "And I love home-made bread."

"It's good to hear laughter in this house again," Lotus's cousin, Will, whispered to her as they both listened to the rousing but good-natured argument Rob and Todd were having with their father about the football of today as opposed to his day.

Lotus could still see the shadows on her uncle's face as he sat at the head of the table in his wheelchair but much of the despair seemed to be gone. It delighted her that the doctors had informed her aunt that he would regain use of his right leg and arm and would be mobile by summer.

After eating, they all moved to the other end of the room so that they could watch the play of the garden lights on the water. Conversation was light as they sipped coffee and tried the dainty finger desserts made by Lotus's aunt.

When Todd suggested that they play charades, everyone looked at him.

Lotus felt her mouth drop. "It's been years since we played charades. I think I've forgotten how."

"Uncle Silas would like it, wouldn't you, Uncle?" Todd quizzed his relative. Everyone looked at Uncle Silas. When he nodded, everyone joined in with alacrity.

"Jeremy can be the captain of one team," Todd said. "I'll captain the other. Stay with your teams. The captains will gather the titles to be used, but let's make it as tough as we can. No one-worders. Let's do quotations and long titles."

"It sounds boring." Lee made a face at her brother, Will, when he told her to shape up.

Lotus agreed with Lee, then she looked at her uncle and picked up a small square of paper to write down her words.

"I like the idea," Dash drawled, bringing Lotus's head around.

She stared at the lazy smile he gave her, took note of the gleam of his eyes, then she nodded. "All right."

Jeremy glared when Todd kept urging him to write down something. Then he looked at Rob.

"Maybe Jer and I don't feel like this game," Rob interjected.

"I'm sure both of you want to do it for Uncle Silas." Todd lowered his voice so that his relative wouldn't hear. "He said he would like it."

Jeremy hesitated. "Of course."

Rob scowled and nodded.

The game began slowly. No one seemed to have the verve, at first, to make it fun. Then little by little as the Sinclairs sensed the challenge and competition, things changed.

"Lotus, stop winking. Use only the allowed signals." Rob pointed to his sister.

"I had something in my eyes," Lotus said loftily, grinning at her uncle before beginning again. "I hoped you stopped the watch on that interruption."

"Get going." Rob shook his head at her.

Lotus played right to her uncle, exaggerating her expressions and being very melodramatic in her gestures.

"Gy–an," Uncle Sila pronounced, his flaccid mouth seeming to drop the words.

"Giant," Todd yelled, jumping to his feet. "You

guessed, Uncle. He's right, isn't he?" He looked at Rob, who was smiling at his uncle and nodding.

"That was wonderful, sir." Rob went over and kissed his uncle on the forehead.

Lotus was right on his heels. "I knew you would guess. We've always been on the same wavelength." She hugged her uncle, feeling the weakness of his crablike grasp.

The game rolled into high gear. When it was Dash's turn to act out one, he looked right at her and grinned, the devil droop in his lids telegraphing to her that he was up to something.

"Don't you dare do anything outrageous," Lotus muttered to herself, turning her cousin's head toward her.

"Did you say something, Lotus?"

"No," Lotus mumbled, keeping her eyes on Dash.

"All right . . . go . . ." Will said, his eyes on his wristwatch.

Dash began a series of gyrations and turns that were aimed at Lotus.

"Whatever he's doing . . ." Lee whispered, ". . . I wish he'd do it to me."

"Don't be silly." Lotus laughed weakly, her eyes glued to the tall figure just in front of her.

"I think it's some kind of message," Lotus's mother mused out loud.

"Yes." Aunt Lela had her chin in her hand. "A love message."

Dash's hand shot out and he pointed at her aunt and nodded.

"Love something . . ." Aunt Lela said in an excited voice, her cheeks pink.

"Love Son?" David Sinclair frowned.

Dash shook his head and gestured more.

"Time's going, team," Todd urged, his eyes glued to Dash.

"Love sonnets," Lotus breathed, making Dash beam. "Shakespeare's love sonnets."

Dash nodded, sat down beside her, and lifted her hand to his lips.

"*Ooooo,* I love stuff like that," Lee said as she watched him. She sat on the other side of Lotus. "Lord, coz, you should have him cloned."

Lotus inhaled and gave her cousin a vague smile.

"Now it's my turn." Lotus's father stood and took one of the folded papers. "I hope I can do this."

As the game progressed, the names became increasingly hard. The sides were almost even after an hour, but the game showed no sign of abating.

Lotus was delighted with the way her uncle seemed to sparkle and how eagerly he would whisper things to her aunt. There was no doubt he was having fun. "Lee, look at him."

"I know it. I wish we had thought of something like this before."

Lotus nodded.

"Lotus doll, pay attention," Rob called to her. "Lee, it's your turn."

"Yes, great and mighty one." Lee jumped to her feet, grabbing one of the folded papers from the dish. "Oh, no, this is awful."

"No talking." Will laughed at her.

Lee grimaced, but started to make signs anyway.

"First word is shake," Lotus guessed.

"No." Lee glared at her, gyrating again.

"Stop talking," Rob said to both girls.

"Crab," Lee muttered, then started moving again, not only with her body but with her hands as well.

"Merry-go-round," David Sinclair said.

Lee jumped up and down and nodded.

"Lee, for heaven's sake, help us. Do something. Don't just stand there, nodding your head and clasping your hands."

Lee glared at her brother.

"Wooden horses," Lotus offered, earning a scowl from her cousin.

"Do more. Do more," Lela urged her daughter.

"Mother, I'm trying," Lee huffed.

"Stop talking," Rob and Will said at the same time.

"Carousel," Dash guessed.

"Yes." Lee looked relieved to sit down.

"Dash, that was good," Lotus told him, so very proud of him.

The game got hot. There were some disagreements among the brothers and cousins.

"Look at those fools," Lee whispered to Lotus, glancing at her brother and her cousins. "You would think tomorrow's breakfast was on the line." She looked at Todd and Will, who were huddling in agitated whispers.

"Lee, get over here. You're on our team." Rob gestured to his cousin to join Jeremy and him.

"Coming, oh, great one." Lee salaamed and rolled her eyes at Lotus, who laughed.

When Lotus was through marking her square of paper with the title of the Hindu book, *Kama Sutra,* she had a chance to watch the others. Uncle Silas was doing his with Aunt Lela's help. Mother was biting the end of her pencil. Todd and Dash had their heads together. She frowned at them. What were they doing? They seemed too serious for a silly game, she mused. She was about to rise and go over to them when Todd turned around and looked over at his brother and Jeremy.

"We're ready." Todd had a zealot's gleam in his eye. "Everyone should initial his work, so that we know whose work we're doing."

"Bull. I never heard of such a thing," Rob said inelegantly.

"Neither have I," Lotus concurred.

Todd glared at her. "You're on our team, sis."

The game was begun after many fits and starts, and small points of order from both sides.

The Sinclairs do everything the hard way, Lotus thought, then she was heart and soul in the fight.

Noisy and raucous, the game would have gone on all night, except that Uncle Silas tired. There was much arguing and rehashing of things done, then it was time to leave.

Lotus was yawning by the time she and Dash reached her house, but she insisted on walking him to his car to kiss him good night. It struck her that he seemed more than anxious to leave, which rankled her. Visions of gorgeous women waiting for him in the foyer of the Strathallan rose in her mind.

She went upstairs to sit on her bed and stare at the wall, not able to quash the thoughts of Dash with other women. "Damn him," she groaned aloud. "I know he loves me."

Wide awake now, Lotus went down to the kitchen in the darkened house. She knew no one would be there. Rob and Jeremy had gone out, her mother and father were in bed, and she assumed that Todd must be with Rob and Jeremy. She was staring out the kitchen window to the road that ran behind the houses, not far from the abandoned Hojack railroad line, when she noticed that there was a car parked down the lane, not far from her uncle's house. The headlights were out, but the interior light was on, showing shadowy figures in the auto.

Not too alarmed, Lotus put down her glass. There were few break-ins in their area. PAC-TAC, Police and Citizens Together Against Crime, was active in their area, and most people had watch dogs and alarm systems. Curiosity won over prudence, and she took off her slippers and pushed on old mocassins she had at the back door to wear to the beach and pulled a sweat jacket of her brother's over her silky pajamas. Then she whistled to Bear, her brother's mixed-breed dog, who would be more of a comfort to her as a companion than a threat to strangers.

She walked out of the house, cursing the squeak of the old wooden screen door that had just been put on for the summer. Her mother didn't like the newfangled aluminum kind, so each year the old wooden one was dragged out of the loft in the garage and made ready for another summer season. "Come on, Bear. Look ferocious."

Bear wagged his head and panted, looking more like a small friendly teddy bear than a dog.

"If you can't look fierce, just throw a mean shadow," Lotus mumbled as she went out the gate between the high cedar hedges to the narrow tarmac row that was an access for the homes along the shore.

The closer she came to the car, the more her hands shook. There were three people in the car! And they were reading something with a flashlight!

Lotus stopped, deciding that caution was the

better part of valor when the light of the flash shifted to a face. "Will!" What was he doing in the back of a Mercedes? A Mercedes! That looked like the car that Dash had arranged to have at the airport!

She squinted, inching closer. That was Todd in the front seat with Dash! What were they doing? She marched up to the car and grasped the handle of the front seat passenger door. It wouldn't open.

The window slid down. "Damn it, Lotus, I thought you were tired." Todd was irritated.

"I should have known she'd sniff out something," Will said from the backseat, slouching down into his lounging position again.

Dash got out from behind the wheel and gestured to her to come around the car. "Your skin is damp." He kissed her cheek, then looked down when Bear growled at him. "Who's your defender?"

"He's a sweetheart." Lotus felt gratified that Bear had done his work.

"Go home, Bear," Will said, and rolled down his window. "Get in back with me, Lotus."

"No. I'll take her up front with me," Dash told him, ushering her under the wheel to the middle of the bench seat of the Mercedes. He followed her back into the car, hooking his arm around her waist and pulling her close to him. "She's chilled."

"Am not," Lotus said, then shivered.

"Don't worry. She's tough," Todd said at the same time.

Dash folded her close to him, then nodded to Todd. "Go ahead. You said you thought you had recognized the handwriting on the folder. . . ."

"Folder? Are you talking about the file I stole from Dash's office . . ?"

"Stole?" Todd and Will gasped in unison.

"Well, lifted, sort of . . ." Lotus floundered.

"I'll explain another time," Dash told them. He turned to Lotus. "I told your brother and Will about the file—and how we needed to match the handwriting. Todd thought it looked familiar. He suggested we do something that would require everyone's writing . . ."

"Charades," Lotus guessed, wondering how Todd could suspect someone so close.

"Right. Stop interrupting." Todd took a deep breath, ignoring it when Lotus poked him in the arm. "Then tonight when I kept all the pieces of paper . . ."

"With the initials on them . . ." Lotus interjected, excitement in her voice.

"Do we have to gag you?" Will leaned over from the backseat.

Dash said nothing but he folded her even closer to his side, his chin on her head. "So you feel you have someone whose handwriting fits the file?"

Todd nodded. "I sure didn't want to believe it, but I think it fits. I brought some other samples of his writing from my briefcase and . . ."

"Someone in our family?" Lotus pronounced in horror. "I don't believe it."

Will put his hand on her shoulder. "Neither did I, but I'm coming around to it . . ." His hand squeezed her. "And if I find out that my father went through this because someone we trusted . . ."

"You'll do nothing," Dash interrupted, his voice like steel. "The police will be called and they'll take it from there. My advice is that you, Will, stay away from the firm tomorrow. Let Todd handle it."

"What are you saying?" Lotus whispered.

"Jeremy." Will choked. "It's his handwriting that seems to match the file. Dash called his people out in Las Vegas . . ."

"I called Hans. He has run an investigation of his own, and it seems that the man who called himself Sinclair had gray hair, but he was quite youthful-looking . . ." Dash paused, looking down at her stunned face. "One of the showgirls remembers him . . . without the wig."

They talked some more. Lotus heard them say that it must have been a wig he wore because he couldn't just dye his hair. She heard their words, but she wasn't really listening. "Could he really have done that to Uncle? To all of us?"

"Honey, having gambler's fever is every bit as deadly and addictive as being a heroin addict or an alcoholic," Dash said in a low voice.

"That's what they say," Lotus answered listlessly. "I can't believe I dated him . . . and never knew him." She choked. "My God, what if I had been serious about him?"

"No chance. We were meant to find each other, angel," Dash whispered in her ear. "I'm going to take her back to the house. Todd, I think you should handle this in the morning and as soon as possible."

"I will. It won't be easy convincing Rob. They were roomies at the university."

"I'll kill him." Will pressed his hand to his eyes.

"Willy, don't." Lotus got out of the car, then climbed into the backseat with her cousin. "Don't be foolish. Uncle Silas couldn't take that, could he?"

"No." Will put his arms around her and pressed his face into her shoulder. "You did it. The rest of us knew he couldn't have done it, but we didn't do anything about clearing his name. You did that. I love you, little cousin."

"Oh, Willy, Willy." Lotus held him.

"Come on, sweetheart." Dash edged her out of the car, then looked over the roof at her brother. "Maybe you should stay with him tonight."

Todd nodded, then muttered something to his cousin, who got out of the car and walked with him toward his home.

Lotus leaned on Dash as he walked her home. "Will thanked me, but he should have been thanking you. Hans took a great deal of time to question so many people, and it was under your direction that it was done. Thank you."

"I knew that you believed in your uncle. That was enough for me."

"I don't suppose you'd believe me when I tell you I love you."

"I believe you, not just because you are a very truthful person but because I find that I have to believe that if I'm going to feel whole."

"I will love you forever, probably."

"Not just probably, I hope." Dash kept his arm around her as they walked through the gate in the hedge. "Love, I know we have to stay here while this mess gets ironed out, but I believe the outcome will be ultimately a happy one. So . . . I was wondering if you would like to marry me before we meet my family? What do you think of that?"

Lotus was going to remind him that they were going to table any discussion like that, but when she looked up at his face, silvered by the moon and starlight, her heart thumped in rough cadence at the look of love on his face. "I think I would like to be married before we go to Boston, or is it Worcester where the fishermen are? Dash? What is it?" She stared at him.

His jaw felt paralyzed, his tongue and lips wouldn't work. He had never felt so helpless in his life. She said she'd marry him. "Darling . . ." he breathed, then swept her up into his arms so that she was high above his head. "Darling. I'll call tomorrow and make the arrangements. Don't change your mind."

"No." She leaned over him, feeling a shivery delight. Could something part them? She clutched him to her, letting her hair swing around his face. "No. I want to marry you right now."

"God. How can I leave you tonight?" Dash groaned, his mouth moving over hers as though by touching her his life would be sustained.

"I think I'll be taking cold showers too." Lotus half laughed, half groaned, pushing back from him.

"I'll be here as soon as I make a few calls in the morning. Will you prepare your folks or shall I? I don't want anyone changing your mind."

"I'll tell them. Father will balk a little, but we'll talk. Mother will listen to Father."

With one last lingering kiss, Dash was gone.

Lotus didn't expect to sleep right away. She hugged her pillow to her, pretending it was Dash. Her eyelids drooped and she was gone.

She heard the voice before she opened her eyes and knew who it was. "Lee! What are you doing here?" She blinked open her lids to squint at her cousin who was crouched on the end of the bed.

"Is it true? Did you clear Daddy, Lotus? Oh, Lotus, he's smiling this morning. He wants to see you. The police were here," Lee chattered, her moist eyes shining with happiness. "I can't believe the nightmare is over. Daddy says that if Jeremy clears out and repays the money, he won't be prosecuted. I think they should throw him in a dungeon. Oh, Lotus." Lee threw herself on the bed, hugging Lotus. "Hurry, get dressed. J.D. is here too."

"What!" Lotus shot to a sitting position but Lee was gone.

She scampered into the bathroom taking a fast shower and shampoo, then scuttled back into the bedroom. She took the time to get out her best ultrasuede vest suit in pink with a pink silk blouse dotted in turquoise to match it. With the outfit she wore medium high leather slings that were almost the color of her hair.

She ran out of her bedroom and down the stairs, taking them two at a time.

"Whoa." Dash caught her as she catapulted down the last steps. He held her and kissed her, then pushed her back from him so that he could look at her. "Lovely. You look wonderful in that color. I have something for you."

"You do?" Lotus felt out of breath with him.

"Yes. Here's part of it." He pushed a filigreed gold ring on her finger, the gold swirled high around one very large round diamond. "Do you like it?"

"It's beautiful. It looks old." Lotus looked up at him, feeling the shimmer of tears in her eyes. "I do love it. Thank you."

"Thank you for wearing it." Dash kissed her

again. "It belonged to my grandmother. She gave it to me after my divorce, and told me to find someone to love." He touched her lips with his index finger. "Now I know what she meant."

"Ahem." Mrs. Sinclair coughed to get their attention. "I don't want to interrupt." She smiled at her daughter who was now in Dash's embrace.

Lotus didn't move from Dash's arms. "Mother, we're in love. We're being married soon."

"Tomorrow. Here. By a judge," Dash stated softly.

"I wanted her to be married in a church," her mother faltered. "But I want her to be happy too."

"I will spend my life making her happy, Mrs. Sinclair. I promise you that."

"You must call me Mother then." Lotus's mother's smile was tentative. "Or something like that."

"I would be pleased to call you Mother," Dash told her.

It delighted Lotus when her mother smiled and nodded. "I never expected it to be this fast." Mrs. Sinclair laughed when Lotus looked puzzled. "I mean that I knew you would tumble into love all of a sudden, child, but you've surprised even me."

"Mother." Lotus went to her parent and hugged her. "I do love him."

"We should tell your father. My goodness we have so much news today." Lotus's mother paused and looked at her. "I must tell you, child, that neither your father nor I ever thought you were in love with Jeremy, but we did like him." She looked sad for a moment. "Rob is very upset this morning."

Lotus felt stricken as she hurried after her mother. She almost fell into the large country kitchen and ran straight to her brother, Rob, who stood in one corner of the large eating area watching her. She threw her arms around his neck. "None of us would have ever guessed it could be him."

Rob sobbed into her neck, hugging her close. "God! I wanted you to marry him someday! I was sure he would make you happy."

"We all liked him," Lotus murmured, aware that the family was watching them, listening. "What will they do to him?"

Rob shrugged. "I saw to it that he had a lawyer. I don't think the family wants to prosecute as long as Uncle Silas's name is cleared and the money is repaid." Rob sighed, his eyes sliding toward the window where a proud, male cardinal sang his heart out in the backyard. "It's been a nightmare, Lotus." He looked back at her. "I should have paid more attention when I gambled with him. I should have checked out his debts and I never did."

"Robbie, don't say that. I was stunned when Todd and Dash told . . ."

"Dash? You mean J.D.?"

Lotus turned around and held out her hand to Dash.

He was at her side at once, taking her hand in his. "What is it, love?"

Lotus reached up to kiss his chin, aware that her cousin, Lee, and her parents were looking at her. She smiled at each of them in turn. "I wanted to tell you this before, but we thought we should keep it a secret. J.D., as we have called him, is Dash Colby, and he owns the Cicero and Xanadu in Atlantic City where Jeremy did his gambling. . . ."

"Oh, dear, she's marrying a gambler, David." Lotus's mother's voice was faint.

"Now, Ginna, he's proved himself a good man. He helped clear Silas," her husband soothed her, but there was a crease of worry on his face.

Todd walked in the back door in time to hear his father speak. He walked over to Dash and shook his hand. "He has my vote, Father. He'll make our Lotus doll happy . . . or he'll have us to deal with." Todd's grin was broad when he said this.

"She'll be happy," Dash said quietly, his arm sliding around Lotus's waist. "But I think you should all get ready, since we are marrying at three this afternoon." While the others gasped, and her father came forward to hug Lotus, Dash turned to Ginna Sinclair. "And if you like, ma'am, we can be married again by a minister if it would please you, but I used all my powers of persuasion to get the waivers for our marriage today. But we could have another ceremony."

"I'd like that," said Mrs. Sinclair, who looked pleased. "Are you to be married in the judge's chambers?"

"I thought that would be nice, but then he said that he could arrange to marry us in the park nearby . . . ah . . ."

"Durand Eastman Park?" Both Lee and Lotus spoke at the same time.

"Yes." Dash grinned when he saw the look of happiness on Lotus's face.

"Darling, that's wonderful. You can wear that dress that Lela made you for the country club dance that you never attended." Ginna Sinclair looked at Dash, her lips pursed. "She came down with the most awful sore throat last spring. She had a fever of one hundred and . . ."

"Mother . . ." Lotus pleaded, rolling her eyes at her father. "Daddy, stop her."

"I'll try. Ginna, dear, we should get this place spruced up a bit. Everyone will be coming back here. . . ."

". . . And when she was a girl she always had things harder than the other children. She had measles in the most unlikely places. . . ."

"Mother," Lotus moaned, glaring at Lee, who was covering her mouth, and her brothers, who were nudging each other.

"Don't forget the time she fell off her bike and had stitches . . ." Rob offered helpfully, earning a baleful stare from his sister.

"Twenty-six stitches," Ginna said stoutly, taking Dash's arm and leading him to the table, then picking up the silver coffee pot that had belonged to her mother and pouring some coffee for him. "Now the boys never seemed to get as badly hurt as Lotus."

"That's because you were usually the cause of my getting hurt," Lotus muttered, glaring at her laughing brothers. Then she implored her father. "Stop her, Daddy, or I won't get married today or tomorrow!"

"Don't stop her, Uncle David. She only has five hundred pages of diseases and injuries to go. . . ." Lee giggled.

"Very funny. Well, if you want to be my maid of honor, you had better stop this," Lotus threatened, looking at her mother as she sat adjacent to Dash at the table, her chin in her hand, her eyes dreamy as she recounted in minute detail all the misadventures of Lotus's life. Lotus rounded on Todd when she heard him guffaw. "Just wait until Kate comes today and you want to make a big impression. I'll get Mother started on the time you and Rob built the tree house and you fell and broke your collarbone."

Todd held up his hand palm outward. "All right, all right. I won't say any more."

When Ginna Sinclair was finally pried away from Dash, he came to Lotus's side at once. "I'll be back in an hour. In less than two hours you'll be my wife . . . and I want that very much." In front of her family he gave her a deep kiss, then sauntered out the back door to get to his car.

Lotus had such a ringing in her ears, she didn't even notice her brothers' teasing.

CHAPTER SEVEN

Lotus's wedding was a rainbow of greenery and pastels. Her dress was almost the same green as her eyes. It was a silk cheongsam that her aunt had made her from material brought back from China by Will when he had been on a business trip to the Orient. Her delicate, fine-boned body seemed to give the silk the essence and mystery of the East. Lee had caught her hair up high on her head in a tight bun. Her only adornment was the ring Dash had given her which she now wore on her right hand, and long twists of gold that had belonged to her Chinese mother. She wore the garter that Ginna Sinclair had worn at her wedding and carried cymbidium orchids on a small bible that had belonged to Great-grandmother Sinclair.

She walked along a lane of dogwood trees with Lee, who was dressed in rose pink and preceded her. Dash was standing under a bower of lilacs, their strong scent filling the air. She took a deep breath and stepped away from her father and took his arm.

She had never met Judge Mitchell before that

moment, but she was entranced with the sacred traditional words he spoke.

Dash felt as though all his life had led him here. He remembered the pomp and circumstance of his first marriage and knew that it couldn't compare with the solemnity of this moment. Nor could the blond ethereal Prue ever have touched his soul like the darling standing next to him. It made his heart lodge in his throat at the thought of having children with such a beautiful woman. He made his vows loud and sure.

Lotus turned to look at Dash when the judge said, "You may kiss the bride."

She took a deep breath. "I'm so glad we're married," she told him in a quiet voice that seemed to bell up into the shrubs and trees surrounding them.

"Are you, darling?" Dash choked, forgetting those around him, and lifting her up to kiss her, their eyes level. "So am I." He kissed her again, a long sweet kiss that seemed to go on forever. He didn't want to put her down . . . ever again!

"Ahem. I am the father of the bride. May I?" David Sinclair chuckled when he spotted the reluctance on Dash's part to release his new wife.

Lotus threw her arms around her father's neck. "I'm happy, Daddy. I love him so much."

Her father's arms tightened. "That's all I've ever wanted for my baby girl."

Lotus was whirled from one set of arms to the other, always aware that her husband was close, but it wasn't until she knelt in front of Uncle Silas's wheelchair that she cried. "Oh, Uncle, I'm so happy." She kissed him, then placed her head in his lap, feeling his shaking hands on her head.

She lifted her face and kissed his knotted hands. "But I do feel you've been idle long enough. Sinclair's needs you and you should get back to work."

"Lotus, darling." Aunt Lela bent over her and kissed her head. "You are a good girl."

"That makes a nice change," her cousin, Will, said, giving her a resounding smack on the mouth. "She was always a brat until now."

Lotus pinched his cheek, not able to wipe the smile from her face because her husband was holding her hand. "You mustn't mind the way they tease me." She referred to Will and her brothers as Dash scowled.

"I don't mind anyone teasing you. I just hate it when anyone kisses you."

Lotus's shout of laughter turned smiling faces her way, but she didn't take her eyes off her husband. "You are one silly man, John Dasher Colby."

"And you are one beautiful lady, Lotus Sinclair Colby."

Lotus stopped dead as they meandered back to the cars that would take them back to the house and the reception for the family. "That's me," she whispered.

"That's right." Dash swept her up in his arms and carried her the rest of the way to the car.

"My goodness, he's always carrying her," Lotus's mother observed.

"Yes," Lee said, and sighed. "I want a man who'll carry me."

"Oh? Are you planning on marrying King Kong?" her brother, Will, teased her.

"Rat," Lee said mildly, punching his arm.

They drove down the winding roads leading through the park, the windows of the autos open so that they could inhale the fragrance.

"It's a beautiful park," Dash told her, his one hand on her knee. "And you looked luscious today in that green dress. I'm going to get you some pink, green, and lavender jade that will suit you, my darling."

"That's nice." Lotus hesitated. "But don't get me too much. I don't want to spoil what we have with material things. Our love isn't based on that." She smiled at him, noting his hot appreciative gaze, feeling her heart flutter in response. She squeezed his hand and looked out her window at the park. "When I was in college, I took some horticulture courses and the professor told us that some of the flora in Durand Eastman Park is unique. It's a marvelous place," she said benignly, resting her head on the back of the seat and looking at him. "Thank you for arranging for us to marry here. I'll never forget it."

"Neither will I," Dash told her.

The buffet that her aunt and mother put out in the enclosed backyard of their home was soon swelled by additional dishes brought by smiling neighbors who were encouraged to stay by both Lotus and her parents.

Dash was paraded from person to person and introduced.

"You're awfully good about this," Lotus told him as she fed him a piece of wedding cake that had been delivered by a local Jewish bakery where her mother bought all her rye bread. Lotus hesitated, before speaking. "I'll bet your first wedding was more elaborate."

Dash saw the questions flitting across her face and took the hand that held the cake to his lips and kissed it, taking a tiny bite of the cake as well. "It was a very emotionless, boring day. I realized not long after our marriage that I had never loved her and that we bored each other to distraction. This day has been beautiful, and I have never been happier than I was when I heard you recite your vows to me."

"Me too." Lotus gulped, snuggling closer to him.

Dash inhaled a shaky breath. "When can we leave?"

"Why, Mr. Colby, are you impatient?"

He looked down at her, her eyes dancing with amusement, her skin luminescent with health, her lovely black hair glistening like satin in the sunlight. "Very."

"Me too."

"Stop that," Dash groaned. He looked down at her, shaking his head. "I just wonder if I'll have the strength to chase after you when we've been married fifty years."

Lotus nodded. "Yep. You'd better or you'll be in trouble."

They made their good-byes in a slow circle round the lawn and the house. Then it was time for Lotus to say good-bye to her parents.

"Dash said you will be staying at the house on Beacon Street for a few days. Then he will be checking on the Xanadu in Atlantic City. From there you may be going to Greece on a wedding trip." Her mother sound ecstatic. "He's so nice."

"Yes, he is." She paused as she recalled what her mother had said to her. "He was joking about the house on Beacon Street, though."

"He didn't sound as though he were." Her father kissed and hugged her. "No matter, I think he will make you happy."

"Yes." Lotus sighed contently. She was sure that he would.

At last she and Dash were alone in the Mercedes driving back to the suite at the Strathallan where they would be spending their wedding night.

Conversation between them was desultory, but electricity filled the air. Small touches of fingers and hands seemed like charges between them. The tiniest looks caused breathing to become ragged, looks to become hot. "I need to live with you just to get my vital signs back to working order," Dash told her dryly as they got off the expressway and took the road leading to East Avenue where the Strathallan was located.

"Fool," Lotus told him when he pulled up in front of the building and hastened out of the car to come around and open her door before the attendant reached them. She smothered a giggle when she saw him glare at the young man who reached out to help Lotus.

They walked, arm in arm, across the narrow paved area through the front door to the lobby. Then they were riding up in the elevator to the suite, their arms around each other. Once in the room, Dash turned to her. "I had planned on saying that we would have a glass of champagne then order dinner. Those plans just went out the window."

"Fine with me." Lotus closed her eyes, her hands coming up to clutch him at the waist.

"Lotus, Lotus. I am going to make you happy."

"You've succeeded already."

"Oh, darling, it has never been like this. You are my life." The words burst from Dash, stunning him.

Lotus felt her eyes fill. "I can't believe what you've done for me . . . and my family. You freed us from a terrible burden . . . and you've made me come alive." She took a deep breath.

"Helping your family gave me great satisfaction because I knew it made you happy. So you gave me much more than you think."

"Ordinary things become extraordinary with you," she murmured, leaning on him as she felt him unhook her dress at the back. "I had always enjoyed kissing, for instance . . ." Lotus began.

"How much kissing did you do before I met you?" Dash closed his eyes and groaned when she laughed. "Don't answer that stupid question! Just try to understand that I'm jealous of every man who has ever kissed you, and I think that includes your brothers and father."

Lotus laughed out loud, throwing back her head. Her eyes, which had been filled with tears, now brimmed with merriment. "Impossible."

Dash shook his head, as he slipped the dress up over her head and threw it to one side.

"Dash! My wedding dress . . ." Lotus tried to glare at him, but she could feel her lips lifting in a smile. She wriggled free of his hold long enough to lift the dress and put it on a hanger. When she felt his arms circling her waist, she leaned back. "Shame on you," she murmured as he kissed her neck. "I want to wear this again."

"On our fiftieth wedding anniversary?" Dash muttered, feeling her heart beat against the palms of his hands.

"No . . . well, maybe if I'm still the same size. But I thought I'd wear it if we go out anywhere in Boston. Do you think your folks would mind if we went to see the Boston Pops or the symphony one evening?"

Dash pulled back from her to ease her around to face him. "They might even go with us. Darling, it's true what I said about them being fishermen. My great-great-grandfather put out lobster pots off the coast of Worcester when Boston was a village. . . ."

"Your family has been in the country that long? I'll bet they've been here longer than mine has." She laid her cheek on his chest, loving the feel of his hand stroking her bare back after he had removed the silky bra she'd worn under her dress.

"I think so." He looked down at her, his mouth grim.

"What is it? Do you think I mind that your family is in fishing? Because if you do, forget it. That doesn't bother me at all. In fact, I might like to learn how to fish off a boat." It flashed through her mind that they might be needy people. "Please, Dash, it doesn't bother me one bit that you have to send your family money. I never wanted nor required a large amount of cash to be happy." She beamed up at him. Then her smile faded when she saw his mouth tighten. She put her hand up to his mouth. "I don't want to hear anything unpleasant tonight on my wedding night, so whatever it is that's bothering you, why don't we save it until tomorrow."

"Darling. I don't want anything between us tonight either, but I do have to tell you that my family is not poor. Their business does very well. . . ."

"Is that what's bothering you? That I might be worried about your family's finances? Put it out of your mind." She put her hand over his mouth when he would have spoken again. "I thought I might give you a massage? How does that sound?"

"Wonderful," Dash muttered, his lips still against her hand. "But, darling, I want to tell you—"

"Tell me later." Lotus kissed him on his bared chest after she unbuttoned his shirt. When she heard the sound emitting from his throat, her smile widened. Her wedding night was going to be wonderful! She took his hand and led him toward the bed. "You can help by removing your trousers, or do you feel shy with me?" she teased, batting her eyes.

"Brat." Dash grinned at her, pushing away the niggling feeling that he should be discussing his family with her at this moment and not put it off. Then his eyes fixed on her rounded breasts, the uplifted softness moving as she breathed. He unzipped and dropped his clothes from his body, kicking them aside, irritated with Lotus when she picked them up and put them on the clothes valet. "Never mind that, darling. Tell me about my massage."

"Lie face downward on the bed. Be back in a minute." She left him for a minute to pick up the makeup case she had brought from the house, taking out the fragrant oil that she always carried with her. Then she took the time to remove the last of her clothes before she went back to him. He had been lying, propped on one elbow, watching her, his eyes never leaving her as she climbed up on the bed next to him. "This is a lovely oil that comes from China. My mother's family manufactured this before the Communist takeover. Then my mother had relatives manufacture it in Japan. I own a small part of the company." She grinned at him as she sat cross-legged next to him. "So you see, I did come with a dowery. I also own some stock in Sinclair's."

"It's a good thing. I definitely wouldn't have kept you without a dowery," Dash murmured, his hand stroking her bare thigh.

"Suspicions confirmed." Lotus choked, feeling her body heat from his touch. "Roll over. I want to start on your back."

"Are you sure you can get an unlimited supply of this oil? I don't want to have to go without my massage." He turned his face sideways as he pressed his body down into the mattress. "*Umm,* this is almost as comfortable as you, Mrs. Colby."

Lotus paused in the act of pouring oil on his back. "I am, aren't I? Mrs. Colby, I mean."

Dash looked at her without lifting his head. "Yes, you are, for the rest of your life you'll be Lotus Sinclair Colby."

"Nice name." Lotus poured oil onto his skin, making him flinch. "Cold?" She giggled.

"You know it was," he grumbled, then his eyes closed. "Ah, don't stop. Your hands are magic, love."

Lotus straddled him, loving the feel of his muscled back between her legs. She squeezed them at his waist.

Dash groaned. "Don't do that, love. Having you naked on my back is putting my libido at rocket speed. . . ." Dash moved as though he would turn.

"No. Stay where you are. I want to show you how well I do this." Lotus could feel her own blood begin to pound as she pushed and pummeled his back and shoulders, stretching and kneading the supple muscles. As she moved lower, her movements slowed, becoming langorous, caressing.

Finally when she reached his calves and ankles, Dash turned and clasped her hands, bringing her up and over his body. "Enough. It's my turn to massage you, my darling . . . but I sure as hell don't know how long I can keep it up."

Lotus smiled, her whole being magnetized by him.

He lifted her gently and placed her where he had been. Then he poured a little of the oil in his hands and turned back to her. He squeezed his eyes shut. "I may have to do this blindfolded. Looking at you lying there is dangerous."

Lotus stretched, her body feeling relaxed and yet alert. "Massage me," she said in a sultry voice.

"Lord, woman, take it easy on me," Dash begged as he turned her over on her stomach. "Damn, this is worse. Now I have to look at your backside."

"Get going, masseur, or you won't be paid."

Dash made long slow strokes on her velvet skin. "I think I'm being paid as I do this. Your skin is wonderful."

"Thank you," Lotus squeaked, the rough satin of his hands raising her pulse beats. "Oh, Dash, that feels so good."

"Enough," he grated, flipping her over, then lifting her up onto his lap. "You have blown me apart, Mrs. Colby. And I love you so much."

"And I love you." Lotus twined her arms around

his neck, kissing his throat. "Lovemaking is so much fun," she breathed when they fell together on the bed.

"Isn't it?" Dash growled, scooping her body next to his, taking her breast in his mouth and sucking gently there. "You taste so good, my own. I do love the taste."

"Dash," she whimpered as she felt his tongue flick over her body. Her eyes felt glued shut. When his mouth touched her in the most intimate way, she heard a keening sound and knew it was her own response to him. "I love you."

"I love you." He slipped her under his body and entered her with a gentle violence that rocked them both.

Love took them away where only they could go. Ice and fire splintered around them as they soared, clinging one to the other. The climax was reached in a shower of comets. Then they settled to earth once more.

"I do like that more than tennis," Lotus said and giggled into his neck, her hand running over his chest, now glistening with love dew.

"I even like it better than racquet ball," Dash muttered, his mouth in her hair.

"No!"

"Yes." He leaned back from her. "Darling, I was going to tell you something . . ."

"Uh-huh." Lotus tried to smother her yawn. "I want to nap." She cuddled close to him, feeling warm and comforted. "Strange," she whispered.

"What is?" Dash asked, distracted by her wriggling body.

"How I can feel so sexy, yet comfy with you. Weird." And then she fell asleep.

* * *

A tickling sensation disturbed Lotus and she tried to brush it away from her nose. "Rob . . . Todd, stop it. I'll hide your baseball mitt. See if I don't . . ." Lotus said sleepily, opened her eyes then closed them quickly. Sunlight was blinding! She squinted and saw Dash leaning over her.

"We should have been packed and out of here an hour ago," he told her.

"I was tired. . . ." She stretched her, body, brushing his, feeling his body tent over hers at once. She smiled up at him. "I feel like the conquered and the conquering both at the same time. Crazy."

"Yes." He kissed her neck.

She chuckled and ducked free of him and rolled off the bed to her feet. "I should think you would have had enough of kanoodling for a while."

"Never." Dash watched her, his hands behind his head, his eyes touching every pore. "We should dress."

"Me first." Lotus turned to sprint for the bathroom, gasping when she was caught around the waist.

"You can't get away from me, Mrs. Colby," Dash whispered. "I will always be right at your heels."

"Wonderful." She turned in his arms. "Carry me."

"I intended to." Dash chuckled, lifting her into his arms.

For almost half an hour they cavorted like children in the bathroom, bumping into one another, laughing out loud when Lotus tried to shave Dash. Then they had to work at breakneck speed to get packed.

"Will your parents meet us at the airport?"

"No, but there will be a car for us," Dash told her as he led her out to the Mercedes.

This time he drove. It surprised Lotus that he needed so few directions to get on the expressway.

"You have a good sense of direction," Lotus told him, sitting as close to him as she could.

"Thank you." Dash paused, then shot her a quick glance. "Darling, I've been trying to tell you something and not doing a very good job of it, but I want to make sure you understand before we reach Boston."

When he stopped speaking, Lotus put her hand on his knee. "Well?" she prodded.

"My family is far from poor, love. They have been on the New York Stock Exchange for years. They have good-sized holdings in real estate. They do have fishing boats . . . fleets, in fact."

"I see." But Lotus didn't really understand. "If your family has so many businesses, why did you choose gambling?"

"I liked the challenge. When I was twenty-five I had the chance to pick up the Xanadu. It was broken down and in shambles. I borrowed money . . . not from my family. Using my own holdings as collateral, I started rebuilding the casino into what it is today. I begged, and bribed with huge salaries, the best entertainers, I stole the best dealers from other establishments. I brought an haute cuisine chef from Maxime's in Paris. I did the same at Cicero's." Dash punched out the words, steering the car onto the access road of the airport.

"You like walking the razor's edge," Lotus stated.

"You could say that." Words dropped between them like stones.

Lotus followed him from the car, and through

the small private terminal to the waiting Lear jet. She paused before entering the plane. "Coldris Limited is the family company?"

"Yes." Dash helped her into the copilot's seat.

She didn't know what to think! Or what to believe! It didn't seem feasible that he would lie about his family, but then why didn't he come out and tell her about them right away? What was wrong with the Colby family that Dash was hiding them? Is that why he married her before he introduced them to her? Was there insanity in the family? No, no one was ashamed of that today. Prison? Were his father and mother in prison and only out for a few days to meet their daughter-in-law? Her imagination ran out of control. She wanted to laugh out loud at her foolishness.

"Darling? Come out of the dream world for a minute, will you?" Dash felt his heart turn over when she gave him a weak smile, then sighed. "My family won't be that hard to take."

"I'll stand by you," Lotus breathed, caught between the sublime and the ridiculous.

"You will?" Dash looked surprised.

"Did you think I wouldn't?" Lotus felt miffed.

"No. I didn't think that."

What was wrong with his family? Her imagination took her away again. She saw a gaggle of Colbys without a tooth in their heads, gumming a welcome to her. She saw Colbys with hot cars lining their driveways . . . She really was letting fantasy control her thinking!

Dash looked at her when her eyes closed. "What were you thinking of, my sweet, that had you frowning so?" Dash shook his head. She would be concocting a nightmare family. He watched her for a moment, then realized she was asleep. He felt his own eyes closing in minutes. He took her hand in his, then he was gone.

He woke as they circled Logan Airport. He looked over at a sleeping Lotus and decided to let her sleep until they taxied to the terminal. As they banked, the sight of the land and water sparkling beneath him gave him a feeling of welcome. Home! Boston had been home to him until he'd left after Harvard to seek his fortune in the world of business.

After landing and taxiing to the small terminal for private planes, he turned to her, shaking her gently. "Wake up, wife. We're here."

"We are?" Lotus woke, rubbing her eyes, smiling at him. "I have to comb my hair."

"We'll do all that in the car. Come along, love."

Lotus watched, bemused as Dash hurried her from the small terminal to the waiting Rolls Royce. "My goodness, look what your folks sent for us. I imagine it costs a great deal to lease one of these for a few hours."

Dash ushered her into the car. "Hello, Timmons."

"How are you, sir? May I offer you my congratulations?"

"Thank you. This is Mrs. Colby. Darling, this is Timmons."

"How can you be sure of getting the same driver every time? Does your family ask for him by name?" Lotus whispered from the side of her mouth.

"He works for us," Dash said abruptly, noting the look of disbelief cross her face even as she nodded. *What in hell is she thinking now? She no doubt has my family selling state secrets to the Russians.*

Dash shrugged, put his arms around her, and clasped her close to him.

Driving through the beautiful New England city that had its origins and fiber in the great struggle for independence, Lotus felt, once more, the spiritual tug she had had the first time she had visited Boston. "Boston, Boston . . ." she whispered, ". . . the land of the bean and the cod. Where the Cabots talk only to Lowells and the Lowells talk only to God." She grinned at him. "Or something like that."

"Close enough." Dash murmured into her hair, feeling an alien nervousness as they approached the beautiful area known as Beacon Hill where his parents had a home. The roomy, six-bedroom row house dated back to the very early days of Boston, and it had been home to him while he was growing up.

As Timmons drove around Boston Common, Lotus craned her neck looking at the Bostonians strolling the lovely area that their ancestors had fought to keep. "It's a trip through our history books, isn't it?" she asked with awe in her voice. "There's Park Church . . ." She pointed out the window. She leaned forward and tapped Timmons on the shoulder. "Thank you for bringing me through this section."

"Beg pardon, ma'am?" Timmons blinked at her over his shoulder, before quickly facing front again.

"She likes the drive," Dash said abruptly as they wended their way through a hilly section leading to Beacon hill.

"Yes, sir." Timmons's smile was fleeting as he turned into the narrow historical section.

Silence filled the car as they pulled up in front

of the brick-fronted home with the black wrought-iron fence in front, brass knockers on the black doors matching the shutters.

Dash opened his door and stepped out, reaching in to help her alight as Timmons opened the trunk and removed the luggage.

Clearing her throat twice, Lotus tried to speak. Before the words emerged, the front door opened, disgorging three tall, slim women with ash blond hair, one of whom carried a baby. "Your sisters?"

Dash nodded, watching her color fade a trifle. He kissed her once hard on the mouth.

"Really, Dash, can't you save it for the bedroom?" One slender blonde ambled down the steps toward him, her amused drawl having a slightly less deep timber than Dash's. She put her arms around her brother and kissed him on the cheek.

"Ann. How are you?" Dash's twisted smile touched his sister, then he reached out and pulled Lotus to his side. "This is my wife, Lotus Sinclair Colby. Darling, this is one of my older sisters . . ."

"How like you to mention that," his sister interrupted dryly.

". . . Ann," Dash finished, even as another sister took hold of him and kissed him. "And this is Jennifer . . ."

"If you say the oldest one of all, I shall hit you," the perfectly coiffed and gowned woman at his side said before she turned to Lotus, who had just shaken Ann's hand and been kissed on the cheek by her. "I'm Jennifer, my dear. Welcome to the family."

"And I'm the baby, Laura, the youngest of this wolf pack," the slender girl holding the baby told Lotus. "But I don't think any of us are as young as you." She held up her baby to Dash to be kissed, then she kissed him herself. "Meet the youngest so far of the clan. This is Henrietta, called Hank by her father, who is a boor."

"Laura, what a hideous name. Why did you saddle her with it?" Dash took the baby and cuddled her.

Lotus felt her heart beat out of rhythm as she watched him with the infant.

"James's grandmother was Henrietta, and since she's the first girl in his family in umpteen years, I gave in," Laura said comfortably, smiling at Lotus as she took her arm. "We always knew that if John Dasher ever married again, she'd be a looker, but none of us expected a beauty. You are very lovely, Lotus. Good heavens, you're blushing. You can't have been around Dash very long or you would be past that."

"True," his sister, Ann, said as she walked on the other side of Lotus as they went in the front door.

Jennifer turned around to look at Timmons. "Put their things in the Rose Suite, please, Timmy." She smiled at the older man, then hefted one of the smaller cases.

"Leave it, Jen," Dash ordered. "I'll be back for it as soon as I take Hank into the house."

"Lord . . ." Laura moaned. "He's going to call her that too."

A tall, dark-haired man bounded out the door. "Dasher, you dog, that's my baby you're carrying. Be careful. What do you think of her?"

"I'm amazed she can be so beautiful with such an ugly father," Dash chuckled, shaking hands, before Hank's father took the cases from Timmons and followed him into the foyer.

"You mustn't mind the way they talk to one another," Laura confided. "They were roomies at Harvard . . ."

"He really did go there." Lotus pushed the words through plastic lips.

Laura looked surprised. "All the men in our family have gone to Harvard. Of course, none of them have had the record that John Dasher accrued, captain of both the crewing and the football teams," Laura announced proudly. "He was such a hunk. I had many girl friends when he was at Harvard and I was at Boston College, and all of them wanted to meet my brother. Even before he went there, Ann and Jen had friends who were interested in him. They were all at his feet. He had such an ego about women."

Laura squeezed Lotus's arm as they walked into a high ceilinged, wainscoted room with a marble fireplace. "Now you've brought him to his knees and we're delighted." She giggled at Lotus's agape face. "He was always so bored when we would parade our friends for him. Took it for granted that they'd all throw roses in his path." She gave a grunt of satisfaction as she urged Lotus toward the older couple in the center of a group of children. "It's wonderful to know he's on his knees for a change."

"But he isn't," Lotus began, then she realized she was standing in front of a tall, gray-haired woman, whose full figure was still graceful and an even taller silver-haired man with a spare, still muscled frame. "Hello." She could feel a smile tremble across her face.

"My dear." Mrs. Colby embraced her. "Do call me Lissa. Everyone does, even my children. You are quite lovely."

"Indeed." Mr. Colby kissed both Lotus's cheeks. "Dash is a lucky man."

"Dasher always had good taste," Lissa Colby told Lotus.

"Especially in women," James Wells said to his wife, who shushed him.

Dash glared at his former roommate when he saw Lotus blush. She'd heard that! Dash ground his teeth. God, what a nightmare it was going to be. None of them would spare her! They would trot out all the things he'd done with names and dates, from the age of six months, he thought bitterly. It tore at him that he didn't want his wife to know what a traveling man he'd been with women, that though he was sure she had guessed about some of his life, he didn't want the lurid details that had meant nothing to him before he met her to be put in front of her now. He went to her side and leaned down to kiss her ear. "Isn't she beautiful, Lissa?"

"Yes," his mother said, giving him a smug smile.

Dash glared at her. She had been plotting to marry him off from his seventeenth birthday when he had been accused of fathering Lydia Helmsley's baby. He hadn't been the father, but only his own father had believed him and extricated him from the predicament. From then on his mother had considered it a mission to get him married and off the streets, since he was a menace to helpless women. Her words, not his. Dash ground his teeth as he remembered the countless times she had told him he must marry and settle down and stop besmirching the Colby name.

"No doubt, my dear, you want Dasher to give up his gambling houses and take his place in the family business," Lissa began, gesturing for Lotus to take her place on the settee across from her as she signaled Timmons to bring a tray of wine.

Lotus stared at the gleam in her mother-in-law's eye. "I have no plans to change Dash's life."

Someone sucked in a breath. Another whispered, "Oh, oh."

Lissa studied the diminutive figure across from her in the petal pink suit, the almond-shaped green eyes unwavering. "I see."

Dash leaned over the back of the settee and kissed the top of his wife's head.

Lotus stiffened. He should have told her! The fact that he had tried to explain his family to her didn't penetrate the haze of anger building up inside her. His family was in fishing! Damn him! They no doubt owned half the East Coast! She was going to punch him in the nose at the first opportunity, she promised herself, taking the wineglass from the tray that Timmons was proffering and quaffing the contents.

"Good Lord, she drinks," James announced, chuckling.

"Honey, you always drink Perrier." Dash took the glass from her, glaring at his brother-in-law.

"I'll have another," Lotus said through her teeth. "Mrs. Colby . . ."

"Call me Lissa, dear."

"Lissa, I come from a very hard-working family in Rochester, New York."

"I've heard of Rochester, Minnesota."

"We have cameras and lilacs in our town." Lotus took a deep breath.

"That sounds like Tokyo," Lissa said helpfully.

"We had them first . . . I think . . ." Lotus blinked at the full glass of wine in her hand. "Where was I?"

"You were telling us how much your city of Rochester is like Tokyo." Lissa helped her.

"Lissa," Dash muttered softly.

"I was not. I can't even remember Tokyo that well. I remember Mt. Fujiyama though. We skied there." Lotus tried to salivate in her dry mouth. *Amazing how wine made you dry,* she mused, sipping hers. Then she looked at her father-in-law. "I've lost my place."

"Cameras, my dear. I own a great deal of Kodak film," Zachary Colby told his daughter-in-law.

"Good." Lotus blinked at him, wishing she hadn't taken another glass of wine on an empty stomach. She swallowed, then set down her glass.

"I'll get you seltzer water, darling." Dash signaled to Timmons who brought her a tall, fizzing glass filled with ice.

"Have I met everyone?" Lotus asked Dash when he bent over her.

"Not everyone. You haven't met Alan or my other two brothers-in-law and their children, but you will," Dash told her. *God, she's a bit tipsy. I had better get her out of here.* "You're tired, darling. Come along. We'll take a nap."

"I've heard of anxious, but this is ridiculous," James said, and smiled at his former roommate, who glared at him.

"I think I would like a nap," Lotus said. She felt as though her smile had turned to rubber bands as she looked at each member of the family, then rose to her feet. "Flying is tiring." She licked her dry lips. Lotus scarcely noticed the chuckles behind her as she left the room with her husband. "It was interesting to meet your family."

"Wasn't it?" Dash grated, leading her up two flights of stairs to the third floor where they would be staying.

Lotus could feel tears filling her eyes as she turned to face her husband. "I suppose you feel like drowning me in the Charles River after the spectacle I made. You see, I'm not much of a drinker."

"I know." Dash went to her, his arms outstretched. He never expected her next move.

Lotus kicked him in the shin, then watched him hop around the room, repeating over and over, "Why in hell did you do that?"

"Because you should have told me that your family was wealthy, and not try to mislead me by telling me they were fishermen and that you were supporting them." She sounded out each syllable of the words.

"I tried to tell you, but you chose not to believe me or accept what I said."

"I was duped," she told him, heaving a big sigh. "I think I'll take a nap. I assume I will meet the rest of that pirate's nest this evening."

"At dinner," Dash said, and scowled as she peeled the clothes from her body. He wished he didn't react so markedly to her.

She turned and saw his arousal. "Sorry. I have a headache." She beamed at him. Then she walked over to the oversized canopy bed, pulled back the quilt, and slid under it. She was asleep in minutes.

"A headache! Damn you, brat." Dash could feel his lips lifting in a reluctant smile. "Kicking me in the leg, then telling me you have a headache, and all on the day after our wedding." He stripped off his own clothes and slipped under the quilt beside her, pulling her curled-up body into his arms.

"Dash," she muttered, smiled, then went deeper into sleep.

"Darling, I love you." He felt her body wriggle against him and stifled a groan.

When Lotus woke, it took her minutes to orient herself. The first thing she recognized was the warmth at her back. Dash was with her! She relaxed at once. Even when she remembered that she was irritated with him about his family, it didn't lessen her contentment at being enfolded in his arms.

"Hello," he spoke in her ear, feeling her body come out of sleep.

"Hello." She turned to face him. "I shouldn't have kicked you. I was angry."

"I guessed."

"Will you forgive me?" Lotus said.

"I'm sorry," Dash said at the same time.

They laughed, holding each other.

When he saw the tiny frown lines in her face, he shook her gently. "Tell me what you're thinking."

"I don't think your family thinks I'm right for you."

"Stuff what they think. Besides, I disagree. I think both my parents were delighted with you. I know them. Mother wouldn't try her verbal sparring with just anyone. She usually reserves that for someone in the family or someone she wishes were."

"Really?" Lotus exhaled a relieved breath. "I don't want to start off on the wrong foot."

Dash kissed her. "I think they like you . . . especially my sisters who are the most critical." He kissed her mouth. "But I also should tell you, I don't give a damn who likes you or doesn't like you. You're mine and I love you. Nothing else is important."

CHAPTER EIGHT

The two days that Dash and Lotus had intended to stay in Boston turned into five.

On the fifth day Lotus decided to take a walk through the historical area called the Freedom Trail. She remembered reading about it in the Sunday *New York Times,* but she had never actually seen it.

She looked out the bedroom window in the suite where they had been staying and thought about the days she had spent with Dash's family. They were as rambunctious and fractious as her own! She smiled to herself as she thought of all the things they'd done . . . even sculling on the Charles River with Alan, Dash's younger brother. She sighed as she remembered the scene when she had returned to the house. Dash had been furious!

"How dare you take my wife out on the river?" He spat the question at his brother, whose eyebrows had risen, but who had shown no agitation at being addressed in such a fashion.

"She was bored. You and Dad spend all your time at his office, and when you're here, you're always calling Las Vegas about the deal you have cooking there. Lotus is on her honeymoon, not a business trip."

Lotus recalled how she had opened her mouth to tell Alan that he was wrong, that she hadn't been bored, but then she had looked at Dash and gasped.

Blood chugged into his face, filling every pore. His hands had clenched and unclenched at his sides. "I fully intend to show her Boston."

"When? Next year? Lissa is up to her hips in the Symphony Ball we are all attending Friday night . . ."

"Don't be flip, Alan darling. You know the girls and I work on this every year," his mother had answered calmly, looking askance at her older son. "I, for one, have never approved of Dasher's way of life. Gambling is abhorrent to me and my family."

"Ah, yes, we mustn't forget the very boring Hathaways, Lotus. You'll meet them Friday night . . . and forever wish you hadn't." Alan waxed dramatic as he rolled his eyes and minced across the room to Lotus. "Dah–ling, what a divine corn you have on your left foot. You must tell where you got it . . . or I shall die."

"Alan." His father coughed reprovingly.

"All of this has nothing to do with you taking Lotus out onto the river in a shell. She could have been dumped into the water," Dash said, white-faced, stopping all conversation when he took two giant strides toward his wife and lifted her into his arms, cradling her there.

"Dash . . ." Lotus hissed, pushing at his chest, trying to free herself. "Nothing is wrong with me."

"Are you sure?" Dash scowled. "You look tired."

"Is she an invalid, dear?" Lissa inquired.

"Of course not." Lotus felt herself turning red. "Put me down or I shall kick you in the kneecap," she muttered at him through clenched teeth.

"What did she say about a cap?" Dash's sister, Ann, walked into the room, two gangling teenagers at her side. "I brought the boys."

"I think she wants a night cap," Lissa said brightly.

"At four in the afternoon?" Dash's father looked interested.

"She didn't say that." Dash glared at his mother. "She said she was going to kick me in the kneecap."

"That I'd like to see."

"Alan!" Ann pursed her lips. "Not in the drawing room."

Alan shrugged. "We can go outside." He rubbed his hands together, making his nephews grin at one another.

"Roger. Delbert. Don't dare enter into any schemes with your uncle," Ann instructed her sons.

The boys looked at one another, then away from Alan.

"You can't keep them from thinking, Annie," Alan jibed.

Roger cleared his throat. "We're on the rowing team, Aunt Lotus. If you would like to go out . . ."

"No," Dash had roared, then put his arm around his wife and led her from the room.

Lotus sighed as she remembered how embarrassed she had been to go down to dinner that evening because of the fuss, but the family not only didn't mention it, it wasn't even alluded to in any way.

Now, Lotus dropped the sheer drape she had

been holding back from the mullioned window, and turned to don her sweats and running shoes. She would jog along the Freedom Trail, perhaps stop at Quincy Market, maybe even have a bowl of chowder at one of the open stalls in the market or have lunch at Durgin Park.

The house was quiet when she descended the stairs from their suite. She had left a note for Dash, telling him what she was going to do, even though she might be back before he returned. The lawyers had called that morning and told him that there was a snafu in closing the deal and they wanted him to hook into a conference call that afternoon with them. That's what he was doing in his father's office.

She left the house and went down into the front yard area to warm up before she would begin. Then she started a very slow jog along the street and down to the area that was marked as the beginning of the Freedom Trail. She moved slowly not only to pace herself but because she wanted to see everything as she moved.

When she came to the narrow alley where so many bakeries were located, and she could smell the warm bread, her mouth began to water and she wished that she had decided to go to Quincy Market first. There she could have sat down at a table.

She ignored the wonderful smells and continued on her way to the Old North Church of Paul Revere fame. After a while she was down near the docks and she could make out the buildings of the huge public market known as Quincy Market.

She paused outside the market to catch her breath, walking the tiled area in front of Faneuil

Hall to cool down. She took a drink at a fountain and with a tissue she dabbed some of the water on her face.

She walked across the plaza and through the doors of the market to the area of shops that lined the inside. As she was bent over a deli case of fresh fruit and vegetables, she felt a hand pat her backside. Fists high, she turned around to belt the nuisance who dared to touch her. "Dash!" she exclaimed.

"Close your mouth," he told her gently, then leaned over to place his lips on hers. "Timmy said you had only been gone a few minutes when Father and I arrived home. I wanted to be with you." He pulled her closer to whisper in her ear, "You look gorgeous in those pink sweats."

"How did you find me in this crowd?" Lotus felt such a surge of happiness that he was with her.

"There will never be a time when I don't find you, darling, wherever you are." Dash looked down at her.

"My goodness, I like the way you look at me, but we might get picked up for indecent exposure . . . or something."

"Funny lady." He touched her nose with his one finger then picked up her left hand. "I do love seeing my ring on your finger. I can't remember anything giving me as much joy as that does."

"I like it myself."

Dash smiled, then looked up and over her head, swiveling slowly. "So you want to see Quincy Market . . ." he said slowly, a smile drifting across his face.

"I hadn't realized it would be so large, so bustling . . ." Lotus breathed, looking round her. "It seems as though persons who work nearby come here for lunch . . ." she mused.

"Indeed, they do. The food is very fresh." He grinned down at her. "And I'm going to take you to Durgin Park for lunch."

"You are? Good. Is it close?" Lotus smiled just because Dash laughed out loud.

"It's very close, but first I want to take you to the boutiques and stalls. I feel like buying. Do you feel like buying, Mrs. Colby?"

Lotus stopped and bit her lip, her glance sliding away from him. Would he be bored doing such a mundane thing as browsing in Quincy Market? "Maybe you would rather—"

"Darling . . ." Dash bent over her. "I'll enjoy being here with you. It makes me happy that you want to see my city."

Lotus lifted her hand to his cheek. "And you make me happy. I guess I'm still a little unsure about what you enjoy . . . but I don't want to change you. I want to keep the man I married. I suppose at some point we'll stop being so sensitive with each other."

Dash shook his head. "I don't think I will." He took her hand and turned her so that they could walk along the open concourse next to the covered section of the market. "That business with Alan taking you sculling proved that to me." His smile was twisted as he looked at her. "It wasn't only the danger that angered me, though that was most of it. It blew me to hell that someone else was showing you things for the first time, and I wanted to be the one to do that."

Lotus pulled her hand free and slipped it around his waist. "I understand that. I feel the same way about you." She leaned on him when they paused in front of a leather-working shop. "When you love someone, all the nerve ends are exposed. Everything quivers in the air and is vulnerable. Love is ridiculous when you think about it."

"My wife, the philosopher," Dash said, kissing the top of her head, his arm hooking around her shoulders to keep her close to him. "Let's buy you one of those suede carryalls with the Indian beading."

"Why? I have room to carry things in my purse." Lotus could feel herself being propelled forward as she gestured to the small leather shoulder bag she carried.

By the time they purchased the carryall, Dash had already spotted the jewelry stall. "I'll be over there. You get the change," he murmured, kissing her cheek, then striding away.

"Wait," Lotus called to him, then the leather stall owner caught her attention. "Oh, yes, the change. Thank you." She put it in her pocket, so that she could give it back to Dash, then hurried after him across the narrow plaza.

"But do you have a pink or lavender jade? My wife looks wonderful in those colors," Dash was telling a goggled-eyed salesperson as he pointed to several things that he wanted.

"Well, sir, just a moment, let me get the owner." The young man looked down the counter and gestured for an older man to join them.

"What are you doing?" Lotus whispered to Dash. "You can't buy all this— " She swung her hand to encompass the earrings and necklaces on the black velvet.

"I can too," Dash told her, then he turned from her to smile at the older man. "I do have a nice coral set that goes with her coloring, but I'm interested in pink or lavender jade."

"No such thing," Lotus again whispered to him out of the corner of her mouth.

Dash looked at her. "Stop doing that with your mouth or you'll freeze that way. Do you want to spend your life with your mouth two degrees left of center?"

"I was trying to be discreet," Lotus answered, lifting her chin, then feeling her mouth drop as the man opened up a square of velvet in front of them. "Good Lord. Is that real?" Lotus bit her lip and smiled weakly when the man looked affronted.

"That's marvelous, Calvin. Louis at VanCleef and Arpels told me you had a fine collection of jade," Dash interjected, throwing Lotus an irritated glance.

"He did? Who's Louis?" Lotus couldn't take her eyes from the richness of pink and lavender jade in front of her.

"Uh?" Dash looked at her blankly for a moment, then looked back at the jewelry. "I can't make up my mind. I like the rings . . ."

"Rings?" Lotus gulped. "Plural?"

Dash frowned at her. "And the earrings, but I can't make up my mind." He leaned his chin on his hand. "That necklace is delicate. I like the dragon motif. Oh, well, we'll take all of it. I'll give you a check."

"No," Lotus groaned. "We can't take all that. Besides, the man would be a fool to take a personal check for such an amount. And jewelers aren't fools." Her fingers twitched at his sleeve, trying to pull him away.

"What is it, darling? Are you hungry?"

Lotus could only shake her head as she watched Dash write the check. "Isn't he going to check your credentials?" she whimpered.

"Just be patient, love. I'll buy you chowder for lunch."

For the first time since she met him, Lotus began thinking of Dash as dense. She waited until they were outside, then she pulled on his arm. "That was extravagant. I don't need so much jade."

Dash smiled at her, then patted her arm. "Indulge me a little, sweetheart. I love giving you things." He kissed her cheek. "Shall we go?"

"But, Dash . . . I . . ." She gaped after him as he strolled across the square. "I think I married Santa Claus," she muttered, nonplussed when he turned and gestured for her to join him. "I really don't think I need so much jade—"

"It looks wonderful with your skin." Dash looked a little bemused as he ran his eyes around the area. "You can forget how alive it is here, yet how relaxed," he said almost to himself.

Lotus was going to say more, but just then he turned around and put his arm around her, his face relaxed, much of the tautness in his frame dissipated. She wanted him to remain that way. She sighed and swallowed her arguments.

"This is fun. Come on, lady. Durgin Park has to be experienced." Dash laughed out loud, turning smiling faces in his direction. He hurried her through the market.

They went into a rather dark small room that

opened off the square and a young man called to them over the bar.

"Going upstairs?"

"Yes," Dash told him. Then he led Lotus up a rather steep flight of stairs to a smoky, steamy kitchen area, where a woman led them into another room.

"Table for two?"

"Please," Dash told her, joy filling him because his wife's head was swiveling every which way trying to see it all.

"They have an oilcloth on the table," she said, grinning up at him.

"Yes." Dash looked around the crowded low-ceilinged room, delighted that they had been led to a table by the window which was open so that the noises from the market wafted up to them. "Didn't I tell you it had to be experienced?"

Lotus nodded, so busy people-watching that she paid scant attention when the woman took the order.

When her chowder came in a huge bowl, she looked open-mouthed at Dash. "Do I swim in it or eat it?"

"Taste," he invited, lifting his spoon.

"*Ummmm.* So good."

They fed each other, delighting in each other's responses.

"I would rather come back to the market than go to the Symphony Ball," Lotus told him, leaning near her husband.

Dash nodded, loving the sparkle of happiness in her eyes. *She is totally unaffected by anything but living, and I love that about her.*

“Tell me about the Symphony Ball. Is it white tie?”

“Probably.”

“You’ll look so sexy,” Lotus snarled at him, snapping her teeth as though she would bite him.

“Love, don’t do that.” Dash looked deep into her eyes. “I wish we were back in our bedroom.”

“Do you think we have time for . . . us before we dress in all our finery?” She bit her lip, then sighed. “I hope my wedding dress will be all right.”

Dash nodded, watching her closely. She wasn’t saying much, but he could tell she was nervous.

When they were finished and it was time to go, Dash led the way down the steep stairway to the street level.

“Love”—Dash kissed her forehead as they ambled back through the market— “let’s grab a cab. I want to go to a store.”

“Is it far?”

Dash shook his head as he urged away from the market and out to the street. He flagged down a cab, put her inside, and followed her. “Charine’s,” he told the driver.

“Charine’s?” Lotus echoed. “Isn’t that a haute couture house in New York?”

Dash nodded. “They also have shops here, and in Chicago and L.A.”

“I didn’t know that.”

The short ride was almost over when Lotus wheeled on him. “Why do we need to go there? Do you think my wedding dress would be outre for the Symphony Ball?”

“No. I think it would be lovely, but I don’t think you feel that way and you seem nervous about tonight. I just thought if there was anything here all made up that caught your fancy we could buy it. But if you don't see anything, that's fine too. Then, at least, you'll be happier with your choice," Dash told her, shoving some bills at the driver then getting out of the cab, his hand holding hers.

When they were standing on the sidewalk together, he put his hand on her lips. "And please don't tell me I shouldn't spoil you. I love getting you things, love. Please indulge me just a bit."

Lotus looked up at him. How had she ever gotten anyone like him? Even at night sometimes when she would wake up in his arms, she could hardly believe that he was hers, and that they were married. She sighed.

"You're in that dream world again, love." He kissed her cheek, then drew her toward the glass-fronted establishment that had beige silk sheers on the door and window and the name CHARINE'S scrolled on the window in gold.

Lotus dragged her feet. "We can't go in there in running clothes. . . ."

"Yes, we can," he told her gently, pushing open the door into the plush champagne-carpeted and silk-walled reception area.

There were two other women waiting as they entered, who looked at them askance. A salesperson crossed the spacious area, her feet sinking into the pale, thick carpet. She smiled at each of the women in turn, then gestured to two assistants who followed her. They took the two women through a door that Lotus surmised must be the fitting rooms. She then turned and looked at them, her eyes icy, her chin raised. "Yes?"

"Charine is sometimes here on Fridays. Is she here today?" Dash's strong voice reached out to the woman, cracking the starch in her demeanor. "Tell her that Dash Colby is here."

"Colby?" the woman's smile widened. "Yes, of course. If you'll take a seat." Her glance slid off Lotus. "I assume you are together."

"Tell Charine we're here," Dash said coldly, making the woman almost scuttle into the back of the salon.

"You were a bit rough on her," Lotus ventured, leaning on him when he put his arm around her.

"I didn't like what I read in her tiny mind. You're my wife. I will not let anyone think of you as anything else."

"Yes, sir." Lotus giggled, without raising her head from his chest.

The curtains were flung back and a doll-like woman tottered toward them, her hair as black and silky as Lotus's, her arms raised. "You dog . . ." Her rather high-pitched voice had a trace of accent. "You are married! I read it in the *Times*." Charine's eyes slewed toward Lotus. "Ahh, so you have chosen well, cheri." The tiny woman looked at Lotus. "You are lovely."

"Thank you," Lotus said.

"Thank you," Dash said at the same time, then laughed and hugged her. "She's beautiful and tonight we are going to the Symphony Ball. . . ."

"Ahh . . . and you expect me to outfit her in twenty minutes," Charine interrupted dryly, shaking her head when Dash laughed and nodded. She clapped her hands, then spoke in rapid French to an attendant who came on the run, then scurried away to carry out the command. "I am not sure it's here," Charine said, talking to no one in particular, a slight frown on her porcelain skin.

"Come, we'll wait in my quarters. Marie will bring it there."

"This number thirty-four you sent her for must suit my wife, I take it, by the way you're pacing," Dash told her when he followed the women into a large studio area and straddled a chair, his chin on the back. He sat very close to Lotus who sat on the edge of her chair.

Charine stopped her pacing and smiled at him. "Ah, your French is still good, I see." She looked at Lotus. "And do you speak the language of the gods, madame?"

"Some. My first languages were French, Japanese, and Chinese. Then I learned English. My father was from the United States, but he was very comfortable with the other languages," Lotus told her.

Dash beamed at Charine.

"You love this lady very much, I think."

"Very much." Dash grinned at a reddening Lotus.

"You must not mind me, *chérie*," Charine spoke to Lotus. "I always speak my mind. It is me to do so." She looked back at Dash. "As for the dress . . . Ah, you have it, Marie." Charine gestured to the girl to bring it forward. Then she turned and gesticulated to Lotus to stand near her. "As I thought, this green silk is the same color as her eyes. Marie, you will help Mrs. Colby and get shoes in her size, please." Her bow-shaped mouth curved upward when she saw Lotus's surprised look. "So you worry about the shoes I tell Marie to bring? Do not. I always keep a supply of try-on shoes for my customers." She shrugged in a Gallic way. "It is more efficient."

Lotus felt as though she had climbed aboard a fast-moving merry-go-round when Marie took her into a dressing room adjacent to the studio. She could hear the murmur of Dash and Charine's conversation as Marie and another woman pulled off her sweats, then had her don nylons and medium-heeled shoes. The dress, in sea foam silk, was slipped over her head. It was strapless except for a long scarf that was tossed over one shoulder, Roman-style. The dress was form fitting from under the bust to the kneecap. There the silk was draped from a point at the knee downward so that it flared back and down like a ruffle. It delineated every curve of Lotus's body and didn't allow for any bra.

"Madame, you have a perfect figure for this gown, but perhaps you should consider not wearing underpants for the evening. The line could show through such delicate fabric."

Lotus stared at herself in the mirror. There was a tiny line where the underpants showed. "I think I would prefer to wear something. I have some very sheer and delicate panty hose I can wear with it."

Marie shrugged. "We have the micro bikini briefs here, madame. They would be less conspicuous."

"Ah . . . well, perhaps. That might be better."

Marie inclined her head then pushed back the curtain of the dressing room. "Madame Charine and your husband are just on the other side of the screen, madame."

"Thank you." Lotus felt as though she had nothing on, the silk was so light. Only the whisper of silk announced her presence as she rounded the screen to where her husband and the diminutive designer were conversing.

Dash turned first. "Darling," he whispered,

breathlessly. "Your eyes . . . your body . . ." Then he frowned. "My God, I won't let anyone else see you like this. She's perfect." He grumbled, rising from his chair almost knocking it over in his haste.

Both women chuckled.

"*Chéri*, a beautiful woman was made to be seen by others," Charine said and laughed.

"No." Dash fired the word like a bullet, making Marie, who had followed behind Lotus, blink.

"I like it," Lotus told him in low tones.

"So do I," Dash ground out the word reluctantly.

"She would be exquisite with a little jewelry here and there." Charine pointed to her ears and wrists. "Nothing around her neck, of course. That lovely graceful neck must be bare."

"Yes," Dash agreed, going over to his sweat jacket and rummaging in his capacious pocket. "These would go with it." He drew the jade, in white, green, pink and lavender, from the velvet case.

"*Ma fois!* I should say they would," Charine exclaimed. She drew out the lavender jade ring and earrings and put them up against the sea green dress. "She will be exquisite," Charine pronounced.

"Yes." Dash scowled when Lotus laughed, then glided up to him to embrace him.

"I won't take it. I like my wedding dress."

"Of course you'll take it. Your wedding dress is lovely on you. But this is magnificent. You must wear it, with me at your side every minute."

"Indeed, you must, *chéri*. You will be fighting off the population of men at the ball." Charine covered her mouth with one hand when Dash looked murderous. "I am sorry, cheri, I don't mean to laugh, but it so funny, the great Dash Colby . . ."

"If you say hung by his own petard, Charine, my love, I shall stuff you in one of your own garment bags," Dash threatened her.

Charine put up her hand palm outward. "I will say nothing."

"Right," Dash agreed, fumbling his hands over his clothes to reach for his checkbook.

"There is no need, my friend. I will bill you for the ensemble"—Charine put her hand on his arm—"but I must insist that she go to Giulio's next door and get her shoes. He will fit her with something that will be even more beautiful and elegant than the try-on shoes here. I am sure he will make sure she is most comfortable so she can dance the night away." Charine kissed her fingers to both of them.

"True." Dash snapped his fingers, not listening to Lotus when she protested.

"I have shoes . . ." Lotus said, bidding good-bye hurriedly to the dress designer as Dash pulled her out of the store.

"Come back again, Madame Colby." Charine's tinkling laugh followed after them.

"Of course she will. Good-bye, Charine," Dash answered for both of them.

Despite her reluctance Lotus was entranced with the tiny bootery that had no frills but a good address. Giulio himself waited on them.

"I do not like to give a woman a ready-made shoe"—he lifted his shoulders—"but of course there is no time to create footwear for the *signora.* I will see what I can do." After rapid spate of Italian, an assistant appeared from the back room, bearing stacks of boxes. First Giulio studied her dress and looked at the many shoes his assistant showed him. Then he lifted Lotus's foot, stripped off the sweat sock, and ran his hands up and down her instep. "Ummm. She has a high instep. We must fit her properly." He jumped to his feet and left the room.

"I feel like a prize mare being shod by the blacksmith," Lotus whispered.

"Darling." Dash laughed. "I assure you it's much more expensive to shoe our horses than it is you."

"We have horses?"

Dash's eyes narrowed on her as he nodded. "One of the mares is about to foal soon. If it's a filly, I intend to call her Lotus Blossom."

Lotus could feel her eyes light up. "Dash, really?" She kissed his cheek. "What a nice idea!"

Just then Giulio popped back into the room, another of his attendants following him with more boxes. He stared at Lotus, frowning. "The *signora* cries. It cannot be my shoes."

"She's happy. *Molto bene,*" Dash responded in Italian.

"You have horses. You speak Italian. Are there no ends to the facets of you," Lotus whispered, feeling helpless as Giulio slipped a nylon stocking on her right foot then removed a rather high-heeled slipper from the box. The plain leather pump was close in shade to her dress.

"That should feel very good, *signora,* though I can see that you are not used to wearing the higher heel."

"No, I'm not," Lotus said, rising to her feet and walking up and down. "This feels like air. It's very comfortable."

"Good. That will be for this evening. I have brought you other shoes that suit your foot for other occasions," Giulio said, rubbing his hands together.

Lotus shook her head. "No, thank you. I never buy shoes without having an outfit for them."

"Let's see them." Dash pawed through the boxes, pointing to some and frowning at others. When he saw Lotus shaking her head, he spoke. "Now, darling, I just want you to have a few pairs of recreational and dress shoes. That will be all. I'll give you a check."

Giulio held up one hand palm outward. "Not to worry. I will bill you, sir." He beamed.

"Fine. Could I use your phone to call our driver?" Dash took only a moment to call Timmons, then he was back at Lotus's side. "Come on, darling. I told Timmy we'll meet him at the corner. No, don't worry, I can carry the parcels."

"Not all of them. You have the dress bag. I'll take some of the shoes."

"I could have them sent to your house, sir," Giulio suggested.

"No, I don't want anything not arriving for tonight. We'll take them." Dash smiled and led her from the store.

"He was positively drooling with glee," Lotus huffed, trotting at his side and carrying two of the shoe boxes. "Maybe his shoes are wonderful, but I don't like people who rub their hands together like that after a sale. I feel uneasy."

Dash chuckled and looked down at her and winked. "This has been one of the happiest days of my life. It is nowhere near the idea I had for our honeymoon—and we will still be going to

Greece—but I have enjoyed this day with you more than I can say."

"Me too." Lotus looked up at him, very aware of the women who passed by and gave her husband more than one look. *They can't have him! He's mine and I will keep him!*

"Ah, there's Timmy." Dash waved and stood at the curb as the Rolls cruised to their side. "Good man," he told the family retainer as he and Lotus settled back against the cushions of the backseat.

"It was fun. I didn't need the dress, but I do love it," she told Dash as she snuggled close to him.

"So do I, but I think Charine was right. I'll be fighting Boston single-handed when they see you."

"Crazy."

When they reached home, only Dash's father and his brother, Alan, were in the drawing room.

Alan waggled his iced fruit juice in their faces. "Good thing you're back. Jennifer was positive you had taken Lotus to Borneo without so much as a good-bye note."

Dash chuckled as his father grimaced. "Getting sticky around here?"

"Bad, my boy, bad." Zachary Colby sighed. "We will be having fifty to dinner and cocktails at the Neptune before the ball."

"God." Dash closed his eyes. "When was that arranged?"

"Who knows?" Alan said. "Father and I found out this afternoon. God, I'll never marry a society woman. I'm going for a peat bog farmer in the auld sod."

"Won't last a week," His father said mildly, "but I applaud your choice." He went over to Lotus and kissed her on the cheek. "And how are you doing, my child? You have color in your cheeks and a sparkle in your eye. It can't be my son that did that, so it must be that you're looking forward to the frivolity this evening." Zachary gave his son a smile when he glared at him.

"Not that you deserve to see them, but before we go upstairs, perhaps you'd like to see what we bought today." Dash was eager to open the package of jade and spread it out on the coffee table.

Alan whistled, setting down his drink, then sinking onto the settee in front of the coffee table. "Beautiful stuff." He looked up at Lotus. "Why are you blushing, lovely sister-in-law? The jade will be great on you."

Zachary Colby saw Lotus's nervousness even when Dash put his arm around her and laughed at what Alan said. "My child, I am delighted that you will be wearing such beautiful jade. It is almost as lovely as you are."

"Thank you," Lotus whispered.

Dash's mother swept into the room, irritation flashing through her smile. "So you haven't even begun to dress, Zachary? Or you, Alan!"

"My fault, Lissa," Alan said, pounding his chest with a closed fist. "I was looking at the jade Dash bought for Lotus."

"Oh?" Lissa came farther into the room. "Do let me see. Jade is a favorite of mine." She bent over the table, gasping. "My Lord, it's lovely. Did you see it, Zach?"

"Yes. It will be perfect on Lotus." He took his wife's arm and led her toward the door. "Come along, love. You can dress me." He winked at

Lotus whose low laughter stopped her mother-in-law in her tracks.

"You do have a sweet laugh," Lissa Colby told her, then her gaze slid to Dash. "And you do have John Dasher by the jugular, do you not?"

Lotus felt her mouth drop open as her mother-in-law sailed from the room, holding on tight to her husband's arm.

Dash cursed fluently and roundly for two minutes. Alan whistled again.

"Ah . . . Dash, maybe we should go upstairs and dress too," Lotus ventured.

"I will, after I have three fingers of Irish whiskey," he told her grimly.

"Do you think a good stiff drink will keep you from strangling Mother?" Alan asked his big brother.

"No, but it's only fair to give her a head start," Dash grated, ignoring his brother's chuckle.

"Dash." Lotus watched him toss back the whiskey. "I thought we might dance this evening, but if you'd rather get drunk, then I'm sure Alan will take pity on me."

"Be happy to help." Alan jumped to his feet and gave an exaggerated bow.

Dash cracked the glass down so hard, it surprised Lotus when it didn't break. "I'll be dancing with my wife. Come along, darling, it's time to dress."

Lotus was almost running as she tried to catch him as he left the room and took the stairs two at a time. By the time she had reached their suite, she was out of breath. "Are we in a marathon?"

"Huh? Oh, sorry, love. We'd better take hurry-up showers." Dash looked at her regretfully.

Lotus wrinkled up her nose at him. "I suppose."

"There's always after the ball," Dash told her, his voice deep and husky.

"I look forward to it," Lotus told him, smiling, then watched him leave the bedroom to go to the other bathroom in the suite.

Lotus knew that she should hurry, but her aching feet demanded the soothing of a bath. She filled the tub with water and dotted it with the bath oil fragrance from the shelf.

She was halfway between sleep and waking when she heard Dash calling to her. Blinking herself wide awake, she watched the bathroom door open. "You're almost dressed," she squeaked.

"Honey, we leave for the Neptune in half an hour."

"No!" She shot to her feet, clambering out of the tub.

"I do love you dressed that way. With just a few bubbles here and there." Dash leaned over her, the crease in his silk evening trousers razor sharp.

"Dash, stop it. I'll be late."

"So . . ." But he stood aside as she scampered into the dressing room, fumbling another towel around her as she pawed through the makeup she'd scattered on the countertop. "This is going to be close," she said after she cleansed her skin, then applied a creamy foundation and blush. She touched her eyes with pale orange eyeshadow, speckled with gold, not bothering to darken her already black and thick lashes and the thin arching line of her brow.

She was busy pulling on the very sheer flesh-colored hose with just a tad of green through it, which she was wearing with her dress, when she noticed that Dash was still with her. She felt that ambivalent shyness and pride she often felt with him. "You should be through dressing by now."

"Almost." His sexy eyes ran over her. "I had most of my things in the other room, but you intrigue me so much I decided to finish in here so that I could be with you."

"Should I think of you as a voyeur?" Sensual amusement bubbled in her as he continued to watch her even while he was tying the intricate white silk bow tie that would match the hand-sewn pleated shirt and cummerbund he was wearing.

He shrugged. "With you, yes. I can't say I ever was interested in seeing a woman dress before I met you."

"Only watching them strip I suppose," she said tartly, sliding the silk sheath over her head and letting it fall down her body.

"Yes," he shouted with laughter when she turned on him, hands curled into fists. He leaned forward so that his face was close to her. "Take your best shot."

"I will if I see you around any women tonight," she blurted then covered her mouth.

Dash preened and thumped his chest. "You Tarzan's woman." He grinned at her.

"I should hit you," Lotus told him as she kissed his chin, then stepped back from him, irritated with herself that she had exposed so much of her feelings to him. Damn him that she should be so jealous of him!

"What are you thinking?" he asked her as he fitted the snow white carnation touched with cream into his lapel. Then he watched her affix the creamy lavender jade earrings into her ears.

"The dashing Dash never looked more dashing," she simpered, her hands still on her left ear as she looked into the mirror, freezing still when she saw his face harden and close as he leaned near her. As he drew back she turned, putting the one earring down on the dresser, her hand reaching out to his. "Wait. I hurt you. How?"

Dash looked down at her hand, for a moment, seeming to studying her wedding ring and diamond carefully. Then he looked up at her. "I suppose it bothers me that you would adopt the sobriquet of the tabloids for me."

Lotus felt her mouth drop as he seemed to move further away. "Dash. I never knew they called you that."

His eyes narrowed, seeming to go over her face in laser study. "That doesn't seem possible," he murmured.

She could feel her nails digging into him. "You don't believe me?"

"Oh, no. I believe you. I just find it incredible. Not that I'm complaining. It gives me a rash to think of you ever reading some of the bull those rags put out."

"Bad?"

"Bad! Trash is the word." Dash spat the word. He bit his lip. "I'm not whitewashing myself, wife. Many women were in my life and that suited me, but now I wish I could erase every moment that wasn't with you."

"Most men love that type of experience," she said sweetly.

Dash felt his mouth quiver with anger and

amusement. She was getting to read him very well! "I liked it myself . . . at the time, but now I hate the least taint of gossip because you're my wife." He bit off the last word. He sounded like a preacher! "We should be going." As she turned back to the mirror and put on the last earring and the thin jade bracelet, he studied her again. "You are so lovely. Your eyes are like almond-shaped emeralds. Your shoulders are like the flower of your name, creamy lotus." He sucked in a breath when she walked away from him and pirouetted, the dress flaring at the bottom and showing the green leather pumps and her trim ankles, her outstretched arms like cream satin against the silky dress. "Mrs. Colby, you are very precious."

Lotus paused in her turn and looked at him. "Thank you. Because you're looking at me, I feel very beautiful."

Dash groaned, closed his eyes for a moment, then crooked his arm. "We are late."

Lotus clung to him as they went down the two flights of stairs.

"I never asked you if you preferred taking the elevator, dressed as you are." Dash glanced at her ruefully as they paused on the first landing.

"No. I need the motion of walking to calm myself."

"Darling. Be assured that there will be no one there who will even come close to your beauty."

"You might be prejudiced."

"Yes." He told her as he hesitated outside the drawing room. "But I also know a beautiful woman when I see one. You're one." He squeezed her hand, then led her into the drawing room.

"About time," Dash's sister, Jennifer, sighed. "We were about to go without you, John Dasher."

"I wish you had," Dash said, ambling over to the small bar after leading Lotus to a chair next to his mother.

"Really, dear, you know you'll have a good time. So many of your . . . cronies will be there," Lissa Colby told her son, sipping daintily at her Riesling.

Dash's hand froze in the act of pouring iced orange juice for Lotus. "What cronies, Lissa?" he hissed.

Silence filled the room like an expanding balloon, pushing the oxygen from the air.

Ann, Dash's sister, swallowed, the sound bouncing off the wainscoted walls. "If . . . if you think, John Dasher, that anyone invited Prue to our dinner party at the Neptune, then . . ." She paused, sipped her wine, her eyes sliding toward her sister.

"We didn't, though I saw nothing wrong with it. I have known Prue since we were children . . ." Jennifer began, two coin-sized spots of color on her cheeks.

"My ex-wife is not a welcome addendum to any party where I am in attendance." Dash fired the words like bullets into the room, his teeth cracking together.

His three brothers-in-law, James Wells, Richard Aylman, and Warren Deitz, looked into their drinks. His sisters, Ann and Jennifer, looked affronted. Laura inhaled, going over to Lotus and standing next to her. His father coughed and took another glass of wine. Alan looked belligerent. Lissa looked benign.

All at once Lotus had the distinct impression all eyes were on her. She didn't look up when Dash strode across the room and handed her the orange juice. She sipped some first. Then she looked up at her thunderous husband, taken aback when she saw his hands clenched, but a flash of hurt in his eyes. "Darling. It's just right. I love it when you take care of me . . ." She batted her eyes at him. "And you always take care of me." She stared up at him until she saw his eyes flicker with warmth, the muscle at the side of his mouth cease its jerking.

"My favorite job." Dash leaned down and kissed her, long and hard. "There was a bit of orange juice at the corner of your mouth."

"How sweet." Lotus looked over at her mother-in-law and sighed. "Isn't he just the dearest person?"

"She'll do," Lissa murmured, her mouth quivering.

Alan's guffaw burst into the room like the popping of a cork.

Lissa's smile widened. "Yes, Dash is unusual."

"Very," Lotus gushed.

"Isn't it time we were going?" Jennifer snapped.

"Right." Zachary Colby came over to the couch where Lotus was sitting and bent toward her. "You must play poker with me sometime, child. You have the instincts of a tigress protecting her young. I like that very much." He turned to his wife and grinned. "Come, my dear, I am sure you will be able to sharpen your sword on fresher game at the Neptune."

"Devil," his wife said mildly, rising from her chair. She looked at Lotus, real amusement on her face. "Dash made the right choice this time."

Lotus didn't move as the others walked toward the door. When Dash came to take her arm and lift her from the couch, she looked up at him. "I'm revising my first opinion of your mother."

His smile was lopsided as he looked down at her. "Darling, I was so afraid they would hurt you. I damn well almost carried you out of here and took you to the airport."

Lotus saw the relief in his eyes. "We have a long way to go, John Dasher, before we know each other, but I'll be damned before I let anyone put barriers between us. We might do it ourselves, but I won't let anyone else."

Dash lifted her ring finger to his mouth and kissed it. "Dad's right. You *are* a tigress. Meow."

"Shame on you, Dash Colby. Tigresses roar." She swept out of the room in front of him, chin high, hearing his shout of laughter.

CHAPTER NINE

The Neptune was a revelation to Lotus. She had been in private clubs many times before but she had never seen anything like the awesome pride that the Neptune's staff carried around with them like a banner.

"If you're thinking that they must be the oldest retainers in Christendom, you're right," Alan whispered as they were being directed to a series of round tables that had been set into a large corner of the oaked-paneled room, the floors covered in ankle-deep Oriental carpeting.

"Shh, they may ask us to leave," Lotus whispered back as Dash seated her between his brother and himself.

"He was asked to leave the premises at one time," Laura said, leaning forward from her place on the other side of Dash.

Lotus looked at Alan. "Not really?"

"True. I put cut-up rubber bands in one of the old duffer's pipes when I was about ten. His grandson ratted on me," Alan chortled. "Old Tyler screeched for a month about his ruined meerschaum."

"And then Al tried to get even by attempting to keelhaul the grandson on his sailboat," Dash finished, laughing.

"That's so dangerous," Lotus said.

"It could have been if it hadn't been a five-foot dinghy sailboat that he sailed on the pond in the park," Dash said.

"I almost did it," Alan said dreamily, spearing a shrimp from his cocktail.

"I think you might be a touch worse than my brothers, but very like my cousin, Will," Lotus told him. "I'm very comfortable with you." She touched his cheek with her index finger. When he looked away and reddened, she glanced at Dash and grimaced. "I've made him uncomfortable."

"You've made a conquest, I think," Dash said. "Stop doing that, Mrs. Colby. I have no intention of battling my brother,"

Lotus's laugh spilled out of her, turning her father-in-law's head.

He sat at the middle table with his wife and older daughters and their husbands. He lifted his glass in a toasting gesture to her.

"See? Even my father isn't immune to your lovely laugh, my dove," Dash said in her ear.

They had lobster for dinner, broiled with pernod and lemon.

"I do like romaine salad," Lotus told him, enjoying the Caesar dressing of eggs and pungent-grated cheese with oil and vinegar and herbs.

"The dessert will be chocolate mousse." Laura leaned forward and said, "I hope you like it."

"I'm a chocoholic," Lotus confessed.

"Oh, sweet heaven, so am I," Laura breathed. "I usually eat my husband's and mine."

"Well, don't ask for mine," Alan told his sister cruelly.

"Monster," she said mildly.

Lotus had looked right and left at all the friends of the Colbys who were dining with them, and though she had been introduced to each one before they dined, she didn't remember one name now. "I suppose all of them trace their families back to the witches of Salem."

"They do," Alan said. "In fact, some of them were present at the burnings."

Lotus chuckled, deciding that she liked Alan and Laura very much.

When they left the Neptune Club, the air was still mild but the breeze had strengthened.

"Darling, you won't be warm enough with just that scarf on you." Dash frowned.

"That scarf, as you call it, is cashmere and very warm," Lotus told him.

Unlike most of his family, Dash had driven himself and Lotus in Alan's car, the Porsche, which gave them a sense of privacy.

The ball was held in an old theater that had been renovated years before by the Landmark Society and was used by them for many of their historical fetes.

They met Alan outside the brick edifice as he was helping his older sisters from a Rolls-Royce. They strolled up the steps and into the huge lobby together.

"My goodness . . ." Lotus looked upward at the vaulted, mosaic ceiling. "It's wonderful. No wonder they wanted to preserve it."

"Grandmother Colby used to tell us that she and her beaux came to the Saxby to see great entertainment," Alan told her as he walked on one side of her as they ascended the sweep of stairs leading to the second level where the ball would be held.

The music made Lotus's toes begin to tap as Dash and Alan paused to speak to friends.

"And this is my wife, Lotus. Darling . . ." Lotus was introduced to someone at every step as they moved toward the cathedrallike ballroom.

"Dasher, darling, aren't you going to introduce me to your charming lotus blossom?" A well-modulated voice spoke behind Lotus's back.

"Prue, how are you?" Dash's voice was cool. "I would be glad to introduce you to my wife, but I don't know what your name is at the present time."

"Touché. You always were a scoundrel, Dasher." The tall blond woman had a strong supple body. Wide cheekbones delineated the shell texture of her skin and the glossy perfection of her makeup. "I'm married to Arnold Case. You must remember him."

Dash shook his head. "I remember the name Case, but I don't think I know him." He looked at Lotus, wondering what she was thinking. His insides sunk at the thought of having her feel uneasy or intimidated. "Darling, this is Prue Case. Prue, this is my wife, Lotus."

"How do you do, Mrs. Case."

"Do call me Prue. Dasher and I go way back. I was his first wife, you know," she told Lotus with great relish.

"How nice for you." Lotus looked up at the woman and smiled. "I'm his last wife." She tucked her hand into Dash's and smiled up at him. "I am dying to dance with you, darling."

"How do you like my sister-in-law so far, Prue, old girl?" Alan asked, chuckling.

"You were always a dirty-faced terror." Prue's icy smile touched Alan.

Alan pointed to his face. "Look. I washed."

The three of them passed through into the ballroom.

"She didn't bother you, did she, love?" Dash leaned over her as they were led to a table.

Lotus stared up at him. The expressionless Dash Colby was gone. In his place was a man who was hanging out his emotions for all to see. "I think I might feel a little sorry for her. How could any woman let you go?" she cooed, feeling strong, confident, and as powerful as Atlas because Dash didn't disguise his relief and delight with her answer.

"That's easy. Until you, she nor any other woman ever had me. And you have me until you let me go," Dash told her, seeming to be oblivious of the people who moved about them, not noticing when the maitre d' indicated their places at a table along the wall.

"Poor baby. You're stuck, then. I won't let you go."

Dash grinned, then lifted his head, smiling at the people at the table, introducing her to the people in their vicinity who were strangers to her, but not letting her seat herself. "I feel like dancing."

"Me too." Lotus looked up at him dreamily. *I wonder what our little boy will look like? He'll be tall and strong with ash blond hair and gray blue eyes. He'll go to Harvard and crew like his father,* Lotus mused as they moved to the dance floor. *Or perhaps he'll go to Cornell like her brothers and their father. Or to the school I went to. . . .*

"What are you thinking?" Dash watched the play of emotions on her face, happiness, wonderment. It tore him up inside that there would be times in their marriage when she wouldn't be happy. He vowed then and there that he would fight against that happening! He had been ready to throttle Prue when she made her clever remarks, yet Lotus had remained serene. In fact, she had thrown a few needle-sharp barbs of her own that had both amused him and made him proud. It was frightening sometimes to dwell on the depth of love he had for her, at how empty his life would be if she weren't in it now.

It suddenly pierced Lotus's cloud of dreams that they had never discussed having children, that there were a great many things they hadn't even mentioned together—things that could profoundly affect their future.

Dash felt her stiffen in his arms as they circled the floor slowly. "What are you thinking now?"

"I was thinking of children," Lotus told him simply.

"Ours?" Dash's pulse double-timed as the picture of a tiny, dark-haired, green-eyed baby leaped into his mind.

"Yes."

"Darling." He hugged her. "You do have the loveliest ideas. This is a project that may take a great deal of work . . . lovely work."

"And you wouldn't mind having them?"

"My love, I can't think of anything that would please me more . . . unless . . ." He frowned.

"What's wrong?" Before he answered a thousand reasons wormed through her brain on why they couldn't have children.

"When was the last time you had a physical? I don't want you being pregnant unless you have a complete checkup."

Lotus was flummoxed. She had not expected him to say that. "Dash. No one has a physical before they become pregnant today."

"You will."

The music changed and Dash let her flow away from his body, the rhythmic gyrations taking them both as they faced each other.

"Darling . . ." Lotus began.

"Yes . . ." Dash kept his eyes on her fluid form as she moved in front of him with incredible grace. "You are such a beautiful dancer."

"Dash . . ." Lotus felt caught between irritation and laughter at the hot look in his eyes. "You're not listening to me."

"I am. Your body language is loud and clear, love." He inhaled a sharp breath when he saw her breasts move beneath the silky fabric. "I am going to take you to Alaska," he said through his teeth as Alan came up to him and tapped him on the shoulder.

"*Tch, tch,* brother. Jennifer says you're making a spectacle of yourself." Alan beamed at him. "You should stop looking at Lotus as though she were the last peanut butter sandwich on the planet. That's a quote, brother. Going to punch me in the nose?"

"Of course he isn't." Lotus laughed at her husband's outthrust jaw, loosening her hand from his grip so that she could dance with her brother-in-law. "I'll be right back, darling."

Dash continued to watch them as they moved out into the center of the floor, dancing apart from one another, but in perfect rhythm.

"You really should get that murderous look off your face, John Dasher. She won't go far, you know." Lissa Colby took hold of her son's arm and urged him to the side of the dance floor.

"Would you like to dance, Lissa?" Dash requested stiffly.

"I don't think so, John Dasher. Why don't we get a frosted orange juice, and you can tell me how you met the tiny Oriental dynamo who has taken over your life."

Dash's twist-of-lemon smile touched his mother, then his eyes were back on the dance floor. "You have a way of hitting the nail, Mother."

"My goodness, you are affected. You haven't called me Mother in years," Lissa drawled.

"I always thought you didn't like to be called Mother."

"I thought so too," she confessed. "Strange how things change in this world."

"True." Dash cupped his mother's elbow as they approached one of the tiny bars set discreetly among greenery in several sections of the huge ballroom. "Two orange juices, please."

Lissa's careful arched brows rose a fraction. "You, John Dasher? Orange juice?"

"I find that I need less and less of either the stimulation or smothering of boredom that I used alcohol for in the past." The words slipped out as he turned his head to watch his wife and brother laughing and dancing on the floor.

"She has taken over your life then?" Lissa moved away from the peopled area around the bar, giving plastic smiles left and right as other guests greeted her and her son, but encouraging no one to approach.

"She is my life, Lissa."

"Darling, boy," Lissa said softly.

"Are those tears in your eyes, Mother?" Dash edged her nearer the wall in the nominal privacy of more of the potted plants that landscaped the ballroom into a "Summer Garden Party," the theme of the Symphony Ball. "I've never seen you cry."

"Most people haven't, but I have cried many tears for you, John Dasher, because I knew how much I helped shape that cynicism of yours, how much I encouraged you to box your emotions away, and how, when I could have warned you what a selfish devil Prue was, I let you marry her anyway because her family was the right one." Lissa looked up at him, her eyes wide. "I scarred you, John Dasher."

Dash stared at his parent, more shaken that he cared to admit by her words. "If I tell you that nothing would have changed my mind about marrying Prue at that time, will that absolve you of the guilt you feel? I really felt at that time that she and I had the best chance of making a marriage. We seemed to have the ingredients of success. We both understood and liked finance and big business. She and I both had money. We knew the same people, had similar backgrounds, and were fond of each other's families. I had no illusions about love, Mother, and not until the moment I met Lotus"—his eyes seemed to have a life of their own as they flitted toward the dance floor—"did I realize that there could be a someone who fits like a glove into your life as she does mine, but I knew it the moment I first held her in my arms when we danced at the casino." He smiled down at his mother. "I developed my own armor in life, which was considerably hardened after I entered the casino business. You had little to do with that."

Lissa put her hand on his arm. "My dear boy, you have always been quick to shoulder the responsibility for your actions, but that does not mitigate my part in your unhappiness. I allowed your sisters to foist Prue onto you." His mother pressed her lips together and shook her head. "I am very grateful that Lotus came into your life. She really is quite lovely."

Dash felt relief when he saw the slight satirical lift to her lips. "What are you plotting now, Mother?"

"Not a thing, dear boy," she drawled. "I was just thinking how absolutely beautiful your children will be."

Dash felt as though his chest would burst through his silk shirt. "I agree. In fact both Lotus and I want children, but not before I know she is able to be pregnant safely."

Lissa's lips parted a bit in surprise. "But, John Dasher, surely you know that most women of average health are well able to carry a child, and Lotus looks of more than average health to me."

"Yes. She seems very healthy, but I want an affidavit from a few good doctors on that," Dash insisted.

"A few good doctors . . ." his mother repeated, then she covered her mouth with her hand.

"It's not funny." His clipped Boston accent surfaced and wiped away his usual drawl.

"No, of course not, dear." She set down her

glass, the ice tinkling in the almost empty receptacle. "That is a very nice waltz, John Dasher. We can dance to that. Surely all those lessons at Madame Duval's dance studio weren't wasted."

Dash smiled at his mother and inclined his head. "I'm not sure, Mother. I played hooky at a few of them."

His mother shook his head. "You were an incorrigible child, but I knew you would grow up just like your father."

"And that would please you. The worst-kept secret in Boston is that you love Dad, Lissa."

She grimaced. "You mustn't shout it about Boston, dear boy. Being in love with my husband could get me forcibly removed from the Priscilla Club," his mother murmured as she lifted her hands to place one in his and the other, most correctly, at the tip of his shoulder. "My, my, this is wonderful. I can't remember when I've last waltzed." She sighed as they moved in rhythm.

Dash whirled his mother down the room, aware that because his wife watched him, his performance was a little more theatrical than it would have been. "Mother, you're as light as a feather. Only Lotus is better on the dance floor," he told her.

"That doesn't surprise me." She laughed as they twirled around the perimeter of the room. "My goodness, is that your father and Alan with their mouths open watching us?" Lissa asked.

Even though she was a little out of breath, Dash could hear the satisfaction in her voice. He slowed his movements just a trifle. "Don't be silly, John Dasher, carry on. I love it," his mother scolded him. "Don't slow down."

Dash grinned and nodded, but he didn't pick up his pace.

At the dance's end Alan and his father approached them with Lotus and Laura, the four of them applauding. "My dear, I've never seen you look more graceful. You showed all those debutantes how it's done." Zachary Colby leaned down and kissed his wife, tucking her hand into his arm.

"It was lovely," Lotus said. "You and Dash looked wonderful out there."

"I'm glad you think so," Dash told her, putting his arm around her and kissing the top of her head. "Because the next waltz is with you."

"Lissa, you looked great. You made the ladies of the Priscilla Club look like old fogies," Alan told his mother.

"And I shall feel like an old fogy when my bunion yells in the morning," Lissa said, and wrinkled her nose when Lotus chuckled.

"Not to worry, my dear. I shall massage your feet before we go to bed," Zachary told her, admiration in his eyes.

"Well, that certainly makes it worthwhile," his wife simpered.

"If you're waiting for me to blush, Melissa, my sweet, forget it." Zachary reached down and gave his wife a resounding smack on the mouth, eliciting laughter from his two sons when their mother looked dumbfounded.

"Don't be such bullies." Lotus pinched her husband's and brother-in-law's arms.

"Ouch, Lotus." Alan glared at her. "You're getting as bad as Laura."

"Don't take my name in vain," Laura said, and

pinched Alan again. "Watch out, everyone, the cavalry is right on my tail."

Lotus saw Jennifer and Ann bearing down on them and lifted her chin.

"Go get 'em, tiger," Dash chuckled at her back.

"Mother, really, we saw you with John Dasher . . ." Jennifer inhaled a deep breath.

"And I thought you looked great, Lissa." Jennifer's husband, Warren, laughed when his wife's mouth opened and closed like a gaffed fish. "You did too, didn't you, Jen?"

"Ah . . . yes, as a matter-of-fact I did, but—"

"But nothing." Ann's husband, Richard, interrupted. "You looked good out there, Mama-in-law." He kissed her cheek. "I'd like the next waltz myself."

"He was better at Madame Duval's than I was," Dash assured his mother.

"Anyone was, Dash. You scared the old girl witless when you climbed down the drainpipe and the damn thing collapsed," Richard stated.

"I banged my backside pretty badly as I recall," Dash drawled, bringing his sisters' eyes on him.

"I'm starved." A bored Alan looked at his relative. "I've done the proper thing, Lissa, now let's get out of here."

"How can you be hungry after the meal you had at the Neptune?" Ann looked at him indulgently.

"That was hours ago."

"We can leave after the orchestra breaks . . ." Lissa stated, ignoring Alan's groan. "Oh, there is that Crawford girl. She needs a partner. Dash, dear, why don't you dance with her?"

"I'll do it." Alan's ears were red when his mother chuckled.

Dash edged Lotus away from the others. "Could I talk you into leaving?"

"After you waltz with me," she said, and grinned impishly. "I wish I could have seen you at dancing school."

"You were a babe in arms then, my dove," Dash said, and gathered her close to him and kissed her. Then he lifted his head. "Ah, that is the 'Blue Danube' they're playing. Shall we, Mrs. Colby?"

"I'd be delighted, Mr. Colby." Lotus put her hand on his arm, feeling the familiar heat flood her as she touched her husband. Oh, how she loved him!

Dancing with Lotus in the centuries-old dance to the three-quarter time of Johann Strauss was a turn-on that Dash had not expected. Lotus was as light as down in his arms. Her not-so-small, uptilted breasts moved when she exhaled with delight. Her curving, slender legs moved through the steps with a minimum of fuss, as though they were not on the floor but cushioned by air.

"Oh, it's so beautiful," Lotus gasped as Dash twirled her. "No wonder so many love songs have three-quarter time."

Dash exulted because she looked so happy, so free. "I wish I could write a love song for you."

"Oh, you have." She took a deep breath and laughed when he looked puzzled.

"Have I?" he whispered.

"Yes. I've been singing some sort of song since I met you."

"So have I."

"See, we write our own music."

"Yes," Dash whispered. "A duet."

Lotus nodded.

Their eyes clung as they swayed and twirled around the floor almost unaware that a great many people had taken to the floor with them, including Dash's parents.

When the dance ended, many persons applauded.

"Even the debs and their escorts were waltzing," Lotus said, leaning on her husband.

"Madame Duval would be ecstatic," Dash announced laconically.

"I would have like to have seen you trying to sneak down the drainpipe . . . then again, I don't suppose I would have been able to stand it."

"No. You would have probably been there with me, going down the other drainpipe."

"I was a tomboy," Lotus admitted. "But what else would I be with two brothers who considered me to be able to play baseball and football as well as any boy? That delighted me and horrified my mother."

"You didn't go to dancing and deportment classes," Dash answered solemnly, his mouth twitching.

"Mother tried, but I was very elusive. She settled for piano lessons, which I liked. She tried not to worry about the rest."

"Wise woman, your mother."

"Yes, she is. I hope I'll be that good a mother."

"You'll be marvelous."

"Pardon me, cousin. But I just have to dance with your lovely bride." A man Lotus had never met whisked her away from Dash before her husband could even speak, let alone introduce them. He swept her down the long room in giant pirouettes.

"Stop." Lotus gasped. "I'm dizzy."

"I'm Dexter Colby, Dash's cousin."

"More Colbys," Lotus said and whimpered, closing her eyes as they stampeded around the room.

Across the room Jennifer and Ann had hold of Dash's arms.

"John Dasher . . ." Jennifer panted. "You cannot make a scene here."

"God forbid," Dash said through his teeth. "I'm going to kill him, not spill his blood and make a mess of course, but I am going to garrot him."

"In front of Boston society?" Ann squealed, rolling her eyes at her husband. "Do something."

"Not me." Richard smiled amiably. "Your brother has a wicked right."

"Not to mention his left hook," Jennifer's husband, Warren, interjected.

Alan ambled over to them, a young curly-headed deb on his arm. "Dash's going to kill Dexter?" he asked his sisters interestedly.

"Monster!" Jennifer seethed, her nostrils flaring as her younger brother laughed.

"Will you two let me go before I drag you out on the floor, clinging to my arms?"

"Not until you promise not to make a scene, John Dasher," Jennifer huffed.

"Swear in blood." Ann intoned each word as she strained to hold him.

"Where did he come from?" Dash grated, nodding at them, finally able to shrug off his sisters.

"Dexter is always around, dear boy." His mother floated toward her progeny, sizing up the red faces and scowls at once. "You mustn't mind him, dear. Besides being an execrable dancer, he's harmless."

"He'll tire her," Dash snarled. "I won't have it."

"Mother! Help us," Ann hissed. "John Dasher has that horrid bull dog look. He'll break Dexter's back."

"Right." Dash bared his teeth.

"John Dasher, you must not kill Dexter. He is family. Besides, we don't want scandal." His mother reproved him mildly.

"Do think of the scandal." Warren, Jennifer's husband, leaned toward Dash.

"Heavens, yes." Richard chuckled.

Dash looked at his two brothers-in-law, then at an eager-eyed Alan. "Well, well, anxious about a brouhaha, are you?"

Warren ignored his wife's outraged gasp and shrugged. "It might slice some of the boredom off this rat's fest."

"How can you?" Jennifer bit off each word.

"I will be glad to break one of Dexter's legs to help out," Richard offered helpfully.

"Outrageous."Ann froze a laughing Laura with one look.

Zachary Colby glanced at his wife, then at his older son. "Ahem . . . my boy, I fully understand your feelings, but I would prefer you waylaid Dexter in an alley, rather than take him and his cronies on here."

Dash's head swiveled slowly away from his wife who was trying desperately to hang on to an energetic Dexter doing the mambo. "Okay."

Ann and Jennifer expostulated, not able to articulate clearly as they tried to expel their wrath.

"Mother." Jennifer tried to appeal to her for help.

"Now, now, girls, your father has settled everything. Dasher won't do anything here . . . and I'm sure we'll all be home and in bed before he's able to get Dexter into an alley." She frowned for a moment. "I can't even think of an alley terribly close to us."

"Mother!" Ann squeaked. "How can you encourage Dasher! He has always been such a—such a—Hun." She finished with a baleful glare at her spouse who was propped against the wall laughing. "And you are as unprincipled as Dasher," she told him.

"Thank you, Annie. That's the nicest compliment you've paid me in a long time. In fact, it may be the only compliment you've ever paid me."

Blood chugged into Ann's face just as a panting Lotus staggered from the floor with Dexter to come to a halt next to her sister-in-law.

Lotus saw the hurt flit across Ann's face, then fade as she looked at Richard. She squeezed her sister-in-law's arm companionably and smiled at her. "Ann, Dexter still wants to dance."

Ann's smile wobbled, then steadied "Thanks. Just what I needed." She held out her arms to her cousin. "Hello, Dex. Just delete the jumps and leaps and we'll be fine." She gave Lotus a weak smile and dragged her cousin onto the floor.

"But I wanted to talk for a while," Dexter complained, looking over his shoulder.

"I think you may have saved his life," Jennifer's husband murmured to Lotus.

"I suppose she has." Jennifer's smile was fleeting, but her husband kissed her on the forehead.

"If you'll excuse us, Lotus, I think I'd like to dance with my wife." Jen's husband grinned when his wife's social smile widened.

"Of course." Lotus stepped back and felt a hard body meet hers, reveling in the familiar strength.

"I felt like dismembering that cousin of mine." Dash gave a rueful laugh.

Lotus sagged against him. "No problem, darling. It was just a dance, but I will admit he's like a dynamo. He would go up and down and sideways all at the same time. It was amazing."

"Devoid of rhythm," Laura pronounced solemnly as she sidled up next to them. "Madame Duval said it many times, but it never penetrated Dex's thick skin. He has always been of the opinion that he's a great dancer." She smiled at Lotus. "I always hide in the ladies' room when I see him coming."

Dash slipped both his arms around his wife, holding her tight to him. "Well, I don't think you'll escape this time, sis. The Menace has just discarded a half-dead Ann and is now approaching."

"No," Laura cheeped, turning to face an ebullient Dexter who took a grip on her upper arm. "I have a broken leg," she told him.

"Nonsense. The exercise will do it good."

"Get my husband," Laura gasped at Lotus, then was dragged away by the inexorable Dexter.

"We have to find him," Lotus told Dash as he was about to walk away.

"I want to leave before I land him one right on that soft chin of his." Dash had a mixture of amusement and irritation in his voice.

"Dash," Lotus cooed. "We'll leave soon."

"Stop doing that. The city of Boston is going to see your effect on me because I don't think my jacket will disguise it."

Lotus laughed, leaning against him, joy spilling out of her.

"Was I that amusing?" His eyes held lazy heat.

"No. But it's wonderful to laugh when you're happy. Next to singing it's the very best thing to do."

"I'll remember that. I feel a little like singing myself."

"You look surprised that you would experience such a thing."

"I am." He looked down at her, studying her. "You have the skin of an angel."

"I think angels are blond."

"Wrong. Angels have blue black hair and almond-shaped green eyes, with wide cheekbones and delicate bone structure. They're doll-like and have great *legs and breasts,*" Dash whispered the last three words in her ear. "And I love them."

"Good." She could feel her heart beat out of control. "Did you say something about leaving?"

"Good idea," Dash said hoarsely, leading her toward his mother and father. "We're leaving," he told them succinctly.

"Your manners astound me, John Dasher . . ." his mother drawled, but when she looked at Lotus, her eyes were twinkling. "I'm sure Lotus would love to stay for another hour or two."

"She wouldn't," Dash said brusquely, making his father chortle. "What's so funny?" he charged his parent.

"I do enjoy seeing you out of stride, my boy." His father smothered another laugh when Dash muttered an imprecation.

"Lotus, you must learn to control your husband." Lissa was chuckling.

"She controls me well enough," Dash said when Lotus started to open her mouth.

"Good night, everyone," Lotus said, then impulsively, she hugged her mother- and father-in-law, taking note that their mouths were agape when she pulled back. "I had a lovely time. Thank you."

"Dash, why don't you move East with your wife and take over your grandmother's house on the Hill? It was left to you," his father stated gruffly, his eyes sliding back to Lotus. "I have a hankering to have my daughter-in-law nearby. I think she's good for this family."

"I agree," Lissa said softly, watching her son as he cuddled his wife close to him.

Dash shrugged. "The business demands a great deal of attention." He looked down at Lotus and smiled. "But I know you would like to be closer to your family. Perhaps we will locate somewhere in the East, if you like."

Lotus wanted to shout at him that she would live on Main Street on the moon if he wished, but instead she quietly nodded.

The other good-byes were quickly made and in minutes they were walking down the wide curving stair to the outside. Dash didn't release his hold on her until he helped her into the front seat of the Porsche. Conversation was fragmented between them, but Dash held her hand all the while they drove. Boston traffic was fairly light at one o'clock in the morning so that they had no holdups on the route they traveled to Beacon Hill.

When they left the car to mount the steps to the front door, Dash had his arm around her waist. He kept it there, even when he unlocked the door so that they could enter the house. When they were standing in the foyer, he looked down at her and smiled. "Shall we have a nightcap? A juice or something?"

Lotus shook her head, smiling when he grinned at her. "It was fun this evening. Even Dexter . . ."

"I was ready to kill him." Dash shook his head as he led her up the stairs to the third-floor suite they occupied.

Lotus was brushing her hair, when Dash came out of the bathroom. He was rubbing his head with a towel. She smiled at him, continuing to brush.

"By the way, darling, what is the birth control pill called that you're using? I think we should tell the doctor the name when we arrange for your physical." Dash disappeared back into the bathroom.

"What pill?" she whispered to her mirror image. "I meant to tell Dash I wasn't on birth control pills . . ." She groaned, her hand, with the brush, falling to the dresser with a thump. She remembered he had been prepared the first time they made love, but they hadn't discussed it since. She straightened with a jerk. "Maybe I'm pregnant now." She pressed one hand to her mouth, the other to her middle, both elated and horrified at the thought. What would Dash say? He would be happy about the child, but he might be irritated with her, that she hadn't discussed the possibility with him that she could get pregnant. Especially since he made such a fuss about her getting checked by a doctor first. She tapped her lips with an index finger. She would find a nice quiet place to tell him. That way they could discuss any disagreements they might have. Yes, that was the best way, she thought, when they were alone, with no interruptions. She smiled to herself. She was probably crazy to act as though it were a fait accompli that she was already pregnant. Yet she couldn't chase the certainty from her mind that she and Dash would be parents.

CHAPTER TEN

The flight to Greece was uneventful, yet Lotus knew that Dash was irritated with her. More than once in the last two weeks, while they were in Las Vegas finishing up the paper work for Dash's takeover of the casino in downtown Las Vegas, he had asked her for more details about her visit to the doctor. She had had the physical. The doctor had confirmed her suspicions. She was pregnant.

Lotus had told him as much as she could without revealing that she was expecting. She knew she was vacillating, but she wanted to tell him when they were in Greece, in pleasant, relaxing surroundings where their privacy would be total.

She had not been surprised when Dr. Ellen Ryan pronounced her pregnant. After the night of the Symphony Ball she had been positive. Not even the fact that she had always had irregular menstrual cycles had shaken that faith. It was fait accompli to have Dr. Ryan concur with her feelings. Before she had taken the test, the doctor had told her that she would have bet money that she was to have a child.

How ironic! The wife of a casino owner would

bet money she's having a child, Lotus mused, her head, lolling against the back of the plane seat as they banked over Athens. Athens! The cradle of civilization! Lotus straightened in her seat as they approached.

"Are you looking for the Acroplis? You can't see it from your angle." Dash's voice had that same curtness she was getting accustomed to hearing since she had been evasive with him.

"Will we see it? Or are we going right to Piraeus and the boat?"

"We'll see it." Dash felt impotent anger. What was she hiding from him? It had put him into a cold sweat when he suspected it was her health. He had called the doctor himself and been assured that Lotus was in excellent condition, but even then he had felt a reserve when he asked Dr. Ryan if it were safe for Lotus to be pregnant.

"Yes, I would say that it is safe for her," Dr. Ryan had answered in measured tones. "If you will excuse me, Mr. Colby, I have a patient."

"Yes. Of course," he'd told her, but he had picked up the restraint in her voice.

Now as he helped Lotus leave the plane and watched her scan everything eagerly, he wished he could read her mind. What was bothering her? Was she frightened of having a family? He could feel his features tighten in anger at being closed out of her thoughts. *Talk to me, damn you, Lotus,* he grated in his mind. He sighed. He would find out what was going on! His mind ticked over the conversation he had had with the doctor. Except for a slight lack of iron in her system, which was being taken care of with iron pills and supplemental vitamins, there was no problem. Could Lotus be worried that he might not be able to impregnate her? Could she think he was sterile? His anger increased.

"Dash? Dash, the customs man said we're all set." Lotus said, pulling his sleeve.

"What? Oh, fine. Let's go. There should be a car out front to take us to the hotel. Then if you like we'll explore Athens this afternoon and take the boat tomorrow."

Lotus nodded. *Oh, darling, don't look so hurt. I'm going to tell you everything when we get to the island. I just want us to be alone when I tell you our good news, with plenty of space in case you decide to blow your stack.*

"What are you smiling about?" Dash looked at her suspiciously as he directed two attendants to see to their luggage, speaking in very passable Greek.

"Where did you learn Greek?" Lotus asked him.

"One of my partners in the Atlantic City casino is Greek, born and raised in Salonika. He taught me to converse in it, so that we can speak privately at times. Athos Paranis is a tough, wily fox, whose body is made of raw hemp and whose soul is tempered steel. He smiles like a piranha and he would literally snap off your head with his teeth, but I'd trust him with everything I have. You're the only person I trust more," Dash said.

Lotus heard the touch of pathos in his voice. "And you can trust me, Dash. You can."

He exhaled a breath and nodded, tossing some bills at the attendants, who thanked him in a spatter of Greek.

"I understood *parakalo*, and *efharisto*, please and thank you, but after that I'm lost," Lotus told him.

Dash settled back against the cushions of the rather battered Rolls-Royce, which he had told her belonged to the Paranis family. "Remember to say *kalimera* for daytime greeting and *kalispera* for evening. Say *adio* when you depart. The rest I'll teach you as we go along. It's a beautiful, convoluted language that's as ageless and interesting as it's people."

"It's very exciting being here, yet somehow I still can't believe it. It's been a dream of mine to visit this country since I used to devour Greek mythology as a child."

Dash watched her, his heart hammering at the thought of being at the tiny Paranis island, alone with her for two weeks. He smothered his irritation and his fear at her evasiveness. "Tonight we'll be dining early, then I'm taking you to a taverna that has all the Greek dancing. . . ." He grinned when he saw the eager sheen to her eyes. It made his heart thud to give her joy! "But first we'll climb to the Acropolis."

Lotus slid closer on the backseat of the car and put her head on his chest. "I'm so happy with you."

"Darling," Dash groaned, his arms folding her closer.

"We are here, *kyrie*." The driver had gotten out of the car and now he held open the back door. His mustache quivered with good humor as he watched them. "Is good to be in Greece and be happy," he told them in halting English.

They went into the house on the hillside, the white limestone almost blinding in the sunlight.

"This home belonged to Athos's grandmother and she left it to him."

"I like it very much," Lotus told him as she followed him up the steep staircase to the second floor.

Later when they began to dress for their excursion to the Acropolis, Lotus felt two arms slide around her waist.

"My good intentions went out the window, Mrs. Colby, when I saw you parade around in that peachy-colored underwear."

She turned in his arms, laughing. "I was not parading, but I must admit I was hoping you would notice me and get some ideas."

He groaned into her hair when she laughed. "I always have ideas about you, Lotus. You could be draped in horse blankets and you could turn me on." He smiled down at her, feeling his heart turn over at the warmth of her eyes. "You look content as a kitten."

"I trust you, Dash." She took his hand and led him over to the bed so that they could sit side by side. Then she turned to face him. "May I tell you a story that you mostly know already?"

"I like you to tell me anything about yourself." Dash leaned over her, wanting to tell her not to speak about the past, but to talk about their present and their future. He held his tongue, wanting her to stay as relaxed as she was at that moment.

"When I decided to take leave from my job and go out to Las Vegas, no one in the family knew anything about my plans, as you know. I was scared, not just about uncle's condition and about the danger in what I would be doing—"

"It was damned foolish. You could have met people who would have hurt you."

Lotus lifted her hand to his cheek. "You have the power to hurt me."

"I never will." His skin and bones were heating to scalding level because she had her hands in his hair and was threading her fingers through it.

"Oh, I think we'll hurt each other a great deal . . . even when we've been married eighty years." Lotus chuckled, edging closer to him so that their bodies were touching.

He laughed, scooping his hand around her backside and bringing her onto his lap. "Eighty years," he said huskily. "What a lovely prospect!"

Lotus put her hand on his to stop him caressing her. "You're not listening to me."

"I'm not?" He felt out of breath. "Sorry, darling. Keep talking."

Lotus clutched her husband around his waist, resting her face under his chin. "It was awful to see our family slowly disintegrating. Each one seemed to become more ghostlike every day. Before the scandal broke, my cousin, Lee, was like sparkling water all the time. Even when we were kids, you could always hear her laugh before you saw her." Lotus spoke with her fingers curling in his flesh.

"Baby!" Dash soothed her. "Don't talk about it if you don't wish, if it makes you unhappy."

She sighed and looked up at him. "I want to tell you everything about me. . . ." She stared at him. "Some of which I'm saving until we reach the island."

Dash's antenna quivered. He felt danger flags flying and his stomach tightened. He had to force himself not to insist she tell him now. "Choose your pace, angel," he whispered to her.

Lotus talked for almost twenty minutes, held close in her husband's arms, drawing him the picture of the clan Sinclair and their closeness to each other. ". . . And so, you see, it wasn't just as though Uncle had been accused and framed, it was as though all of us had been accused." She swallowed. "I had the awful feeling that if we didn't do something . . . that . . . all the Sinclairs would die one by one, beginning with Uncle."

"Darling." Dash felt a wrenching pain when her body clenched. "I understand."

Lotus lifted dewy green eyes to him. "I know that."

"God, you own me." Dash's body trembled in answer to her smile.

"Dash, I have to tell you." Lotus took a deep breath.

"What?" Years of hard dealing in business steeled the fear that tremored through him.

"I don't have any strong clear memories of my own parents, except that there was laughter and a great deal of love. With my Sinclair parents, I found that love again. I was always happy as a child and as I grew older. I suppose it sounds as though I lived in a fantasy and maybe I did, but I tell you I never expected, not in ten lifetimes, to find a love like ours."

"Neither did I," he whispered.

"I love you. I have never loved anyone the way I love you, and I never will, and I want to stay with you for eighty years." Lotus smiled up at him, feeling both sadness at giving herself over completely and the ineffable joy that it was to Dash.

"Only eighty years?" Dash croaked, burying his face in her hair, feeling as though the pounding in his blood stream would break through his skin at any moment. "I want more." He lifted his head and looked at her.

"More?" Her voice was barely audible as she stared up at him, seeing the moistness in his electric eyes. "Can there be more than all there is?"

"How philosophical you're getting, wife!" Dash lifted her and swung around so that they were lying side by side on the bed facing each other. "Do you suppose it's the Greek influence?"

"The Acropolis?" Lotus ventured weakly, her eyes fluttering closed as Dash began to kiss her toes. "We were going to see it," she reminded him.

"There's time, love. I just have good priorities." Dash turned her over on her stomach, letting his tongue trace the fine veins behind her knee. The merest trace of salt on her skin set his pulse in double time. His mouth traveled up her body in slow gentle forays that had him trembling when he felt her body spasm in response. When he heard her breathy moans, low growls were torn from his own throat. "Lotus! I love you."

"Thank you," she responded as he lifted her around to face him. "I must . . . tell you . . . I like this . . ."

"Do you, my baby?" Dash's words were slurred as he slid up her body. He lifted himself above her, noting with great satisfaction her rapid breathing, the feverish glitter to her as she clutched at him. Nothing on earth gave him more satisfaction than to give her joy, and sensual delight as well. It made his heart thunder to watch her rise to fever pitch, his own libido racing hers.

When he took her, it was with a gentle violence

that lassoed them to each other, that took them away, emotion to emotion, love lashed to love.

Dash sighed, gathering her closer into his arms as his breathing settled into normal rhythm once more. "You are beautiful, Lotus."

"You too." She yawned, then chuckled. "Just a short nap," she mumbled, then closed her eyes.

When she woke she heard the water running and knew that Dash must be getting ready for their trip to the Acropolis. She heard him whistling and assumed he was shaving. She laid out the clothes she would wear, then pushed open the door of the bathroom. She looked right into his eyes, that were squinting into the mirror. "Hi."

"Hi. Come in, Mrs. Colby." Dash watched her in frank enjoyment. "Your body is perfect."

"Time to get ready for the Acropolis." She laughed at him and hitched herself next to him, doing her own washing up, feeling very comfortable with him.

"Did I ever tell you I love you?" he murmured, wiping the rest of her face, grinning at her when she nodded.

"The Acropolis," she repeated.

'I think I've heard that before," he crooned, rinsing her hair and body.

"Soap in my eye," Lotus sputtered. "Stop laughing."

"I'd never laugh about that." Dash chuckled, making her fume.

"Monster!" She gulped as he swathed her in warm towels. "Put a towel around you. You'll catch cold."

"I'm never cold around you."

They dressed in a slow fashion, despite Lotus's urgings to hurry.

"If you keep looking at me like that, we'll never leave this room," Lotus argued.

"*Ummm?*" Dash watched as she lifted her arms and let the white eyelet sundress slip down the front of her. "Honey, I think you've gained a little weight . . . here." He pressed his hand on her middle, a slight crease in his brows before he smiled at her.

"Have to get my shoes." Lotus broke free of him and raced across the room, for the low-heeled white slides she was going to wear with her dress. He was just too smart! He already noticed the change in her body and was putting the information into that computer brain of his. She would just have to hope that he wouldn't add everything together and come up with the answer before she had a chance to talk with him on the island.

She reached for a flimsy silk scarf that Dash insisted she would need, then they left the room, her hand held tight by him.

Athens! The most colorful composite of ancient and new in the world. They traveled to the marketplace first, because Lotus had to see firsthand what so many of her friends had described to her. The cacophony of traffic and voices, speaking, singing and bartering, assaulted the ears, yet was not unpleasant. There were times that Dash had to shout to get her attention and there were times when she had to read his lips to know what he was saying, but still it delighted her.

Lotus smiled at the people and they smiled back. She said *kalimera* over and over again, laughing out loud when persons returned the greeting.

"I think I may have to buy you a house in Greece. You like it, don't you?" Dash loved watching her in the market, but he finally had to edge her away and up the hill. "We have to get to the Acropolis."

"Where?" she quizzed him wide-eyed, still looking all around, not wanting to miss anything.

"Follow me." He chuckled as she looked over her shoulder, then began waving to people along the way. He flagged down a battered cab and gave their destination.

"All right, *kyrie,* I will do it," the driver said in a broken Brooklyn accent. "I know America. I drive a cab in New York three years."

The car shot around corners, and up alleys so narrow that if anyone stepped out a door as they were passing, there would have been an accident.

"My goodness, I think he received his taxi driver training in Manhattan." Lotus closed her eyes for the third time as they weaved around a push cart, the vendor shaking his fist at them.

When they reached the area, filled with tourists on that warm day, Lotus knew that they had arrived at their destination. What surprised her was the number of steps they had to travel to get to their destination. In her eagerness to reach the ancient Greek edifice she tripped, and Dash had to catch her.

"Take it easy, darling. We're getting there." He frowned down at her. "You could have fallen."

"Don't worry."

"I do worry about you."

"I know." She loosened her hand from his grasp and slipped it around his waist.

In companionable silence they covered the ground that took them to the Acropolis.

Lotus was in awe. She spoke to Dash in whispers

as they moved slowly through the structure, the wind an eerie voice in the stillness.

When they were through, and retracing their footsteps, there was silence between them at first.

"You liked that."

"Oh, yes, husband, I liked that." Lotus looked up at him. "Thank you."

"Thank you. I don't think I've ever looked at it with such intensity before, so I thank you."

They ambled down to the streets. Then Dash waved at the taxi driver to follow them.

Finally Dash was able to get her into the car and he gave the driver directions in Greek.

"The taverna?"

"Of course."

Lotus nodded and looked around her, craning her neck, stretching, looking out her window and out Dash's.

"You'll have a sore neck."

"I don't want to miss anything."

He laughed.

When they reached the taverna, Lotus was disappointed. "It's so small."

"Yes. But this is not one of the tourist traps, either. This is the taverna where Athos told me he and his father learned the ancient dances."

"Oh. Should we go inside?"

"Not yet." Dash ordered ouzo for himself and retsina, the local wine, for Lotus. "Ouzo over here does not taste like the ouzo you get in New York." He held up his glass and let the rather viscous liquid slide around it. "It is here in Greece that ouzo is at it's best."

Lotus made a face over her retsina, but she

wouldn't let Dash get her anything else. "Are you sure this is the local wine?"

"Does it taste like turpentine?" Dash asked.

Lotus narrowed her gaze on him. "Is this a trick? This isn't even wine, is it?"

"No tricks, my love." Dash leaned across the tiny round table and kissed her, oblivious of the people passing by on the street that ran in front of the taverna. "That is the local wine. I like it, but I have heard people say that it tastes like turpentine. Let me get you something else."

"No. I want to try the local things. Let me taste your ouzo."

Dash looked skeptical, but he lifted his glass to her mouth, and watched her swallow.

"Good Lord," she wheezed.

"A unique flavor," Dash assured her.

"Yes. That must be what nitroglycerin tastes like." Lotus coughed, then sipped her retsina and grimaced. "This is getting better."

Dash put back his head and laughed, not noticing the admiring glances of a woman who passed.

"I wish you wouldn't do that," Lotus said crossly.

Dash looked puzzled. "Do what, love?"

"Women are looking at you," Lotus informed him.

"Huh?" Dash looked around him, then back at Lotus, his smile building slowly. "Jealous?"

"Yes. So watch yourself."

"I will," Dash answered, not able to stem his contented smile.

"And you needn't look so pleased with yourself. I'm sure there are other gorgeous, sexy men in Athens."

"But none of them for you . . . except this one."

"Thumping your chest?"

"Yes," Dash growled back. Then he looked over her shoulder and smiled. "Dmitri."

"Yes, my friend. I knew that was you. Athos has told us you were married and that you would be coming to Greece."

A bear of a man lifted Dash out of his chair and hugged him, pounding him on the back. Then he turned to Lotus. "So you are the beauty who has taken the beast, eh?"

"I'm Lotus Colby." She held out her hand. It stunned her when the man ignored her hand. Instead, he lifted her out of her chair and embraced her also.

"Dmitri Amopoulos would never accept just the hand of Colby's wife, eh?" His booming laugh brought heads around, smiling and chortling as they watched Lotus being bear-hugged. "Why is not the big Dasher Colby laughing, eh? You, who used to wrestle Graeco-Roman–style with me and a few times win. Just what is it that makes you frown, my friend? You like no man to touch this very special woman, is that it?"

"That's it." Dash fired the words through tight lips.

Dmitri's booming laugh filled the air once more. "Is good. You have been well and truly taken, my friend." Dmitri looked down at Lotus whom he'd barely released. "Yet you are so small to have such power, my little flower. You are much like your name. My friend Athos told me of it. Lotus, eh?"

"Yes." Dash managed to free Lotus and pull her back against him.

"*Umph . . . mumph* . . . Dash . . ." Lotus gasped,

moving back from him a fraction. "You're smothering me in your chest."

"Oh. Sorry, darling." Dash glared at the Greek who was laughing again. "I think it's time you and I had another go round on the mat."

Dmitri's eyes had a zealot's glitter. "Where? When?"

"Never." Lotus clutched Dash's waist and looked at the Greek. "I prefer him in one piece."

Dash kissed her head as Dimitri grimaced. "These women, they do not want us to play."

"Breaking Dash's ribs wouldn't be play to me," Lotus said tartly, making both men smile at her.

"You are a lucky one, Colby, I will say that. I wish that I had seen her first. You would not have had a chance."

Dash grinned, but his arm tightened. "It would have been war, my friend."

"So it would." Dmitri read the challenge. Then he shrugged. "But for now we will watch the dancing and maybe do it ourself, heh?"

Lotus looked at the reckless gleam in Dash's eyes and felt her heart thump. "Can you do it?"

Dash nodded.

Darkness came quickly. One moment the sky was colorful orange, purple, and blue and the next it was deepest night.

Inside the taverna was cool, but as the music began and the dancing started, the coolness was replaced by a moist heat.

Lotus became so caught up in the slow fever of the rhythms that she wasn't even aware of the light sheen of perspiration on her own skin. When Dash rose to his feet to clasp arms with the other men in the dance, she felt such a rush of excitement she had a hard time breathing. She sipped the tall glass of iced lime juice Dash had gotten for her. Lotus had laughed at him when he had made a small fuss about assuring himself that the ice cubes in the glass were made from bottled water.

The throbbing beat took the dancers around the floor in slow, measured steps first, then they broke apart in leaps as the music quickened. Lotus was on her feet, clapping as were the other patrons as the men gyrated and spun. Then with a rousing flourish it was over and Lotus was cheering with the rest. "Darling . . ." She threw herself at Dash when he came from the center of the floor, feeling the wetness of his body. "It was so beautiful. Here, take my juice."

She watched him swallow the liquid. "*Whew.*" Dash grinned at her, then made a face. "Warm work." He exhaled a deep breath.

Lotus embraced him. "You were so graceful." She looked up at him. "I love you," she whispered, satisfied when she saw his eyes darken. He would make love to her when they returned to the house! She frowned for a moment, looking up at him. "You might get chilled and catch cold."

Dmitri laughed as he wiped the sleeve of his cotton shirt across his forehead. "He will not catch cold, little flower. Sit down. We will have chilled retsina and ouzo."

Lotus drank fruit juice and watched the men. Though Dash drank his share of the Greek liquor and so did Dmitri, neither man seemed to be much affected by the alcohol.

"Come, little flower, it is time for you to dance."

"Ohh." Lotus felt herself lifted out onto the

floor as the music was beginning again. She sensed rather than saw that Dash was right at her heels. At first she stumbled and felt very gauche, but gradually, with the smiling encouragement of Dmitri and Dash and the other Greek dancers, she was able to overcome her shy awkwardness and begin to take part. The music entered her soul and took over her nerve ends. The throb of the bouzouki became her own pulse rate, and her legs bent and swayed to the ageless chords.

Finally Dash decided it was time to go.

Lotus felt like a wet noodle. "It was wonderful," she told Dmitri. "I do hope we meet again."

"We will, my little flower. Each time you come to Athens you will see me. And sometime when I come to your Atlantic City, you will see me then. I will teach you to speak Greek, *kyria*." He swept her up in another hug, then shook hands with Dash and was gone.

"Isn't he interesting?" Lotus quizzed her husband.

Dash shrugged. If Dmitri had kissed Lotus one more time, he would have torn his head off! He could feel his jaw grinding at the thought.

"Hey, Silent One, I think we've arrived."

"Huh?" Dash looked at her, then at the taxi driver who's head was cocked quizzically. "Oh, sure."

Lotus watched her husband as he led her into the house, his arm around her. "I don't know about you, but I'm anxious to make love to my husband."

Dash's head shot around to her. His smile was slow in coming. "Good idea."

They hurried through a shower to rid their bodies of the sticky feeling after dancing.

"Darling . . ." Dash breathed as they made their way, arms locked around each other, to the bed, their bodies still damp from the shower. "I love you."

"And I love you."

That night their love was an explosion of gentleness and delight. To Dash's joy, Lotus took the initiative and began an aggression of her own that turned his bones to jelly and made him feel as though his heart was fibrillating.

"That's it. No more." He growled, turning her on her back, both their bodies having a love sheen. He entered her with a gentle thrust that had her gasping.

Then there was only oneness with no single Dash or Lotus, just the oneness that only love could bring them, the marriage of the spirit that made their blood boil, their skin freeze on that very special journey into physical love.

They fell asleep with their arms around each other.

The next day they woke and made love again, showered and dressed with their eyes meeting constantly.

They breakfasted, feeding each other wedges of orange, bits of egg, pieces of toast, sips of coffee.

As they packed their things, both of them kept looking at the bed.

Lotus laughed. "We had better run, or we'll never catch the ferry."

"Just wait until I get you on that island. The beach is so private that we'll make love there."

"Sounds good," Lotus croaked, feeling her hands tremor as she carried the overnight bags and Dash managed the heavier luggage they took down to the cab waiting outside the house.

The ferry was a delight. It was old, but the very clean and the plain food that was served as the craft wended its way through the lustrous water was a delight to Lotus.

"I can't believe you're eating again after the breakfast you had." Dash cuddled her, laughing as he munched a very sweet orange, licking the juice from her lips himself. "*Umm,* I do like doing that."

"I think the Greeks are suspicious of your mental stability. You show too much interest in your wife and not enough in their beautiful scenery," Lotus told him, hazily, feeling once more the need to love her husband. She put her free hand to his cheek. "Have I told you that I love you?"

"Yes," Dash answered hoarsely, his body bent over hers. "But feel free to repeat yourself . . . every hour."

"Silly." Lotus wiped her hands on the damp towel an attendant handed her then let herself lean against her husband as he pointed out the many small islands they passed. "I can't believe your knowledge of this wonderful country. How many times have you visited Greece?"

"I don't know the actual count, but the first time I visited here was the summer between my freshman and sophomore years in college. I was working on a steamer for the Amopoulos family for the summer."

"Oh. Were you an officer?"

"No." Dash chuckled. "I shoveled coal into the furnace that heated the boiler. Hot work."

Lotus grinned at him. "Poor baby."

They talked and bantered back and forth, until the moment that Dash pointed past her cheek. "There. That's the island. We'll be there in fifteen minutes."

The island was a chunk of rock in the sea with a hilly, grassy plateau. A tiny white village huddled near the harbor and a twist of road rose up from the sea into the high meadow.

Dash pointed to the house as they debarked from the ferry. A battered car and grizzled driver, who glared at Dash and called him a name, were there to meet them.

"What did he call you?"

"*Filos,* meaning 'friend.' He told me he remembers the friend of Athos." Dash grimaced. "Don't laugh. He's liable to order me out onto the fishing boats for a day or two, just to make sure that I'm not out of condition."

Lotus laughed, making the grizzled driver grunt in her direction, his face not changing but his eyes twinkling.

When they arrived at the villa, Lotus was too awed to move, much less hear what was said to her. The view of the sea and the other islands was magnificent. The breeze had the fragrance of blossoms she couldn't identify, with a touch of the saltiness of the water.

"Yannis said good-bye to you . . ." Dash said in her ear. ". . . But you didn't hear him." He chuckled, his insides melting at the happy look on her face. "I take it you approve of our view. Now come in and see the inside, then we'll go to the beach."

"Yes," Lotus breathed, turning to look at him, then blinking. "Oh, dear, I'm sorry I didn't say good-bye to Yannis. I hope he won't think me rude."

"No, he was very pleased with your reactions to his island."

They walked arm and arm through the six-bedroom villa. Lotus admired the terraced gardens she could see from the windows and the master suite of bedroom, sitting room and two baths that they would be occupying.

"There are two custodians, a man and wife, Stavros and Maria, who care for the property," Dash told her as they donned their swim suits and took towels and a blanket with them. "The beach is quite a climb, down a path, then a stairway, but the beach is worth the effort." Dash led her out to the kitchen where he filled a bag with bottled lime juice and several oranges. "Sustenance for the lady with the big appetite."

And wait until you find out why, Lotus thought as she followed him out of the house and down the circuitous path to the stairway, then to the beach. "It is worth it." Lotus inhaled the sweet air, then she dropped her towel. "Race you to the beach."

Dash was open-mouthed as he watched his nude wife run to the water. *Little witch! I thought she had her bikini!* He felt his body harden as he watched that tiny but well-formed body hit the water in a clean surface dive. Then he was off and running right behind her into the waves, his long sure strokes carrying him to her. He dived under the surface and caught hold of her lissome form. "Where do you think you're going?" He held her easily in the deep water.

"Did you like my suit?" She smiled impishly at him.

"No wonder you came out of the bathroom with your robe on. Shame on you, Mrs. Colby. I think you're a wanton."

"Right you are, Mr. Colby." She swam closer to him and pressed her mouth to his, letting her tongue touch his teeth, then enter his mouth.

"Stop that. I'll drown," Dash gasped, feeling his muscle tone disappear as she continued to caress him.

"I'll save you," Lotus murmured, feeling in that moment that she could have saved him from anything, that she could have prevented the Empire State Building from falling on him.

They played in the water for a long time, but Dash seemed to sense before she did that she was tired and insisted that she get out of the water.

"Are you my keeper too?" Lotus asked him as he kept his arm around her as they walked across the sandy beach, then dried her with a towel.

"Yes. I'll always be that. Besides, didn't we say that maybe you could be pregnant very soon after we married?" He inhaled. "You do think I'm able to impregnate you, don't you, darling?"

Lotus covered her mouth to smother her giggles but she couldn't. She made an effort to stop when she saw a flash of hurt on his face. "My love, sit down next to me." She put her arm around his neck and climbed into his lap when he sat. "I'm not laughing at you. I'm laughing at us. I have very special news for you, Mr. Colby. We are expecting a baby. . . ." She put her two fingers over his lips when he gasped. "I've talked to Dr. Ellen Ryan about it, and I have figured it happened the second time we made love. I knew you were very concerned about me getting a checkup with a doctor before I became pregnant, so I didn't want to tell you until we were absolutely alone on this island."

"I talked to Dr. Ryan—" Dash shook his head. "She said you were capable of having a baby."

"I wanted to tell you myself . . . have it be my surprise to you. That's why she didn't tell you." Lotus stroked his cheek with her hand.

"Are you well?" Dash croaked, cradling her close to him.

"Very well. Strong as an ox."

"And with the same-size appetite. . . ." Dash's smile was crooked as she nodded.

"And no morning sickness, nothing but blooming good health."

"Oh baby . . . baby . . . baby . . ." Dash held her, feeling his body tremble with need and happiness. "I didn't expect this. From the moment we met you've been bringing me happiness and now this. I love you, Lotus, and if I live a thousand years, I will never be able to tell you how much. Never leave me."

"Never in this life or any other, because if I leave you, then I leave myself. Love has made me yours."

"And I belong to you." Dash made the covenant, then pushed her gently back on the blanket to make slow, sweet love to her.